09-BTJ-431

EMBRACE ME

OTHER NOVELS BY LISA SAMSON

Quaker Summer

Straight Up

The Church Ladies

Tiger Lillie

Club Sandwich

The Living End

Women's Intuition

Songbird

EMBRACE ME

LISA SAMSON

THOMAS NELSON
Since 1798

NASHVILLE   DALLAS   MEXICO CITY   RIO DE JANEIRO   BEIJING

Published in Nashville, Tennessee, by Thomas Nelson. Thomas Nelson is a registered trademark of Thomas Nelson, Inc.

Thomas Nelson, Inc., titles may be purchased in bulk for educational, business, fund-raising, or sales promotional use. For information, please e-mail SpecialMarkets@ThomasNelson.com.

Scripture quotations are from the King James Version of the Bible and from the HOLY BIBLE: NEW INTERNATIONAL VERSION®. © 1973, 1978, 1984 by International Bible Society. Used by permission of Zondervan Publishing House. All rights reserved.

Publisher's Note: This novel is a work of fiction. Names, characters, places, and incidents are either products of the author's imagination or used fictitiously. All characters are fictional, and any similarity to people living or dead is purely coincidental.

Library of Congress Cataloging-in-Publication Data

Samson, Lisa, 1964–
  Embrace me / Lisa Samson.
    p. cm.
  ISBN 978-1-59554-210-6 (pbk.)
  1. Women circus performers—Fiction. I. Title.
PS3569.A46673E47 2008
813'.54—dc22   2007048456

Printed in the United States of America
08 09 10 11 RRD 6 5 4 3 2 1

FOR BILL, VAL, LIAM,
FAMILY AND FRIENDS

"To love means loving the unlovable. To forgive means pardoning the unpardonable. Faith means believing the unbelievable. Hope means hoping when everything seems hopeless."

—G. K. CHESTERTON

"He who is devoid of the power to forgive is devoid of the power to love."

—MARTIN LUTHER KING, JR.

ONE

DREW: 2002

It's amazing how good a priest looks when you've got nobody else to turn to.

The sign says he should be here. The front doors are unlocked and I walk right down the aisle. It feels creepy, despite the white walls—that Catholic, old world creepiness cemented by the statue of Mary standing on the earth, stepping on a serpent whose mouth stretches wide in agony.

Good for you, Mary. We've never given you enough credit. Not that we'd overdo it like these guys. I shove my hands in my pockets, looking around at the altar, the stone baptismal font, two pulpits—one big, one small—two rows of pews, a side altar with a statue of Joseph, I think. The doors at the back, another side altar with the statue of Mary.

But I see no carved wooden booth with a curtain hanging down like they always show in the movies. So I call out, my voice reverberating against the stone walls of the small church. "Anybody here?"

No answer.

Thomas, his stained-glass face eating up the late afternoon sun, looks doubtful of my presence and I can't blame him.

I sit on the front pew, my gaze resting on the rack of votive candles flickering in their red cups and then skating up to the round

1

glass window in the back wall where Jesus—hands spread wide and welcoming, a dove above his head, beams of light shining—looks out over the room.

A small man enters the room—much younger than I expected.

"Hello there."

"Are you the priest?" Great. I'm in the greatest inner crisis of my life and God sends a guy fresh out of seminary who probably doesn't know a thing about the real world. Fitting.

"Yes. Sorry I'm a little late. There's always so much to do before mass begins."

"I understand. I hear the priesthood is waning."

"An understatement. Too much to give up these days. Are you here for confession?"

"Yes."

"Are you visiting Ocean City?" He sits down next to me, laying a comfortable arm across the back of the pew.

"Sort of. Extended stay. My mother and I used to vacation here when I was younger. I'm not Catholic."

He stares at me, brown eyes calm as he rubs the five o'clock shadow on his chin, then straightens his short dark hair. "Well, God isn't choosy about who's allowed to confess their sins if they are truly repentant. Are you a religious person?"

"I used to be a pastor—nondenominational."

"Oh my. Well, I won't hold that against you." He chuckles then settles into something more relaxed. I'm not a priest but apparently he recognizes someone else willing to answer a call. "Forgive me. I sometimes say too much. So what's on your mind? And just to reassure you, this will still remain confidential."

"Bless me, Father, for I have sinned."

"You're not Catholic. This isn't the movies. No need to go with such formalities." He waves it away. "But you did say it so heartfelt. I'm not used to that these days. Vacationers. You know, they went out the night before and committed all manner of mortal sin, and they're planning on doing it again. Thankfully, God is the true judge of the heart, not me. I only do what I'm supposed to and leave the rest up to Him. It's all any of us can do."

"I wish someone would have told me that a long time ago."

"So, tell me your troubles. I'm Father Brian, by the way."

Brian? I smile.

"Yes, I know. The trials of being a young priest with a youthful name."

"I don't know where to begin."

"Repentance goes a long way in the saving of our souls. Anywhere is fine. God knows the end from the beginning anyway. Unless, of course, you're an open theist. Are you an open theist?"

"No. That never made any sense to me."

"Nor to me. Sorry for interrupting. Go on ahead. Just talk to me."

I try to form the words on my tongue. Nothing comes. I imagine the surf pounding outside. Seagulls circling above a piece of trash. I picture sunbeams and Bibles and Jesus dying on the cross. Even picturing the Resurrection and the anticipated gathering of the nations does nothing to resurrect my tongue from the bottom of my mouth.

He leans forward slightly. "Are you ready for this?"

"I don't know."

"Tell you what. Write it all down, then come and see me. Be assured that God is waiting to forgive you. He joys in a repentant heart." He taps the back of the pew three times. "Even if you're not Catholic."

"All right. That's what I'll do."

"Then come back. If you make an appointment, I can give you all the time you need. Do you mind telling me your name? I'll pray for you in the meantime."

"Drew."

"Good, Drew. Come back soon. In the interim, pray like your life depends on it. And would you pray for me too?"

"I've forgotten how."

"There's no trick to it."

"I don't need a rosary or anything?"

"No. Correct me if I'm wrong, but I'm not quite picturing you as the kind of man who's used to asking a woman for anything. Oh there I go again! Forgive me."

He doesn't realize he just landed a firm punch to my jaw. "Thank you."

"Feel free to stay and pray."

"Thanks, but the statuary kind of gets to me."

He laughs. "A common response from protestants. No worries. Just call me when you're ready."

The priest rises and walks toward a door at the side of the church. A minute later a young woman stops before a door right next to it. Oh, that's the booth. Her head is bowed, perhaps beneath the weight of her sin, and her hand trembles as she reaches for the knob.

I can't watch another second of this.

I trudge back to my room, stopping at the pharmacy for a notebook and a pack of pencils. Maybe I shouldn't plan on doing a lot of erasing, but I'd like that option.

I came to Ocean City because I couldn't think of another place I wanted to go. Chapel Hill? No way. DC? Definitely not. That town killed me before I ever had a chance.

The Dunesgrass Hotel where I'm staying is scheduled for demolition come spring. My mother and I stayed here for a week every summer, just her and me, tanning to a ruddy brown and reading books on the beach, walking the boardwalk every night, eating caramel corn and pizza or pit-beef sandwiches. Not exactly a vacation that suited the tastes of my father. This hotel smells old now. The sconces that lit the hallways don't work. The threadbare maroon carpeting is curling at the edges.

You can pay by the month, by the day, or by the hour if you're in good with the desk guy who works eleven to seven. Most people live here year round. Four blocks from the ocean, miles and miles from proper society.

I arrange the bed pillows against the headboard, pull the lamp forward to illumine the pages of the composition book, and set the tip of the mechanical pencil against the top blue line of the paper.

◆◆◆

Father Brian,

I begin with thoughts that it would just be easier to give up altogether.

Hermy says more men actually succeed at suicide than women.

I guess when we stand upon that precipice, perhaps we've exhausted all other options. No one can help. We've sought help already. Nobody came running; or if they did, it didn't stick. That's about it. One place left to go.

Assuming there'd be no going back, I'd opt for a good shot in the mouth. Quick. Efficient. Not likely to result in survival. The spot of self-execution would be easy for me to choose. Someplace no one would ever look for me, miles back into the woods, off the trail I've come to use as solace. I thought of tying cinder blocks on my feet and jumping into Lake Coventry where I'm from, but drowning to death takes too long. Leaving little trace of a body is, I have to admit, a favorable element in either of these scenarios.

I'd leave a note to my congregation, of course. And it would writhe and teem with lies about Daisy's disappearance and my own. I'd blame Trician, just as guilty in the mess as I, and never once would I come right out and admit my own complicity.

This is exactly why I don't deserve to even kill myself at this point. Or ever, really. I'm not the type. Just wish I was. And it seemed like a dramatic way to start this. The fact is, I haven't begun to exhaust my options.

◆◆◆

I slide my arms through my jacket and head down the stoop, out the back of this old hotel. Old hotels aren't choosy about their occupants. They seem relieved somebody showed up inside their dim recesses, hoping maybe a bit of their former grandeur will shine through, maybe somebody will see them for who they really are. Or were. Or something. Even when Mom and I came, it wasn't all that nice. But we were never in our room anyway—we were always on the beach or the boardwalk.

I light up a cigarette, inhaling and looking around the alley where Glen sleeps bundled up in blankets and alcohol near the back stairs of the pawnshop. Glen has drug-induced dementia. He told me this the first day I found him back here. I tuck a five in his pocket then sit down on the back steps of the hotel.

Pulling up the sleeve of my jacket, I press the burning cigarette butt into the flesh atop my wrist. My breath catches. I lift up the cigarette and the cold December wind whispers over the scorched skin.

After the initial release, the inevitable thought arrives. *What did you just do, you idiot?* It makes me feel better. I don't know why. I don't care why at this point. There are, as they say, bigger fish to fry these days.

Well, Father Brian, let's get back to it. The morning is young and I am running out of time. A man can't live between sin and redemption for long, can he? I might die in an accident, choke on my food. Or the Rapture might happen any day.

I stuff the pack of smokes inside my jacket and walk toward the beach. Yeah, it's winter. It's cold. But it's our beach. I could use a walk in the sun. I look like I'm made out of school paste right now.

◆◆◆

My room looks extra dingy after the sunlight burned into my retinas. I sip on a cup of coffee I bought at the 7-Eleven and pick up the composition book again.

◆◆◆

When Daisy and her mother walked into the sanctuary, the crowd's attention was locked on the young pastor working his deal on a central stage amid the encircling padded chairs. *I'm from the town of Mount Oak, Father. I doubt you've ever been there.*

The year was 1999, the primaries for the presidential election were already heating up, and I was joking about the candidates who would receive my vote.

"Look at this tie. Look at this fine suit. What party do I look like I belong to?" I didn't believe for a second that if we were in power, America would become a holy nation and God would look past our sins, but we had that kind of congregation, and right then, they laughed. I laughed with a soft bit of snort, rolled my eyes, shook my head, and held my arms wide. "Hey, I am who I am. The apple doesn't fall far from the tree."

They laughed some more. I didn't have to fill them in on my father. Everybody knew Charles Parrish, political pundit, lobbyist, and general DC mover and shaker.

My people just wanted to feel at peace in their own hometown, in their own houses, their own church. I guess I wanted them to feel that way too.

Peace? Peace—when there is no peace? you ask, Father Brian? Granted.

I pulled a swiveling barstool from off to the side, made sure the wireless mic unit held tight to my belt, and sat down. Utilizing these downbeats, I could work theatre-in-the-round style church better than anybody I'd ever seen, making eye contact with at least half of the nine hundred people gathered every Sunday morning. In my less than gracious moments, of which there were many, Father, I thought of it as a feeding trough, people gobbling up their weekly plate of spiritual quiche, eating just enough to get themselves through the next seven days, or until they met with their small groups, but not enough to share *with anybody else. In my gracious moments, I realized deep down they were truly looking for the peace of Christ. And I was giving them the same old answers that hadn't been working for a good long time.*

But even if I'd wanted to serve them up a meaty stew, I wouldn't have known the recipe back then. I still don't.

I smiled and said, "I was reading an old book by Dr. Susan Gordon—anybody remember her radio show back in the eighties?" Of course I was a child when she was so popular.

I pointed to a woman in her fifties—Maggie Reynolds, I think— and buttered on an even bigger smile, making that longed-for connection. Longed-for on her part. A hundred other Maggies sat expectant in the congregation just begging to be noticed—by someone. I wasn't idiot enough to take this personally, nor was I idiot enough not to realize women like Maggie were the key to my success.

"Dr. Gordon used to say we have to take care of ourselves before we can take care of anybody else. Amen?"

"Amen!" she shouted—they all shouted. Oh, I could elicit amens.

"God wants us healthy and whole. He doesn't endorse suffering. Amen?"

You see, the more amens you ask for—the more you get. No, Father, I don't suppose there are many amens echoing in the rafters of St. Mary's.

The congregation, too busy trying to hear that someday life wouldn't hurt so much, didn't see Daisy and her mother enter. I knew what they wanted to hear. Exactly. Because, you know what? I wanted it too, Father Brian. More than anything. If I could spread that message far enough and wide enough, maybe it could come true.

God doesn't want you to hurt—ever. Never mind that "tribulation worketh patience," as Paul said to the Romans. Who wants to hear that? I sure didn't. Do you?

Looking back, I realize I must not have given one whit about my congregation. I wanted my words to be true for me. I believe that's what drives a lot of preachers. Not all. I've met some true believers, men hand in hand with Jesus, shepherds who love their flocks more than themselves. Good men. Kind men. Men who look a lot like Jesus, but without the robes and beard. But the gospel I've seen peddled most is usually cut-to-size, a perfect fit for the purveyor. Which pretty much ruins it for those people who don't exactly cotton to a three-piece suit, or a cassock, or even jeans and a polo shirt.

At least you all keep it pretty consistent, Father. I'll give you that.

If somebody could just tell me what the gospel really is these days, I'd leave this hotel room and never look back. Where I'd go wouldn't matter as long as it wasn't Mount Oak.

If I don't figure out this gospel, then there's nothing left for me. Professionally speaking.

Anyway . . .

I was good at the rally cry.

"The days of the long-faced Jesus are over!" I raised a fist, my smile wide and thankful for those tooth-whitening strips. "Over! Can you say it with me?"

Over. Over. Over. Over. Over.

Never mind He was a man of sorrows.

Never mind He was acquainted with grief.

"Over! Over! Over!" they chanted. One lady stood up, raising fists of joy and victory, shuffling in her high-heeled pumps.

Daisy looked for a place to sit down.

I settled the crowd. "Glory to His name. The One who banished pain and sorrow and death."

It wasn't so much that what I said wasn't true. I just failed to flip the coin over and expose the rest of the picture: the bloodied Christ, the dirty hands of service, the dusty feet with miles of calluses, the bruised heart of making oneself vulnerable for kingdom come. Whatever that is.

I had rehearsed my message ten times, so seeing her didn't cause me to misplace a single syllable. I was that good. I planned on heading to the top. A publishing contract and a few New York Times best *sellers with my picture on the cover. A huge church and a television ministry. The televangelists had already garnered a bad rap, but Drew Parrish would change all that. I could do it. It wasn't all selfish. Or . . . well, I don't know. I think I convinced myself a small portion of me desired the growth of God's kingdom.*

Whatever that is. I didn't understand it then either, but I knew it was something attainable if you could even semi-understand it. Jesus said it was among us and within us, and yet we still pray for it to come. How could it be all of that?

Yes, I know the seminary answer, Father. But look around you. Is it really playing out that way? I don't think so.

I knew measurable success. I knew seats filled and cash in the drawer and if both of those were overflowing . . . kingdom come it is.

You might call it greed. In fact, you'd probably call it exactly that here in your small parish in Ocean City, Maryland. You'd be right.

Pride too, you say? Okay. Yes.

When I came to Elysian Heights, there were only one hundred and fifty members.

Her mother pointed to a seat and Daisy sat.

Just like a hundred other late people. Their hair caught my attention, I suppose, and the bright pink of her mother's suit. Nothing more.

I moved forward in my message, seasoning it with jokes and shrugs, half comic/half friendly professor, never too close to the bone. Never talking about sin. That just wouldn't do—I had them right where I wanted them, the closing prayer, the final flourish, "Thanks be to God who gives us the victory. Amen."

Only I pronounced it Ah-men.

And they gave it to me, the last note of the service, as planned. "Amen."

Only they pronounced it Ah-men.

Normally, due to our numbers, I couldn't stand at the back of the sanctuary like an old-time preacher or—perhaps like you do, Father Brian—shake hands with the Mrs. Grandys of the world who hold their Bibles like treasure chests, eyes crinkling at the corners when the pastor mentions something personal about their lives, something to let them know I care. How did that outpatient surgery go? Your daughter fly in safely? I've got a copy of that book we were talking about for you over at the information desk.

No, those personally delivered sentiments jumped ship a few years before. Collateral damage I called it. It should have been a warning sign. I see that more and more.

But Senator Randall, a friend of my father's, was visiting, so instead of heading to my study in the office area behind the sanctuary, I walked down the aisle amid the confused stares of those who expected the same thing every Sunday. I winked as if I was letting them in on it all.

The senator was one of the first to leave and we talked for a minute or two. I'd been raised in politics. It was all second nature. But I couldn't very well leave upon his departure so I stood at the door to the worship center, smiling easily because I had a lot of practice at it. What a church Elysian Heights had become under my watch. The board loved me and maintained high expectations. I delivered.

What a place for God's people!

The gray-green carpet, the cream walls, the plain windows of the vestibule all served as a backdrop for bulletin boards, the information center, the coffee and juice bar, and a sweeping staircase up to the balcony which housed more seating, the projection and sound systems, and the choir. We called them the Community Singers, because choir sounded so old-fashioned. We kept them out of sight.

No crosses to be found.

Shocking to you, Father, I'm sure. "Ashamed of the cross?" you ask. We just didn't want to be offensive, even though—yes, I admit it— the Scriptures themselves claim the cross is an offense.

Folks milled around the coffee bar, the aroma of freshly ground beans perfuming the gathered ones. People can slam down the idea of a church coffee bar all they like, but when we installed ours the year before Daisy came and stuffed it with good beans and syrups, the congregation grew by twenty percent. That was a great move.

We were set to start our own sports league the next fall. Plans for a Christian school were already on the drawing board. The more we had to offer, the more likely they'd be to come and then to stay.

I didn't have a huge organization like the Catholic Church behind me, Father. We were pretty much on our own.

"I saw your father on TV just last night!" Lacy grabbed my hand and shook it like thunder. Lacy volunteered for nursery every month even though she had no children of her own.

"Good! Good!"

"He was really giving it to, well, the other guy on that talk show. The one with the two guys? I can't remember their names, but it's on after the eleven o'clock news."

I smiled. "He has that way about him. Have a good week!"

I smiled. I smiled. I smiled so much I often wondered if it would divide my head in two.

Fred Hastert was next. "How're ya, Pastor?" Needed to bleach his teeth what with all those cigarettes he smoked, but he worked wonders with our budget and headed up the men's prayer breakfasts early Tuesday mornings.

"I'm fine, Fred. Take good care."

Raynelle Pierce came after that. Enjoyed her fruit salad at church dinners. And she always showed up for cleaning days. Unfortunately she was sleeping with our janitor. No wonder she showed up for cleaning days. I know. I know. I kept meaning to talk to them about that. I pushed her along through the line as well.

Maggie Reynolds stood there next.

"Maggie! How's the new job?"

"Great. A lot of travel. Was in DC this past week for several meetings with the FCC."

Maggie worked for a media conglomerate. She was nobody's fool and we were lucky to have someone of her caliber coming to Elysian

Heights. I kept trying to get her to help with the vision or financial committees, but she was always strapped for time.

She and the other big timers rushed off to other commitments and the humble backbone of the church filed by. They offered their compliments onto my altar and I nodded, smiled, and pressed their hands lovingly, accepting their adoration if not their affection. Always looking slightly over their heads for the next bigwig about to step in line.

"Fine sermon, pastor."

"You gave me a real word from the Lord."

"Anointed. You're anointed."

I smiled. I smiled.

Yeah, it kinda makes me sick too. Hopefully that's a step in the right direction.

After ten more such interactions, the tardy pair made their way toward me. Daisy wore a light brown sitcom-lawyer suit, complete with a short skirt, but she had a few more curves than that skinny actress with the strange name who popularized them a few years before. I loved something about that actress, her taut skin stretched like latex across the bridge of her nose and her cheekbones, those dowel legs that seemed almost like a fairy's, able to be broken by a harsh glance.

She changed the look of Hollywood. One person. I admired her.

I smiled. "Hello there! Good morning! Thanks for coming today!"

Trician, the mother, hair frosted the same color as Daisy's but a little shorter and half again as big, smiled back. "Wonderful sermon, Reverend." Her jewelry jangled and sparkled, pushing a heavy, cloying perfume my way.

A country accent contrasted with the glitzy getup. You can take the girl out of the hollow . . .

"Oh, I'm just Drew." Nerdy charm engaged, I turned to Daisy.

She thrust forth her hand, manicured tastefully, and shook mine with a firm grip. Well. That surprised me a bit. I took her for the same sort as her mother.

"This is my daughter Daisy."

"Nice to meet you, Drew."

Well, she might not have been stick thin, but her shocking blue eyes and ample chest said hello in ways skinny legs never would. Just couldn't help noticing. She had an allure about her that any heterosexual male would pick up on if he had decent vision.

"Thanks for coming today."

She withdrew her hand, and in the withdrawing I saw the truth. She dropped her eyes and smoothed her jacket. So the bravado was learned, practiced, perhaps thousands of times in the full-length mirror on the door of her bedroom closet.

Too bad.

"I'm Trician." The mother leaned forward, a glint in her eye even a monk would recognize. "Trician Boyer."

She's coming onto me! I wanted to laugh. This used-up thing who'd obviously been tugged and pulled by a surgeon into some sort of Kabuki mask?

I whispered, "Nice to meet you," and then turned toward the next member in line. But I caught Daisy's eye and winked. She winked back and scooted through the door, squeezing her behind in between two of the elders.

Just before she disappeared onto the patio, she turned back around and caught my eye. She was swallowed by the crowd.

But she stayed behind in my second layer of vision, trapped in a greenish freeze-frame. Huh.

I escaped soon after, pretending to hear my name from someone in the stairwell. I waved with a smile to the people remaining in the lobby. What a nice guy, that Drew Parrish. What a really nice guy. Always so clean-cut and presentable. Never a hair out of place or a crease not ironed.

They had no idea.

Hiding in my locked office until the building quieted down, I held a decorative orb carved of rose-colored marble. It calmed me, the smooth coolness reminding me of my mother who left the orb behind.

Footsteps approached, knocks vibrated the wooden panel of the door, footsteps retreated. I pretended I was gone. Sitting there, staring at the reflection of the lamp on my desk, getting ready for my father's Sunday call. I wished I truly was ready. I was never ready. Not once.

12:59 p.m. The alarm on my desk clock beeped three times. One minute until the most calculating, ridiculously sleazy, and perfectly groomed man in existence would call me on the phone and grill me as to the productivity of my week. And numbers, son, how are the numbers? Any new people of importance?

I know, it's hardly respecting one's parent, is it? Another sin on the list.

I picked up the phone upon its third ring. "Dad."

"Drew."

Yeah, but I admired the guy nonetheless. He had the ear of the president, congress, and every major preacher and Christian ministry leader in the United States. And while his clients spouted Scripture, he knew the Word of God was of little value on Capitol Hill, where he tucked himself away with representatives and senators.

At least he called once a week. How many fathers failed to do that once their sons were on their own?

"Happy Birthday, Drew. Did you get my card?"

"Yes. Thanks, Dad."

"Thirty is a big year for a man. No excuses left, full forward from there on out."

"Yes, I believe you're right. So will you be coming down sometime soon?"

I always fell into the formal tones of my father.

He remained silent, for he knew I already knew the answer so why ask a worthless question? It was his way, my father, of reprimanding me for being foolish. He'd always been that way. I'd come home from school with a new idea. If he didn't agree, he said nothing. If he didn't like my clothing, he'd drip a silent stare down my frame.

No wonder my mother committed suicide.

How's that for a confession? Nobody in the world knows this but my father and myself. And now you.

"So are you traveling this week, Dad?"

"Yes. To Lynchburg, Virginia Beach, and then out to the Springs."

"The big three."

"I've planned a new strategy. You won't recognize things in a decade. It all hinges on the gays. They should have never opened up this marriage can of worms. I think we can use it to the hilt."

The man's nerves would bong like a gong if you struck them with a tire iron.

"Won't that bring up other marriage issues that people don't want to think about?"

"You're talking about divorce?"

"Yes."

"Well, that's a separate issue."

The last thing my father wanted was for any of his candidates' supporters to think about sanctity in marriage across the board. My father understood that people used votes to express a morality their lives didn't mirror. They count on hypocrisy in politics.

Outside the window snow fell, and I said I had to go. I'd never cut my father off before. But I couldn't listen to one more word.

Twelve noon and all is well. I lean over and grab the bottle of gin beside the bed. There's a bullet hole in my nightstand. A bullet hole. What's next? Roaches? A severed head?

I take a sip.

The phone rings. Gotta be a wrong number, but might as well get it.

I reach over.

"Is Drew Parrish there?"

"Yes, I'm Drew."

The woman hangs up.

I feel almost scalded.

So familiar. I give my ear a good rubbing with my index finger. Can't place the voice.

And how did she know who I was and where I was? I thought I was pretty good at covering my tracks.

TWO

No kids I ever knew pictured themselves being sideshow freaks someday. I didn't either.

I pack away my costume, folding it in tissue paper and laying it gently into a shallow plastic tub. The sequins wink in the illumination from the hood light over the stove where a pot of chicken and dumplings simmers, almost ready. Atop the gown I lay the iguana green evening gloves.

Lella watches as I do the same to her costume. "Valentine, you surely pack more neatly than anybody I've ever seen, even my mother, God bless and rest her, and that is truly saying something." The dinette made into a bed, Lella lies with her head propped on two decorative pillows.

A cold snap woke us up this morning.

"I'm glad the last show is done, Lell."

We'll get on the road this afternoon, and then Mount Oak, here we come. I hate Mount Oak, but that's where Blaze lives, and Lella loves staying at Blaze's during the off-season.

A knock shudders the door to my truck camper in which I've traveled with Roland's Wayfaring Marvels and Oddities for the last four seasons. We're a freak show, or sideshow if folks prefer. Most prefer sideshow and I don't blame them. I'm off base calling us freaks, but I can't help it. I look at myself in the mirror and I see a freak and that's all I see, all I'll ever see.

"It's Roland. That's definitely his knock." Lella.

I get the door. Lella can't. She's our legless-armless woman. She's not a freak. She's disabled but has been doing this for so long, the thought of getting government assistance hasn't occurred to her, and I'm not about to clue her in.

"Hey, Roland. Come on in. You're in time for grub. As usual."

"I could smell it all the way in my own trailer! Smells like chicken."

"Chicken and dumplings!" Lella announces.

"It's not bouillabaisse or anything."

Roland, dressed in his usual jeans, flannel shirt, and quilted jacket of completely non-coordinating plaids moves Lella over a bit and sits down on the end of the bed. "The circus is already gone."

"I figured. Those guys are good."

Sometimes we set up our own circus tent for smaller venues like county fairs and carnivals. Sometimes, like here in Omaha, we join with Max's Magical Circus, setting up along the midway, our acts leading folks into the tent to view Max's offerings. Mixed in with the usual circus fair, the magic acts keep folks gasping. Little do they know how many people can actually swallow a sword.

"Did Buddy leave?" Lella asks with a shake to her voice.

Max has the requisite clowns too. Including Buddy. Buddy's been eighty-sixed from our campsite.

"Yeah." Roland rubs a hand over a short, gray crew cut. "Yeah, thank heavens. What a jerk."

"How somebody that mean can be so funny in front of a crowd is beyond me, it truly is." Lella closes her eyes. "I mean it's one thing to be gawked at by the crowd as they file past us and get the occasional insult, but from one of our own?"

"He's not one of us." Roland. "Not even close."

I give the stew a final stir. "No, he's not one of us. Just think,

Lell, in a few years we can leave all this behind." I pull three bowls down from the small cupboard over the small sink in the small kitchen.

Hey, it's home.

Roland holds his heart. "I know you two girls can't be on the road forever, but at least have the heart not to talk about your end game with me around."

I slide a ladle out of the drawer. "You'll be fine without Lizard Woman and The Human Cocoon. Besides, the days of our kind of attraction have come and gone."

"People are curious. They're always gonna look."

"We cause discomfort now, the way we remind people that life sometimes isn't perfect. People years ago understood all that."

Lella and I have this conversation all the time. I guess we think if we talk about it enough, some vibes will go out to the general public that we're glad they look at us. We need the work. We understand.

Roland nods. "That's right. Too bad you girls aren't like Clifford. I'd have you around for a good long time."

I hand Roland a bowl of stew. "I think he enjoys it a little too much."

"Oh, but Clifford's a dear!" Lella.

Clifford's our Human Blockhead. I swear he'd perform his act in the middle of McDonald's if they'd let him. Lella's right, though. He's a good guy. He's fixed my truck a few times and always changes the oil for me.

I feed Lella her stew while Roland eats his. It was a good season. Nice weather a lot of the time, no highway accidents or mishaps, and lots of melt-in-your-mouth funnel cake.

"You make a lot of money this year, Roland?" I ask.

"It wasn't the best year. But it wasn't even close to being the worst."

Roland pays us well. I've got no complaints there. And he's doing all right himself. Maybe he's got plans he's cooking up too.

He finishes his chicken and dumplings and sets the bowl in my sink. "We'll head 'em on out in about an hour."

"Reginald packed and ready?" I ask.

"Yep. Both heads and all six legs."

Reginald's one of Roland's crazy stuffed animal oddities. He has his own platform. The other exhibits include a giant toad, a 600-pound squid, and Henrietta, the four-legged duck. Okay, Henrietta is still alive.

"You all need help packing up?" he asks.

"We'll be ready."

"Lell? You gonna ride with Valentine?"

"Surely I will. We love playing that license tag game, don't we, Valentine?"

"We sure do."

He lays a hand on the doorknob. "Okay. Rick'll just pull your trailer without you."

"Give Rick a thousand thanks."

A little over an hour later, the meal cleaned up and put away, Lella, having thanked me a hundred times for feeding her, sits on her donut, strapped in the passenger seat of the truck. We pull onto I-80 south of Omaha. Another season over. Another year closer to a little house near the water. I always picture yellow siding with sherbet colors for the trim.

"So, Lella, where do you want to live someday?"

"Well, I do know you'd like to live on the water."

"I like the sound of the surf."

"I do as well. It's going to be expensive if we settle right on the beach. But surely there's still a patch of undeveloped shoreline we can find on the cheap."

"I'm hoping. I'm going to make more jewelry this winter than ever before, Lella. We'll get there. You and me. Five years . . . seven years, tops."

How many times we've had this conversation? I have no idea.

We drive for another hour without speaking much. The road tumbles beneath the wheels of my dark green truck, and I put in Lella's favorite CDs. George Winston, John Tesh, and some other haunting solo pianists.

"Valentine, I need to ask you a serious question, if you don't mind."

"Go ahead, Lell."

"Why do you want to live your dream with me in tow? I'm so much work. Feeding me, taking me to the bathroom all the time. I'll just tie you down."

"You're my friend, Lella. And who wants to live alone? My face already isolates me. We need each other."

I glance to the side and I'm not surprised a tear falls down Lella's cheek. She waits until it makes it to her jaw, leans her head over, and wipes it off with her shoulder. "I'd like five minutes with the woman who burned you, Valentine. Surely, I would."

I fail to remind her she has no arms or legs. But I guess with a heart the size of Lella's you can get along without them.

I lean out my bedroom window despite the chilly morning.

We winter in the town of Mount Oak because that's where Roland grew up. His sister Blaze owns this huge, crumbling white house here in town, on those fabled "other side of the tracks." It's not literally on the other side of the tracks—the Chessie lines run a couple of blocks south of here. This used to be a nice area a century ago, but now, well, this house looks like a boarding-house for the bedraggled and the slightly stunned, a place where people end up after they've reached their pinnacle and come back down. The shutters are painted a dark green, and the shrubbery hugs the stone foundations and the lattice under the square front porch.

I live in the back room on the third floor. Used to be a sun porch. I'm flooded with light early in the morning, which is okay. I've always been an early riser. A night owl too.

The nights feel cold with all the drafty windows on three sides. The one brick wall somebody painted black. That wasn't nice.

Unfortunately winter gives me more time to smoke, and I'm up to two packs a day.

Blaze calls up the steps. "Valentine! Are you smoking out that window again?"

"Sorry!" I grind out my smoke in the ashtray on the window-sill and shut the window.

Rick the contortionist enters my bedroom, sits down on the desk chair, and holds out a magazine. He's about 120 pounds, long-legged, short-waisted, narrow-hipped, and his ice blue eyes tell you he's the kind of guy who can keep a secret.

It's a body modification magazine. Piercings, tattoos, and whatnots. "Look, Val." He points to a picture of some weirdo with a forked tongue.

And I'm the freak?

I sit on my bed and he hands me the magazine. "What do you think? It would make the Lizard Woman angle complete."

"It's bad enough that I look like a reptile with my burnt face, Rick, I sure don't need to look like an evil reptile. This guy looks satanic."

"Sorry, Val. I just thought maybe you'd be interested." He gingerly lifts the magazine from my hands.

"I am still human you know, Rick. Forked tongues are fine on lizards, but I'm not really a lizard, remember?"

"Sorry, Valentine." He presses a hand down on his dirty-blond hair and closes his eyes.

"Just like you're not really made of dough, like you're not really a pretzel. Got it?"

"Sorry, Valentine. I'm really sorry."

He slinks off, feet splayed outward, a little like Gumby, only with pockets. He sinks his hands in them. I feel bad, but you have to make some people remember you're a human being. It's an occupational hazard, I suppose.

"I just didn't think I'd have to do that with Rick," I say to Lella after telling her all about it as I brush her auburn hair back into a high ponytail. Lella is stunning. I've never seen anyone prettier.

"Valentine, were you nice to him?"

"Not really."

"Be gentle with his heart. Even a three-year-old could see that Rick is awfully fond of you."

"Which leads me to believe he stretches his optic nerves out of shape as well."

"Oh, Valentine!" But Lella laughs.

I finish her hair, pat on some light makeup, and dress her in a yellow fleece top and a pair of sweatpants I cut off and sewed across the bottom. "I'll go get dressed and then bring you down for some breakfast."

"I'm not at all hungry yet. Would you mind just turning on the TV? Robert Schuller is on soon. I dearly love that man."

"Lella, you and your TV preachers."

"Now, Valentine, don't begrudge me my pastors."

I turn on the TV and find the right channel. "He looks like a leprechaun."

She just laughs.

"They all look like leprechauns."

"Oh, Valentine, that simply isn't true. I can think of at least two that look like trolls."

I back into the hallway, leaving her door open.

Blaze calls up two flights of stairs. She's that loud. "I'm going to church! You want to come?"

"Yeah right!"

"Just figured I'd ask!"

"I'll make dinner tonight!"

"Thanks!"

I watch her back her station wagon out of view.

Lighting a cigarette, I head to the bathroom. It's a cramped space under the attic stairs in the hallway. The door's in my room, thus making it my own commode. It's a good thing, having my own commode. Just before entering the glorified closet, I start up iTunes on my laptop and the tones of my favorite song enter the quiet space beneath the steps.

"Embrace me, my sweet embraceable you."

Lady Day, sliding up and down the notes, swings the words in the gentle circles of a parent grasping the hands of her toddler and twirling around like the swing ride at the fair.

I grab a pot of Ponds and look in the mirror. Imagine a purpled-red alligator purse. I have hardly any lips left, except on the left side. My skin is dry. I rub in the moisturizing cream, sighing with a small relief.

It's too bad I didn't have insurance when it all went down.

After I dress I head down for breakfast. I'd like to detail a quaint B&B or farmhouse meal, but I'd be lying. Breakfast at Blaze's table consists of a gallon of milk, a box of shredded wheat—the big biscuits you break up with your fingers—and a pot of coffee.

She doesn't mind if we use her kitchen as long as we clean up the mess and whatever you do, don't leave the metal cabinets open. I don't feel like cooking, so I shred up a cereal biscuit, pour on the milk, and let it soak while I fix a cup of coffee. I load in cream and sugar.

I eat all the sugar I can.

It's hard to chew without showing the world or dripping, so hot cereal or sopping shredded wheat, as long as nobody's around to watch me drip, works.

I pull a straw from the bag I keep in the second drawer down next to the fridge. I sip my coffee, eat my cereal, and read the Sunday paper, poring over the real estate insert, looking for good ideas. Lella and I will need a rancher. I won't have the strength to carry her up and down the stairs forever.

Four cups of coffee later, a fresh pot almost brewed, the clop of feet vibrates the outside stairs leading to the kitchen—wooden stairs, sixth step a little wonky.

The kitchen door swings open, the curtains on the half window flying out like a dancer's gown. I quickly pull the green scarf from around my neck over my nose to cover my face from the eyes down. You gotta pay to see Lizard Woman.

Blaze, Rick, and some guy I've never seen before butt their way into my Sunday ritual.

Now Blaze should be an overweight redhead wearing too-tight sweaters and floral pedal pushers. But Blaze looks rather funereal. Not after the Morticia Addams fashion, but like a funeral parlor. White skin, white blouses, white legs. Dark hair, dark brows, dark skirts, dark shoes, because funeral parlors are almost always black and white, and is there some kind of code about that, some kind of association morticians belong to that tells them how to paint their establishments?

Blaze works down at the local life insurance company, reminding us further of our own mortality and that accidents can happen. As if we'd somehow missed that.

She sets down her purse. "What a gathering!" Blaze is a Jesus freak, which is probably why she relates to us. She's been going to a new church. "Sit down at the table with Valentine, Gus. Is there more coffee, or did you finish it up?"

"There's more."

Rick pulls out a chair for the guest who takes off a leather jacket that goes perfectly with his gray biker beard. Although it does looked combed. He smoothes a faded red T-shirt. He adjusts a pair of glasses with lenses so thick his eyes look like they're sitting behind him in the next room. Graying dreadlocks hang halfway down his back, and heavy, stainless steel hoops pull down his earlobes. And tattoos . . . everywhere.

"You vying for a spot as the tattooed man?" I ask, pointing to his arms covered with intricately patterned tattoo sleeves. Not the usual skulls and naked bimbos for this guy. Swirls of flowers and vines on the right with a couple of woodland creatures peeking out. Kelp in a current and a rainbow assortment of fish on the left.

He smiles. Shy. "No. Just like tattoos, I guess."

His voice is husky and scratched, higher pitched in a damaged way. He either smoked his voice away or something else took it. It's pleasant though, nonthreatening, even if it is hard to hear. His build is a little husky too.

"How come you went so pretty?"

"Reminds me of beauty."

I look away, pick up my coffee. "Oh. Right."

He rushes in. "Because beauty, real beauty, is usually hidden, right? It's like the animals and the fish. They're looking out, kinda shy, right, from their hiding spots?"

"Yeah, I can see that."

Blaze picks up the coffeepot. "That's what I love about human oddities. Same thing."

The man reddens.

Rick gets a couple of mugs down off the shelf over the stained porcelain sink. "So this is Augustine, Valentine. A good friend."

"Then why hasn't he been here sooner?"

"Blaze just now invited me." Augustine shakes my hand. "Valentine. There's a name you don't hear often. Not that I can talk."

"You don't look like a saint to me," I say.

"You know of Saint Augustine?"

"Nah, not really. Just the name."

Rick pours the fresh pot of coffee into the mugs. "He was a good guy. A real hellion in his younger days. I can relate."

I set the sugar bowl on the table. "Yeah, I'll bet, Rick. If, oh, say, staying out after midnight on a school night can be considered raising hell."

"I'm guilty of a little of that." Augustine. "In my own way."

"Me too," Blaze joins in.

"Not Valentine!" Rick raises his hands. "Clean as a whistle."

"Yeah. But you'd kinda expect that, looking as I do."

"Hey, none of that around this house." Blaze opens the refrigerator door. "So Augustine's our pastor."

She's got to be kidding.

"Do the neck tattoos hurt more?"

"Yeah. Kind of a tender spot." Augustine sits right around the corner of the table from me.

Blaze turns around with a bowl of eggs. "Hard-boiled. Egg salad for lunch. What are you making for dinner, Valentine?"

"Pot roast."

"So he's a pastor. You hear that, Valentine?" Blaze.

I roll my eyes. "I heard. I gotta have a smoke."

Augustine hops to his feet. "I'll join you."

"You smoke?"

"Used to. I just like smelling the secondhand smoke now."

"You're an odd bird."

Blaze begins peeling an egg. "Take it out on the porch, please."

"Yeah, yeah. Hang on. Let me put some real clothes on."

I hurry back up to my room. Yanking open my suitcase, I

decide to go for warmth. With the snow falling outside, a wet November snow, the kind with pillowy flakes, I don't have many options. A pair of jeans, my fleece-lined moccasins, and a sweatshirt from Oxford will do.

Augustine follows me out onto the screened porch off the dining room at the back of the house. "You go to Oxford?"

"Yeah, right. Thrift store." I light up my smoke. "This has got to be quick. I'm going to have to go up and get Lella soon."

"Blaze has mentioned her."

"Pretty weird for you visiting the freak house, huh?" He winces. "You known Blaze long?"

"Just this summer."

"Rick?"

"Met him last winter. He's a good guy."

"You know, he really is." I light my smoke, turning away from him so he can't see me as I lift the scarf I tied under my eyes. "He's not a total freak though, you know?"

"I guess not. He feels like one though. Does that count?"

"You asking that for Rick or for yourself?" I mean, look at the guy. He's so weird!

"You're pretty quick, aren't you?"

"No. It doesn't count. You made yourself look that way. Take Lella. She was born like she was."

"What about you?"

"This woman burned my face. I was dating her ex-boyfriend and she wanted some revenge."

"You're kidding!"

"Yeah. Right here in America. So, technically, I'm not a born freak, I'm a made freak too." I turn away and inhale. "Just made by somebody other than me."

"No kidding. Man."

"Tell me about it. It puts me in a unique position."

"How long ago?"

"Too long."

"How long until the pain was gone?"

"Months and months. I still get twitches of pain every so often. Nerve damage. I couldn't get to a hospital right away so it ate down way too far. I'm lucky I can even see. I guess I should be thankful."

He breathes in my smoke and closes his eyes for a second or two. "You don't have to play that thankful game with me."

"I thought you said you were a preacher."

He shakes his head. "That's what the neighborhood calls me. I just hang around is all. They expect some kind of 'message'"— he does the quotation thingee with his fingers—"each Sunday, so I speak a little something, which they can barely hear anyway with my voice the way it is."

"Huh."

He breathes in deeply through his nose. "It is what it is, right?"

"Guess so. That's what I say about my situation. It is what it is. What happened to your voice anyway?"

"Motorcycle accident. Bad tracheotomy at the roadside. Destroyed my vocal chords." I inhale on my cigarette. "So what made you go on the road with Roland?"

"No place else to go."

"Parents?"

"Gone."

"As in dead, gone?"

"Mother's dead and not a minute too soon. Dad lives in Kentucky. Like, who moves to Kentucky? Not me."

"You got that right."

"Your parents?"

He shrugs. "See my mom occasionally. Lost touch with my dad."

"That's too bad."

"Yeah. He's an addict. It happens."

"I'll bet your mother hates your hair."

He laughs. "What woman wants to see her baby boy turned into this?"

He pulls a smile out of me. But it's underneath my scarf and a good thing that is.

After I stub out my cigarette, we climb up two flights to Lella's room. Her face lights up. "Valentine! And who is this with you?"

"This is Augustine. I didn't think you'd mind meeting him."

"Is he going to be our new tattooed man?"

"Nah. He's a preacher from around here."

Her eyes widen. "Oh my! Why, I would never have guessed, no siree! I love preachers! Truly, I was just watching Robert Schuller followed by Adrian Rogers."

"I'm a sort-of preacher. More of a minister if you have to categorize me. Just try to be around for people."

"Isn't that what ministers should do?" she asks.

He pockets his hands. "I guess."

"Do you prepare a sermon each Sunday?"

"Sort of. I just call it a talk. Sermons, well, I guess my stuff doesn't deserve that dignified a title."

"Well, Pastor Augustine, I'm sure you're selling yourself short. I'll bet you're a fine preacher."

Does Lella not hear the guy's voice?

"Can I help you downstairs?" I sit on the edge of her bed. "Egg salad for lunch."

"Wonderful. Augustine, it was delightful meeting you, but would you mind extending us a bit of privacy?"

"Oh. Yeah. Sure. I'll be downstairs."

He shuts the door softly upon his exit.

Lella's face crinkles. "He's a darling, even with all that accoutrement."

I pull down my scarf. "Yeah. Do you need to use the bathroom?"

"Sorry, but I do."

"No prob."

I lift her out of the bed. She only weighs around sixty pounds, and I carry her into my bedroom commode under the stairs. I pull down her sweatpants and set her onto the toilet, leaning her trunk against me, her forehead resting on my shoulder. Lella goes both ways, and I wipe her gently.

"I thank you, Valentine. I do."

"You're my friend, Lella."

"You take good care of me."

"That's what friends are for, right?"

"Valentine, would you mind terribly if I wore my new vest today for Sunday dinner?"

I carry her back into her room. Over her head I pull a yellow T-shirt, then a navy blue vest I decorated with broad yellow rick-rack and a couple of floral appliqués. I don't know why Lella likes vests so much, but she does.

"You look pretty, Lella."

"Thanks to you. Now let me kiss your cheek."

I lean forward and place my purply, scarred cheek near her angel lips. She kisses me softly, then I raise my scarf back over my nose. I circle my arms around her, lift her, and carry her down to the rest of the gang. Of course not everyone stays at Blaze's. Even Roland lives in Florida for the winter.

Clifford, aka The Human Blockhead, pulls out Lella's chair with a flourish. He can drive huge nails up his nose. Looks like the spike is going right into his brain. First time I saw him do it, I sneezed involuntarily. No infections in those sinus cavities, not with all that fresh air circulating all the time. Swallows swords too. Divorced. Pays child support for two kids down in Florida. He'll go and visit them soon. Until then, he's busy writing the Lord's Prayer on a grain of rice.

Darby Joe Brown, aka Rubber Girl. She has that skin without much connective tissue. The woman can actually grab the skin on her upper chest and pull it over her forehead. She does this while belly dancing. She's only twenty and she's taken a shine to Rick. If they have kids, I swear, they'll be like those Stretch Armstrong dolls. I swear it's true. Unfortunately for her, Rick's not interested. But he should be. She's really a cutie with black Snow White hair and glowing hazel eyes. She has the tiniest hands and feet! Her parents are coming to pick her up next week, and she'll head back home to Minnesota for the winter.

Bindy and Mindy are conjoined twins unified by a liver. Or something. Those sisters are the meanest people to ever walk, walk, walk, walk the face of the earth. Though they shuffle along at a snail's pace, nobody's out of their reach. I swear they should give a pair of legs to Lella, but they never would, even if they could, just for spite. Nobody's coming to pick them up, much to everybody else's chagrin.

There are a few more of us, but that's the sum of the gathering today. Jake the fire-eater visits his sister across town on Sundays and works at the bowling alley. Miranda McLeod, another contortionist, works as a clerk at the local department store's music section.

We're a rather low-key group off-season.

"Where'd Augustine go?" I tuck a napkin into Lella's collar.

"He seems like such a lovely person." Lella. "Thank you, Valentine."

Rick reaches for the egg salad. "One of his people came by. Trouble down the street. Maybe an OD. The guy couldn't say."

Lella gasps. "Oh, dear!"

Bindy grabs the bread plate. "Another junkie off the street would do us all good."

"Yepper." Mindy. "That bread looks stale."

Blaze sits down. "That's enough, you two. Now let's thank the Lord for the food. Thank You, Lord. Amen."

Blaze doesn't waste time with peripherals.

I make up a sandwich for Lella: egg salad, a crisp leaf of iceberg lettuce on lightly toasted white bread. She bites down after I lift it to her mouth, chews, then says, "Thank you, Valentine."

Bindy bites down on her own sandwich, then shoves the food into the side of her mouth. "Good grief. Do we have to hear your sorry thank-yous after every bite, Lell?"

Lella tosses her ponytail. "Indeed you do. Every single bite."

"You really don't have to, Lell."

"Why not? I'm grateful for each one."

"This is going to be a long winter." Mindy.

Blaze screws off the top of the mustard. "For once I agree with the woman."

Again I hold the sandwich up to Lella's lips, and again she bites and thanks me after she swallows.

I mash my eggs with a fork, break the bread into tiny bits, and mix it all together with a spoonful of mayo.

"I'm sorry," Lella whispers so nobody will hear. "I'm sorry you can't eat sandwiches, Valentine."

I rub a circle between her shoulder blades and place a potato chip on her tongue.

I call my dad.

He picks up right away and I ease myself down into the quilt on the single bed in my room. "Hey Daddy." I try to speak extra clearly. My pronunciation isn't what it used to be.

"Honey pie! How are you this week? Settled in yet?"

"I haven't unpacked my suitcase, but I'm ready to get back into my winter routine."

"You'll need me to send you supplies."

"Twice as much as last year. I'm going to be a production machine this winter."

"You got it."

My father, a wholesaler of beads and jewelry-making supplies, sells the majority of his wares over the Internet. I not only make jewelry to sell on the road, but on his Web site and on a few other sites that specialize in the artsy/crafty.

"The usual assortment?"

I ask him to load me up a little heavier on the freshwater pearls. "All types. You wouldn't believe how the wire bracelets went. Had a lot of e-mails from brides-to-be requesting if I could do it with pearls and amethysts, garnets and stuff."

"Nice."

"Even made some bridal veil headpieces."

"You don't say? That's great, honey."

"How's Jody?" My dad's new wife. She's exactly his age, same birthday, same year. That's where any similarity ends. He's a foot-and-a-half taller than she is, he's white and she's Vietnamese, he's Pentecostal in a quiet way and she's Episcopalian and proud of it. My dad is a bead-seller who's never made a piece of jewelry in his life, and Jody makes homemade greeting cards. She sends me one every week. Messages including:

You are loved.

Somebody thinks you're special.

It's not the same without you.

Even though I've never been to their home.

"Jody's good. Still praying for that River Jordon healing experience for you. Can't seem to talk sense into her, but Jody's got the best of intentions. She's got her cards into that new-age store sqecial in Lexington. And down at Third Street Coffee. She's been cutting and pasting like a nut."

"How are you feeling?"

"Tired. I got the flu a couple of days ago."

"Well, I may just look like you feel."

"Honey . . ."

"Sorry, Dad."

So we chat about his job, about the crew here at the house, and when will I visit, which, basically, Dad, will be the fabled Twelfth of Never.

Imagine me stopping for gas along the way without Rick to do the pumping.

THREE

◆◆◆◆

DREW: 2002

If there's a smaller room than mine here at the hotel, the occupant must sleep standing up. I'm guessing mine served as a storage closet at one time. To the left of my bed the wooden floor forms a narrow aisle between my single bed and a grid of rough shelving that checkers the wall. Linen storage in the old days, maybe? Cleaning supplies as well? I could use some cleaning supplies. Today I'll find some, and I will scrub this place from floor to ceiling. Maid service is extra.

After that, I'll head out to take care of business: Pay for my night in this room, buy cigarettes, some cheap gin, and a box of cereal. I prefer Count Chocula, but Life will do if it must.

A guy named Hermy rents a room down the hall. Hermy hangs out at the library all the time, forsaking the computer terminals to wander the stacks in search of interesting statistics. He reminds me of a stand-up comic: short, disheveled, with spiky dark hair and brown eyes with bright flecks of gold near the pupil. Painter's pants, long-sleeved T-shirts, and a bomber jacket hide his fair skin along with black Reeboks and a red bandana tied tightly around his neck. He's always licking his lips.

Usually people with nervous ticks drive me nuts.

This morning he catches me in the hallway on my way to the

shower, which for the sake of all humanity I will not describe. "Hey, did you know that 33,183,000 beef cows had calves in 1988?"

I lay my towel on my shoulder. "No kidding."

"I absolutely kid you not! Milk cows? 10,311,000. That's a lot of calves."

"You said it."

"Gotta get to the stacks. You writing today?"

"Yeah." I told him yesterday I was a writer. High respect, low expectation. Good reason for reclusivity. He asked what I was writing and I said a memoir. That took care of that.

"You guys have the life. Want me to look up writers?" He scratches his nose.

"No thanks. I like to keep the mystery alive."

He shakes his head. "Why?"

"Tell you what. I need to know a little something about the best treatment for cigarette burns."

Some of them are looking punky.

"You know it. Gotta have that telling detail."

"Whoa, Hermy. Nice."

He hefts his rucksack over his shoulder and makes for the stairwell. When he opens the door, the smell of urine seeps into the hallway. I literally hold my breath and run for it when I leave this place, which I do every morning at ten for my daily needs. I could stock up, but if I do that, I'll die here.

And I'd much rather die someplace else. I mean, who wouldn't?

Although death by Count Chocula, gin, cigarettes, and disillusionment doesn't sound half bad.

An hour later, supplies bought, including a folding chair, I sit on the boardwalk just down from Ripley's Believe It or Not! Museum. It's mild for December, a salty humidity in the cool breeze, and the beach lies in such desertion it's hard to imagine that in seven months you'll hardly be able to find a spot to set down your towel.

When Thanksgiving came the year Daisy showed up, I did what I always did: told my father I had plans with church people, told the church people I planned to celebrate with my family. Holidays were useless in trying to further the church. It was more effective to leave everybody alone with their families to feel good about the true meaning of life without me getting in the way.

I went camping on the Appalachian Trail. Packed my tent, a single person job, a sleeping bag, some canned beans, dry cereal, water, booze, and cigarettes. I didn't drink much back then, only on camping trips and only by myself. And I only smoked in my apartment, to which I never invited anybody. Except Daisy, later. The testimony to uphold never left my shoulders. I had to keep up appearances, and I didn't mind doing so. All part of it.

You all don't major on the minors like we do, and I like that, Father. Of course we don't have to cross ourselves with holy water and the like, and we're not worried about purgatory. That must be a little like having a rain cloud over your head twenty-four hours a day. On second thought, maybe you do know about heavy expectations.

On my way out of Mount Oak I stopped downstairs in Java Jane's. It wasn't quite what it eventually became, a posh yet whimsical place that catered to moms, students, and artsy types. Back then it looked more like the old general store it used to be. The golden wood emitted a sort of glowing comfort, and I could imagine myself as just a regular guy, sidling up to the counter to get my mail.

"Hey, Al. How's it going today?" I'd ask.

"Not bad, Drew. Not bad at all."

"Give my best to Dorothy."

"Will do."

And nobody would judge me on my diction or my tie. And more importantly, I wouldn't judge anybody else on their diction or their tie.

You priests have it right with your black shirts and collars. Just takes all that personal preening right out of the equation from the start. Then again, it must get a little boring at times, and there's no hiding, is there? No hanging out incognito in a smelly old hotel for you.

I think there's a portion inside all of us that wants a simple, straightforward life where people aren't commodities and we can just be free to love them without putting them into some hierarchy based on their clothing, their speech, their table manners.

Sitting at the table in the bow window, Harlan and Charmaine Hopewell, the celebs of Mount Oak, sipped hot drinks and shared a slice of apple cake. With Harlan's TV ministry thriving on cable systems all across the country and Charmaine singing like an angel at his side, you'd think they could each have had a piece of their own cake. Have you heard of her? When Charmaine sings, something starts to glow all around her and inside of you. My father couldn't stand watching her, but the power she could wield if she wanted to—with her Dove awards and sold-out concerts—he sure appreciated that!

I did too.

We'd met a few times before. Nothing more than hellos and how's-it-going-over-there—at-your-church type stuff, not real conversation. Very friendly. Very cordial. Very in the club. I suspected there was no other way with this pair, highly refreshing at the time, but then, they could afford to be that open and kind. They'd paid their dues years before.

I walked toward their table.

"Drew!" Charmaine called and then turned to Harlan. "Oh, Harlan, it's Drew Parrish, from down at Elysian Heights Church. Remember?"

Harlan wiped his mouth, stood to his feet, and stuck out his hand. "Of course I remember. Well, hey, Drew."

Harlan's toupee is the talk of our town. It just gets bigger and bigger like some sort of reaction in a chemistry class. "Reverend Hopewell, nice to see you. Cold day."

"Same tomorrow. I always did love a cold Thanksgiving Day."

Charmaine nodded. "Over the river and through the woods and all of that."

"I saw your CD in the music store, Mrs. Hopewell. How's it doing?"

"Pretty good. Why don't you have a seat with us after you order? In fact, you just sit down and I'll get you something. What would you like?"

"Just black coffee."

Harlan nodded. "Now that's a real coffee drinker. Good boy."

I actually took it with cream at home, but black puts you on top at the coffee shop.

Charmaine scurried up to the front, her cloud of red hair giving fair warning to anybody in her way. I could have learned a lot from her if I hadn't been so bowled over by her fame, a fame, I admit, that she herself didn't give even a thought to.

Charmaine drank her coffee the way she liked her coffee.

I set the pen and notebook on the boardwalk, light up a smoke, and close my eyes against the noontime sun. We never came here in the winter, and I don't know why not. This beats the crowds of summer hands down. Maybe this would be a good place to start over. A beach ministry. Trade power for cool. It could work.

Rolling up my sleeve, I inspect the slight festering on the circular sores. But I can't seem to stop the burning. I don't know, I should probably ask Hermy to find out why I do this. Tell him it's for research for my writing, that I'm taking a break from my memoir to write a story about a self-mutilator. That seems to be all the rage these days. Only I'm not a teenager. There's the hook.

Instead of lowering the glowing cigarette I reach for my pen. Seagulls pull apart a Burger King bag that blew out of the trash can.

So Charmaine returned with a coffee and set it down. "I got a carry-out cup because you look like you're headed somewhere, and I don't want you to think you have to sit here and while away the day with old Harlan and me."

"Thanks. I'm just headed out of town for the holiday."

"Family?" Harlan forked up some cake.

"Yes."

There you go, Father Brian, another lie. The sins are starting to add up, aren't they? And a willful lie at that. That's got to be a mortal sin.

Charmaine settled herself into her chair. Very slim-figured, almost boyish, zinging with energy and power—maybe not the way I'd come to value power but a sort of tough-skinned quality, a rootedness that wouldn't budge easily. "This is providential because you've come up in conversation around the Hopewell house lately."

"You sure have," Harlan said. "Quite a bit."

"Good stuff, I hope." Dorky card played nicely.

She batted my arm. "Of course, you silly. What's not to like about a nice guy like you?"

Even she was fooled. Good.

Harlan wiped a crumb from his mouth. "Yep. We were talking about needing some new lifeblood on The Port of Peace Hour. You ever watch the show?"

"Sure. Almost every Sunday night."

"You do?" Charmaine's brows rose. "Oh, that's so good!"

Harlan scratched his head, digging deep to get the itch beneath the grid of his wig. You know how rumors go about a small town. I'd heard from several sources that Charmaine tried all the time to get him to ditch the thing, but he refused. I also heard that at least he takes it off in the house now.

Do priests gossip like we do?

My red hair was such a calling card and the women in the congregation seemed to like it. People think redheads are nice for some reason. You have to go out of your way to offend people.

Harlan said, "So, Drew, we were talking about having you come on The Port of Peace Hour at least two or three times a month. We're going to start taping segments on a living room-style set that we'll insert between the preaching segments and Charmaine's musical numbers. Just kind of informal, chatty stuff. We need to give our viewers something new. And we think you're it."

Some of the locals call it The Port O Potty Hour.

"I see. Well, sure. Glad to help."

"See, Harlan? I told you he'd do it." Charmaine leaned forward. "You have that hungry look about you."

It felt like we stood in a tunnel together, just Charmaine and me, the air a chilly knife between us, the bricks glaring white in fluorescent lighting.

Just as I was about to excuse myself, the door to the coffee shop swung open and two women entered to the clanging of Indian bells against the glass and the smell of fresh air and perfume.

Charmaine stood to her feet. "Miss Mildred!"

The older of the two women, both black and stately, turned her head in our direction. She smiled, lifted a hand, and slightly wiggled her fingers. "Charmaine Hopewell. And Reverend Hopewell. How're you doing?"

Harlan stood to his feet, a real gentleman. I stood to mine. "Mildred, this is Drew Parrish, pastor over at Elysian Heights."

"Oh, my, yes! I heard good things about you, Reverend. Good things!"

That day, Mildred gushed over my church and all that had been happening there. She praised the choir and the children's ministries; she lauded our women's Bible studies and our men's groups.

I drank it all in, the last thing I needed in a million years.

But she couldn't have known that. Miss Mildred just encourages people.

◆◆◆

Later that night I head over to the rectory. Father Brian answers. Recognition dawns as I step into the porch light. "Drew?"

"Good memory."

"You okay? Wanna come in?"

"No. I don't know what I want. I was out walking, having a smoke, and I saw the rectory. I don't know. It's late. I shouldn't have bothered you."

"Let me get my jacket. I could use the exercise."

He appears a minute later in a green down jacket, a black skullcap, and a pair of black knit gloves. He looks seventeen. The pressed grey slacks are the only giveaway he's not entirely what he seems.

We head south on Baltimore Avenue, past bars, music stores, and T-shirt shops.

"So what's on your mind?"

"I don't know, just writing all this stuff down is like dragging up a bucketfull of slop, and I haven't begun to reach the dregs."

"Repenting is never easy."

"Don't give me too much credit. I'm at the confession stage. I haven't said I was sorry to anybody."

Father Brian shoves his hands in his jacket pocket. "Okay, so you're confessing, but not repenting."

"That's right."

"Usually the two go together."

"I'm not ready to ask forgiveness."

He nods. "Got it."

We turn on First Street, head toward the beach in silence, and finally step onto the oceanfront porch of The Plim Plaza. Father Brian points to a couple of rocking chairs and we sit watching the frigid breakers on the wide beach in front of us.

"You're pretty hard on yourself. I can tell," the priest says.

"You don't know the half of it."

"You almost done writing things down?"

"No. It's a long story."

"They usually are. If you start at the true beginning that is. So, your congregation. Do they miss you?"

I shrug. "Don't know."

"Did you just pick up and go?"

"Yeah. About a month ago. I mean, I was going through the motions. I'd been doing that for years, actually, but it was finally starting to bother me."

"Conviction of sin will do that."

Well, he doesn't mince words. "I couldn't go through the motions anymore. So I left. Called it a sabbatical."

"It is one. You were right to do that. We all need breaks."

"It's more than just a break."

"What made you finally crack and get out of town?"

"There was a pipe burst in my apartment building, ruined most of my stuff, put me out. Seemed like a sign."

"So it seems. And what of your faith?"

"I don't know."

"That's a good first step."

"I don't know if I believe in the kind of God I preached about anymore. Maybe I never did to begin with. Is that a sin? I just don't know."

"Were you raised in church?"

"Yes."

"Do you remember who you thought God was back when you were a child?"

"My mother taught me about Him. She was the prophetic sort."

He nods. "And your father?"

"My father saw Mom as his chief embarrassment, his cross to bear."

"What of his faith?"

I just shake my head. "He's a complicated man."

"Ah."

"I mean, who are we to judge, right?"

"It's a hard call. On the one hand we are told we will know the followers of Christ by their fruit. On the other hand, only God knows the heart and many shall say, 'Lord, Lord.'"

"Exactly. So what's the answer?"

"I think Jesus said it all when the other disciples grew angered at James and John for asking to sit at His right hand and His left. Do you remember what He said, Drew?"

"'You don't know what you are asking. Can you drink the cup I drink or be baptized with the baptism I am baptized with?'"

He waves a hand. "No, not that part. The next part."

"'To sit at my right or left is not for me to grant. These places belong to those for whom they have been prepared.'"

"In other words, mind your own business. Your father is in God's hands."

"And if you know my father, you'd have to wonder what God thinks He's doing."

◆◆◆

Over on my nightstand a small loaf of bread soaks up the warmth from the lamp, a milky dotted-glass affair. Blessed bread from the rectory. Father Brian sent it home with me. He asked if I had food and I told him about my current diet.

◆◆◆

I said my farewells to the Hopewells and drove for several hours to the Trail. In the dark I pitched my tent, climbed into my sleeping bag, lit a cigarette, and downed a thermos of coffee laced with whisky. Not used to much alcohol, I slept until long after dawn.

Happy Thanksgiving, Drew.

When I awoke, I thought about calling my father, wishing him a Happy Thanksgiving, and telling him about The Port of Peace Hour. *Small potatoes, that show. He'd think that, even though his words would be, "I see."*

You might be tempted to think I'm feeling sorry for myself about having Mr. Freeze for a father. I'm not. I dislike the man. I didn't want to talk about it earlier, Father Brian. I don't want his love or his approval anymore. These days, if he approved of me, I know I'd be doing something desperately wrong. At one time I would have sold my soul to have succeeded in a way that would impress Charles Parrish. Maybe selling one's soul is what it really takes to gain the approval of people like that. Let God be the judge on that one. Not you, Father. Not me.

I remember that morning on the mountainside, looking out over a hazy vista of the Shenandoah River. A few tendrils of smoke strung their way up into the atmosphere from down below. I read a book about church growth that weekend and outlined a plan to bring in congregants from other churches because I knew we weren't the type of church to make converts. Since my people couldn't procreate that fast, we relied on the whole grass-is-greener mentality. Sure, we'd tried to institute Friendship Evangelism but only a few people showed up for the first meeting. I only wanted to buy more pews and fill them. And having done that, do it all some more, bump out walls, build more buildings. If I'd had a better motive maybe—providing a place of heal- ing for those who'd been in abusive churches, reaching out to those in need—I might have some excuse. But I didn't care why they came, I just wanted more of them.

Covetousness? Yes, I guess it was.

We needed to break ground on an activities building, I realized. That would open up even greater opportunities for our congregation to recreate and fellowship.

At least Ed Phelps was into discipleship and I let him have free rein. People needed to know that as soon as their lives calmed down and they stopped running their kids around to play dates and every kind of lesson in the world, they could always do the work of the gospel. But before they came to that conclusion, I needed money, and they had loads of it sitting alongside piles of guilt. It was the perfect combination.

I realized politics was one of the keys as well. A surefire way, judging from some of the big-time ministries, to build up a following. I'd start showing up at political functions, form a committee for Christian legislation at church, take the bull by the horns.

And I did just that. It was almost as effective as the coffee bar.

You see, people like being frightened in large groups. It legitimizes the fear.

The phone rings. After the eighth ring I pick it up.

"Drew?"

"Yes, this is Drew."

"The Lord is calling you."

My first thought, *He is? On this phone?*

"Who is this?"

That voice. Come on, Drew, think.

"I'm praying for you. You are at a crossroads."

The line goes dead.

FOUR

◆◆◆◆

Valentine: 2008

I lift Lella up from underneath her arms and place her in the stroller for one of our midnight walks. Lella hates wheelchairs. "They make me feel so vulnerable and loosey-goosey."

The stroller hugs her more securely and—just in case somebody comes upon us on our walk—makes for less stares. Thankfully, the only people who see us are usually blinded by the bottle. She looks like a child with her feet tucked up beneath her. Lella always asks me to wrap her up in several blankets, her sweet face peering out, eyes bright and hopeful.

Of course *born* without arms and legs, Lella hasn't experienced life any differently.

"I don't know what I'd have done without you tonight, Val."

"I'm sorry I didn't hear you call sooner."

"You're my angel."

Lella got sick earlier and threw up on herself. I feel so sorry for her when that happens. She has a delicate stomach, and sometimes Blaze lives up to her name when she cooks.

"So where are we walking tonight?" I buckle the seatbelt over her waist.

"How about over to the newer section of town? I've heard

◆◆ 49 ◆◆

about Elysian Heights Church's new education building. Rick says it even has a swimming pool and exercise room!"

"All right." I grab the handle and begin to push. "I don't trust that church though, Lella. I saw right through all the feel-good stuff and the politics, even though my mother swore by the ministry after that pastor went on the air with that clown of a woman by his side. She got scarier and scarier looking every second. Those two should have taken a lesson from *The Port of Peace Hour* and Charmaine Hopewell—there's a woman who knows how to do TV. I admire her, that's for sure."

"Oh, me too! Charmaine's a dandy, isn't she? I can't believe you've never introduced us."

"I just see her out on my dock, Lell. I don't have the heart to ask her back to the house."

Sometimes I head out to Lake Coventry in the middle of the night and sit on the same dock each time. I don't know who owns the house, but I've come to think of the dock as mine.

We navigate Mount Oak, first walking by Love's Rib Room. "Do you like ribs, Lella?"

"Oh my, yes."

"I'll get Rick to get you some."

Maybe I can't chew the meat, but I can sure lick the sauce off my fingers after holding them up to Lella's mouth.

"I'd love to go swimming sometime." Lella's words puff in the chilly darkness, backlit by a haloed streetlight. "My mom and dad used to take me when I was a little child. They'd hold their hands underneath me and let me float, right there atop the water. It felt just delightful. Maybe that church would let us come in late some night."

"I doubt it. Rules are rules are rules at places like that. They'd have to go through three committees and ask somebody to stay up late and it would just be too much trouble."

"Valentine, I wish you'd allow yourself a little belief in humanity."

"Lell, if we were all like you, that might actually be a possibility."

"Now that surely isn't true."

Next we cross the town square. The moon hovers still and bursting over the silent grass.

"Walking in sunshine is so overrated, isn't it, Lell?"

Lella laughs.

The bandstand rests in the intersection of four pathways diagonally crisscrossing the park. Lella hums "Seventy-six Trombones."

I roll my gripped hands on the stroller handle. "I always think of that song when I see a bandstand too."

"Would you like to watch a movie when we get home?"

"Sure. Rick brought *Meet Me in St. Louis* from the library."

We pass Java Jane's.

"I remember the days I'd go into coffee shops thinking I'd always be going into coffee shops, sitting down and sipping a hot drink. Even as a teenager I liked the stuff." I point into the coffee shop window, the large pane of glass surrounded by pink twinkle lights. "Isn't it odd, Lella, how the mundane is so spectacular for us?"

"And conversely, how the spectacular—us oddities, the glittery circus life—has become so mundane?"

"Right."

She turns her head and tries to look at me. "You'll never feel at home among us, Valentine, will you?"

"I don't know how I can. You were born the way you are. Others make themselves the way they are. My situation leaves me in a peculiar place." At least for Roland's shows. I think of Mary Anne Bevans, an old-time freak who got elephantitis as an adult. That happened to a lot of people back in the day.

"Surely we're your friends. And when a person starts to live for their friends, the people they love, and not worry quite so much about the people who laugh or look away in disgust, they find a home." She cranes her neck, trying to look back at me. "Is it all still an embarrassment?"

I stop the stroller and kneel down next to my friend. "Yes. But I wish it wasn't."

"I'm sorry. It's something you'll have to come to grips with eventually. We all do."

"I try not to think about it."

"Do you ever just sit and think, Valentine?"

"Not really. I get angry if I do."

"I sit and think all the time."

Yes, Lella, sweet Lella, I know.

She laughs her musical laugh. "I suppose you might think it's because I have nothing else to do! But . . . I've come to a lot of conclusions in the silence."

"Like what?" I stand up and we continue walking along the sidewalk.

"Well, mostly that the silence isn't so bad after all. I know you feel sorry for me, Valentine, but it isn't so bad. And when it's not silent, you're there, and the others are too. I go from one sweetness to the next, and maybe that's better than having arms and legs."

I round the corner by Love's Rib Room. "What about Mindy and Bindy? They're not exactly sweet."

"Oh dear me, no! I can't stand those two."

We window shop on our midnight walks. As we loiter in front of one of those trendy new paper stores, lots of dots and lines and pinks and greens and friendly flowers splashed across the surfaces, a light snow begins to fall on my scarves and Lella's blankets.

"You look like a Russian peasant in the snow, Valentine. How lovely."

"I'm not sure if I should take that as a compliment."

"The Russians have the best fairy tales."

"So there we have it."

"Precisely."

Twenty minutes later we stand before the edifice of Elysian Heights Family Ministry Center, lots of blondish brick, large, single-paned windows in black metal frames and nothing to let you know it isn't a school or, say, a social services building, except the word *Ministry* in plain brown letters near the door. Cabbage-like perennials dot the gardens.

"Maybe we can ask them about the swimming, Lell. You want me to get Blaze to find out?"

"Only if you'll swim with me."

"Oh, Lell. Nice try. Let's walk over to Clearview Street. They have the prettiest little houses."

"Like ours someday?"

"Hopefully."

The week before Thanksgiving I'm plotting to get my hands on the holiday meal.

"Come on Blaze, you can't cook! And you know I can. Why in the world do you want to spend all that time doing something you hate and doing a lousy job of it when I can give you a shopping list, send you off to the IGA, and we'll have ourselves a meal like you won't believe?"

"I don't know. I've got that great stuffing recipe, and it's easy as pie. Just a few boxes of Stove Top, some cream of chicken soup—"

Unbelievable. "Come on, let me do it." She places her hands on her black-clothed hips. "Hey, nice red nails there, girl. And you're wearing lipstick too. You got a date, Blaze?"

"Naw!" She waves one hand. "There's a little girl down at Gus's place. She loves painting my fingernails after I help her with her homework."

"Gus?"

"Augustine, Val. Good grief."

"What's his deal anyway?"

She shrugs. "Don't know if he has a deal, per se. Showed up in town one day. Said he got out of a monastery or something."

"A monastery? No way."

"Or some sort of missions training program. I don't know, Val. Why don't you ask him if you're so interested?"

"I didn't say I was interested. Don't go assuming a bunch of interest on my part, Blaze. You're the one who brought him up, not me."

"So if I say yes to Thanksgiving dinner will you shut up?"

"You got it."

"Then yes."

I head upstairs to Lella. "Wanna help me make the list for Thanksgiving dinner?" Lella's eyes widen. "Never thought I'd win that one, did you?"

"I'm surely glad you did."

And Lella dreams out loud of a time long ago, before her parents died, when they'd gather in their trailer and cook up a feast for all the circus people. They'd line a picnic table outside with a paper cloth and all the food. She named each dish and described its taste exactly. In her bedroom the walls close in snugly around us, and I can smell the warm heat of the stove, feel the steam from the turkey, taste the butter melting on the mashed potatoes.

"So you want mashed potatoes?" I ask.

"Oh, yes. And sweet potatoes and stuffing. Oh, Valentine, you'll be able to eat until you're stuffed! Won't that be glorious?" She smiles. "What would you think of a cup of tea right now?"

"I'll go make us some. Let me put on my scarf."

"Why, Val? It's just us."

"Blaze brings home too many people—you never know who's

going to show up. I sure don't want that Augustine weirdo seeing this face. Unless he's paid his five bucks like everyone else."

"You know, it's okay to be happy right now, Valentine. You're going to cook us all a lovely dinner for Thanksgiving. You don't always have to be so crotchety."

"You're right, Lell. But I kinda like the crotchety me. It fits right now."

"Suit yourself." She laughs.

The next morning somebody knocks at the back door. Looking out the kitchen window, I tie a blue scarf just above my nose and rise to my feet. Three people wait outside. That Augustine man, a woman with a red cloud of hair—yes, it's Charmaine Hopewell—and another woman with short brown hair—a little chubby I think, judging by the contours of her face. She's pretty, though.

"Hang on!" I carefully swig the chilled dregs of my coffee, set my mug in the dishwasher, and plan a quick exit.

I yank open the door. "Hey, come on in, I'll get Blaze."

The three people file inside.

"Coffee's fresh. Mugs are on the shelf. Help yourself." I head for the doorway.

"Wait!" Augustine steps forward. "We came to see you."

"What?" I turn back around. "Now why is that?"

He grabs the coffeepot and heads for the shelf. "We heard you were cooking up a big Thanksgiving dinner for the household."

"And?"

"First of all, let me introduce these ladies."

I cross my arms and lean against the doorjamb.

"This is Charmaine Hopewell." He touches her shoulder lightly.

"We've met. Hey, Charmaine."

"Really?" Augustine asks.

Charmaine gives a little wave. "You know me, Gus. I don't let any grass grow under my feet. I met her on one of my midnight ramblings when I just couldn't sleep."

"And this is Poppy Fraser."

"Hi, Val. Great to meet you," Poppy says. She's obviously not from around here. She speaks too northern.

"Hello. Nice to meet you. Thanks for coming." I look at Augustine. "So what does our Thanksgiving dinner have to do with you and these women?"

"I'm a lousy cook. So is Charmaine. And Poppy needs a little help."

"Doing what?"

"Her church is putting on a big Thanksgiving dinner downtown. I heard about your dinner here and thought you might make some extra." He pulls down some mugs and hands them to Poppy, who sets them on the kitchen table.

"Doesn't she have lots of church ladies to help her cook?"

"Yeah, I do. Not to mention that you probably don't have time." She turns to Augustine. "I told you she wouldn't buy it."

I point to Charmaine Hopewell. "What does she have to do with it?"

Charmaine laughs and winks at me. Augustine pours the coffee and lets Poppy explain.

"Charmaine just likes to be in on the action, whenever and wherever she finds it. She happened to be at Java Jane's with me when Augustine came in with his bright idea."

"Ouch, Popp." Augustine hands the ladies their coffee.

"Thanks, Gus." She cradles the mug in both hands. "He told us about your burns and all, and I said I didn't think getting you in on the dinner was such a good idea."

"Why? Because I'll make people lose their appetites?"

"Oh, shoot no. Because I've never seen you around, so I figured you were reclusive about it."

"You're right." I turn to Augustine. "Nice try, but no deal. Spooning up sweet potatoes on the street isn't in my usual routine. You could learn a lot from her."

"Yeah, you're right. Plus that would be a lot of cooking for you."

"Oh, I can cook for crowds."

"It's okay. Don't worry about it." He lifts his drink and takes a sip, then points a finger at me. "I'm not done with you, though. This was more of a fact-finding mission anyway."

"What? As in, you want to see if I'll reach out, go outside of my comfort zone sort of thing?"

"Exactly."

Charmaine laughs. "Augustine, honey, that was the lamest thing I ever heard." She looks at me. "Valentine, forgive the man. His intentions are pure."

"Yeah, okay. He does seem like an innocent despite all those tats."

Augustine hoots a laugh. "Will you at least sit down with us and have a cup of coffee?"

"Oh, I get it. If you had come in here just asking for a nice chatty coffee time, I would have balked. But in the face of cooking and serving up Thanksgiving dinner to the less fortunate, a cup of coffee seems like nothing."

He nods.

"You want to get me in with some other women so I'll make friends, be sociable. I'm your new project. Is that it?"

Poppy sits in a chair. "Hey, Gus, you're smarter than I thought."

Augustine pulls out a chair for me. Oh, what the heck. It's Charmaine Hopewell after all. And this Poppy person seems okay.

"Wait!" I say. "Let me get Lella. Charmaine, she's always wanted to meet you." I turn to Poppy. "She's our legless-armless woman."

Poppy gasps. "Was she born that way? Or was it an accident?"

"Born that way. Don't worry, it's not contagious."

Augustine winces.

A few minutes later I carry Lella down in my arms, her eyes closed at my request. Augustine's already brought in her special chair from the dining room. I gently settle her atop the donut and push her close to the table, then arrange her prosthetic arms, quite useless in function but not so in form.

"Okay, Lella, now who were you just saying you'd like to meet? Last night on our walk? Open your eyes."

She does. "Charmaine Hopewell! Oh, my!" She'd raise a hand to her breast if she had one. "Oh, Valentine, did you arrange this?"

"Nah. Augustine showed up uninvited with Charmaine. And Poppy Fraser here. Folks, this is Lella."

Lella glows as the greetings fly back and forth.

"I dearly love your show!" Lella. "And I've got several of your albums."

"That's wonderful, honey. Thanks so much!" Charmaine.

"And how's your husband, Harlan?"

"Still preaching up a storm at church and on the television. That man!"

Earlier in the day I'd scraped back Lella's hair into her signature ponytail, and she asked me to make her up in a more Audrey Hepburn fashion, with slightly Egyptian eyes and red lips. She is easily the prettiest person in the room.

Charmaine takes to Lella right away, answering all of her questions about *The Port of Peace Hour* and her gospel concerts. So Poppy asks me about the road, what it's like to be in a sideshow these days.

"Well, folks still enjoy it. We're pretty politically incorrect now as you could probably guess. But who can resist a human blockhead or a fire eater?"

"Do you mind telling me how you came to be Lizard Woman?"

"Physically?"

She nods.

"I was in India and somebody mistook me for a relative that had brought dishonor to the family and threw acid on me."

Augustine jerks his head up. "But didn't you say—"

"Yeah, it was horrible. We all couldn't believe it. And so I ended up here."

He pushes his glasses up further on his nose.

Poppy asks, "What about your parents? Didn't your mother want to take care of you? Why did you end up on the road?"

"My mother couldn't stand to look at me anymore. And that was fine with me. We never got along anyway. My father isn't the strongest guy in the world, and I didn't want to burden him. I was just as glad to find Roland's sideshow, believe it or not."

Charmaine hoots a "Well, praise the Lord!" at something Lella says. "I swear I haven't felt this good about life in several years." She lays a hand on Lella's shoulder. "I'm always battling the dark monster of depression."

"Oh, no!" Lella. "I'm so sorry for you!"

I say, "I know a thing or two about that."

Poppy shuffles in her seat. "Charmaine takes care of her paranoid schizophrenic mother who deserted her when she was eleven years old."

"Oh. Right."

"Poppy!" Charmaine hits her upper arm. "Valentine's got enough on her already."

I tap the table. "So honestly, Poppy. You need help with the food? I can make something here at Blaze's, I suppose. Like I said, I can cook for a crowd. What's a little more?"

"Valentine makes the best mashed potato casserole you've ever tasted!" Lella licks her lips. "She whips potatoes with cream cheese, sour cream, and softened butter, then places it in a casserole and pours melted butter over it."

I don't notice Rick standing at the door until he says, "And then she bakes it in the oven and it gets all brown around the edges. Mmm!" He rubs a stomach flatter than a first-round contestant on *American Idol*, a show Blaze never misses, darn her.

"It's one of the few things I can eat myself."

Augustine smiles. "Yeah, then. Potato casserole it is. For about hundred people?"

"You got it." I look at Lella. "Will you keep me company while I peel the potatoes?"

"I'd be honored." She turns to Augustine. "That counts as helping, doesn't it?"

"Of course!" Charmaine cries. "Oh, Lella! Being company is the best thing anybody can ever do."

"Valentine's my company, Mrs. Hopewell. Valentine's the best friend I've ever had."

Rick clears his throat. "I'll help peel, Val. If that's all right and you don't mind."

"For a hundred people? I'd be glad if you would."

He whips around and hurries up to his room.

"I'm telling you, Rick is crazy to be fond of a woman like me," I say to Lella later that afternoon.

"Oh, surely not! You're undoubtedly a prize, Valentine."

I can't help myself. I laugh and laugh.

Lella and I sit in front of the TV in her room and watch an ancient episode of *The Galloping Gourmet*.

"Oh, Valentine, don't you just love that man? His smile is so bright and toothy. And that complexion! Do you think he uses makeup?"

"Lots of it. My skin feels dry. I'll go get my Ponds."

Someone knocks on the door.

Lella says, "Come in!"

Rick enters with envelopes in his hand. "Sorry, Val. Nothing for you."

"Big shocker."

"Here, Lell. For you."

"Junk mail?" she asks, even though she reads every word of every piece of mail she gets. Believe me, I know as I'm the one to arrange the pages on the hospital-type tray she has by her bed.

"Don't think so." He hands it to me.

"No, Lella. It looks personal. See?"

She scans the business-sized envelope. "It's from my Aunt Dahlia."

I jiggle it. "Want me to?"

She nods. "I haven't heard from her in such a long time. You'd like her, Val. Have a seat Rick, if you please."

Rick sits on the end of the bed. "I hope it isn't bad news."

I slide a thumb inside and rake open the envelope. "Let's see." After slipping out the paper and unfolding it, I hold it up to her face, about eighteen inches away. Lella has perfect vision.

"Oh!" she says and keeps reading. "Oh! Oh dear."

I know better than to ask what's the matter. She hates being interrupted when reading a letter. Rick opens his mouth and I shake my head. *Don't.*

She turns to face me. "Well, that surely is a surprise."

"What happened?"

"Yeah, Lell." Rick brings his feet up, folding his legs into the lotus position.

"Hold it back up in front of me, Valentine. If you would."

She begins to read aloud. "'Dear Ellen.'"

"Your name's Ellen?"

"Yes. I couldn't say Ellen when I was first beginning to speak. I said Lella."

"How did I not know that?"

"Okay, let's continue. 'Dear Ellen, I wanted to tell you all this sooner but I didn't know where you were. I figured you'd be in Mount Oak now and if you're reading this, well, I guess you are.

"'Your Uncle Joe passed away a couple of months ago. And though I can't say I'm as sad as I should be (he always was as mean as a mountain lion with a toothache), I'm not enjoying being alone. Not even a little bit. It's not so much that I miss him, I just don't like wandering around in this house all by myself. I'm still in great shape, healthy as a horse and clearer thinking than ever.

"'So this letter comes not only with all this information, but an invitation. For years I've wanted you to come live here with us. But I would never have suggested that with Uncle Joe around and him being so unaccepting and all. I'm sure you understand. It was better for you on the road and with that nice friend of yours than here with that man.

"'So what do you say? Why not come off the road? Why not come and let me take care of you. Family is family, I always say. I think your mother would be glad for it. I've always been sorry I couldn't do it sooner, for my sister's sake if nothing else. Now your parents were a great couple, weren't they?' "

Lella nods and I set down the letter. "The rest is news about the ladies in her card club and her neighbors. And she promises a visit soon."

"That's great, Lell. What a nice invitation. You gonna take her up on it?"

"Oh, I don't know, Valentine. I just got the letter."

No downright refusals.

"Here." I take the letter off her lap and put it back in the envelope. I set it behind the floral arrangement on her dresser.

"Remind me to write her back tomorrow. I'll be thinking about what I want to say."

Rick stands. "Sounds like it could be good news, Lell."

Her eyes sparkle. "Yes, it does."

I leave to get my Ponds. Rick follows me.

"Why couldn't she have just thrown the letter down in disgust? Figuratively speaking, of course. I mean, it's a preposterous suggestion, right?"

"Well, you know Lella's never quick to judge." Rick stuffs his hands in his pockets. "Wanna take a walk or something?"

"Hello, Rick. It's still light outside."

"Sorry, Val."

"Yeah, yeah. Me too."

FIVE

◆◆◆◆

DREW: 2002

The mirror in the hall bath is flecked with black spots left behind from the vacating silvering. A bare bulb hangs over my head, shining down on my red hair.

I hear an imaginary member of my congregation in my mind. "Oh, that nice red-haired young man, that Drew Parrish. He just wants the best life for everybody, doesn't he? Freedom and wealth and blessing."

Forget about that Jesus fellow who said take up your cross and follow me. The one who was stripped naked, scourged, and nailed to wood when what He really deserved was a palace, a convertible Mercedes, and a Nobel Prize. Is all the deprivation and gore really necessary?

Monks and nuns used to shave their heads. As a sign of humility? I guess so. And boy, do I need some of that.

I pull an inch-thick section of hair out from atop my head and raise the scissors, anchoring the blades as close to my scalp as possible.

Did the Son of God care about His hair so much? Before the lepers approached Him, did He whip out His mirror and make sure His bangs were out of His eyes? Did He adjust His robe, say, "Hold on a sec," and squirt some breath freshener into His mouth?

I grind the blades together, then throw the dismembered lock of hair into the toilet. All the artifice I employed. Even down to how I fixed my coffee. Makes me want to put more than hair into the john.

Would Jesus take His coffee just the way He liked it?

Repeating the process over and over, I wish I had a video camera here now. Wouldn't the fans of our television show have loved this? A certain sense of satisfaction froths up inside of me. Why are people so willing to cast their fishing nets on the same side of the boat, over and over again, the side where a man points and says, "Hey, fish over here!" Meanwhile, Jesus's fish bubble in writhing profusion on the other side, but, well, Jesus is kinda smelly if you really imagine Him accurately, and He's poor, a failure in our definition of the word, and He's just not enough anymore. It doesn't make sense to *really* follow Him in this day and age. We couldn't feed our children and give them the latest sneakers so they wouldn't be made fun of at school. We'd let people walk all over us if all we did was turn the other cheek. So instead of taking Him seriously, we fight for the Ten Commandments even if we can't recite them ourselves. They're our good luck charm even though we are adulterers, liars, and have thick calluses on our hearts; our way to fool God, to show Him we haven't become the people of Malachi or Amos.

Our holy covering. Our holy hair.

More hair. More hair. Air works its fingers next to my scalp. I nick the skin near the front.

Who'd believe a *word* that guy in mirror would say?

Blood trickles down my forehead and beside my nose.

My father would have laughed in Jesus's face if He appeared before him today and said, "What do you mean by all this garnering of power and wealth for yourself, Charles Parrish?"

"Well, there's where you're wrong, Jesus. This is for you."

"When on earth did I ever do anything utilizing political power or wealth?"

"It was the time period. Everybody was poor and downtrodden. You made us children of the King, don't forget. And maybe you're really not Jesus at all if you're such a pansy as all that. Be a real man! That turning the other cheek stuff is highly impractical. See, Drew?" He'd turn to me. "It's up to us to keep things the way they ought to be. Jesus doesn't have an English accent anymore. This guy needs to go away."

Maybe Jesus needs to go to one of those "Hooray for Men" conferences, which have always seemed a little strange to me even though I encouraged our men to attend. I mean, aren't they basically a stadium-sized coffee-klatch for men? How manly is that?

I press the top of the shaving cream can, depositing a mound of foam in my hand. Skimming it over my head, I imagine the apostle Paul. He'd do something categorically crazy like this. The man had a glint in his eye for sure.

The razor slices off the remaining stubble, taking bits of skin with it at times, and after I'm finished, the face staring back at me is crowned by seams of foam, blooms of blood, and nakedness.

The blooms gather strength and turn to rivers as I pick them raw. Naked isn't enough. I stand beneath the bare bulb, lined in scarlet.

Being a pastor affords the greatest excuse in the world if you have a parent you can't stand. Yeah, that sin's still with me tonight. The Christmas season filled up with activities, each small group and sub-ministry scheduling a party, the Christmas concert that all of Mount Oak seemed to turn out to see and, hey, some turkeys for the poor people none of us knew personally except Patsy Barnhouse, who at least gave our church a little bit of clout in the social justice arena.

I hear you laughing, Father Brian.

"Dad, I'll be stuck in Mount Oak for Christmas again this year."

"Oh, we'll be all right. Senator Randall and his family will be celebrating at the house."

"Great." I'll miss you too.

Back to the Trail for Christmas, I decided a few days before. Because if I stayed home, I would awaken Christmas morning, make some coffee, and turn on the television. And with my luck the choices would be It's a Wonderful Life *or* The Longest Day. *Most of this existence, although I didn't know it then, is lived somewhere in the middle.*

This whole exercise seems apropos, Father, in a way. My mother encouraged me to write.

She gave me a blank book my tenth Christmas. "You're a person of words, Andrew." Each week she'd give me an assignment I'd dutifully complete. We'd read them together on Saturday, and most often, our talks would turn to the Lord. That's what she called God. The Lord. She had the utmost respect for Him.

Monica desired only to fit in with God's plan—unlike my father, who wanted God to fit in with his.

"Just your father?" you ask, Father Brian?

I'm not ready to go there.

It's late Christmas Eve. Tomorrow I'll reshave my head and see if Hermy wants to go down to KFC and get a meal with all the sides. But the walls are closing in on me. Catholics have midnight mass, right? Isn't that some sort of obligation or something? Maybe I'll fall asleep before then. That would be a good thing too.

An hour before the Christmas Eve service an inch of snow fell. I remember losing myself in the view out the window. Mount Oak made

a picturesque scene around Christmastime, wreaths on almost every door—each one competing with the next—garland, tasteful white lights. Except for Charmaine Hopewell's place. She loved colored lights. Strung them from the roof, the chimney, around every bush and every tree. Motion figures waved or swayed as they sang carols. Santa and his sleigh landed on the roof. Cars filled their cul-de-sac to get a peek from December first forward.

From my second floor apartment window over Java Jane's, I watched the town square slowly disappear under the soft flakes. I wondered why the world couldn't always be like that, but like everyone else, I felt clueless how to make it happen.

A hunched figure crossed the perfect white surface, marring it. Dressed in layers, he or she shuffled alone. And I felt a strange stirring inside of me I couldn't, and still don't, understand, Father. I ran down the street but the person had disappeared. I stood in the cold, my tracks a mess behind me.

By the time I realized I'd zoned a little, I was fifteen minutes behind schedule. I hurried back up to my apartment, threw on my suit and tie, and sped over to the church as the snow died down.

I snuck up a side aisle and sat in the second row. Christmas Eve lay completely in the hands of Jim Ignowski, our music and arts director. But I had to show up. Jim wasn't someone to cross lightly. Our financial pastor had basically strong-armed me into suggesting a love offering for the evening, and Jim put his foot down, almost on top of my own. In return he agreed to do a Christmas in America segment despite the fact he didn't see what the two had to do with each other and didn't mind saying so. I knew I had to watch him closely or up his salary. Either one would work.

It was the usual fare besides the Christmas in America segment. Olde English choral numbers and a few from Handel's Messiah. A fun interlude where people strolled arm-in-arm down an avenue singing "It's Beginning to Look a Lot Like Christmas" and "Winter Wonderland." Kids singing Baby Jesus-type songs. Jim knew how to put on a show, get people in the door, and keep them coming back. Well worth the lack of an offering to showcase our talent and goodwill.

My favorite part always closed the show—Mary and Joseph in a darkened stable with the silver beam of starlight shining on the Baby. Our sound effects guy piped the breathing and muffled sounds of barn animals, crickets, even a breeze around the auditorium. We paid a fortune for that sound system.

We sat in the stillness of those effects, a Bethlehem stable becoming reality in that auditorium. Sort of. For about twenty seconds the starlight collected into a stronger beam, then lying down upon the scene like a dove alighting on a rooftop, a single note of a violin. Then light taps on the bongos and Mary sang "Lullay, Thou Little Tiny Child."

Even during my most determined times, Father, the seed my mother left behind didn't die. It was a miracle, I know. But I sat there and yearned to be a better man, a better Christian, more like Mary who wasn't proud and who gracefully shouldered a full load of shame.

Mary sang. The notes filling the air with power and grace, much like the real Mary's life must have done around those who knew her.

And I'd never heard a voice like that before. It was perfect. That's all I can tell you. Clear and perfect. No former Mary had sung like that, and nobody ever will again.

I quickly turned to the cast list at the back of the handout.

That Mary was Daisy. I didn't realize she was still coming to the church. Good for Jim for finding her talent. I knew we'd hired the right guy for the job! She wasn't a beautiful woman, but she had an undeniable presence.

At the closing prayer, I left my seat and made right for the green room. We actually called it the green room.

I found her, already dressed in her street clothes. Plain khakis and a Christmas sweater. Her hair was still pulled back in a simple ponytail for the veil she wore onstage. She looked much better like that, without all that teasing and hairspray.

She smiled, right into my eyes, like she'd known me all of her life.

It's the rare person that can make someone feel so comfortable right away. And I'd seen the congregation's reaction to her as she sang. She pulled them right in, caught them in a spell. She was amazing. Maybe it was the fact that she had such a beautiful voice, but it was more than that. She could minister.

You saw all that right then, you ask, Father?

I did. I'd been sizing up people for years. I'd learned from the master. And I knew we could use her. She'd be in my hands. Together, we'd figure it all out. What surprised me was that I hadn't realized we needed a major female player before that. She had something this male-heavy church needed, a woman up front, someone they could relate to.

"Hi, uh, Daisy, right?"

"Uh-huh."

"Beautiful job. The best Mary we've ever had."

"Thanks."

She still exuded that bit of confidence, but like before, it came from a surface place, the same place where you learn nobody with class wears white shoes after Labor Day or if you really love the Lord, you'll dress in only your best clothes for Sunday worship. Moldable, moldable, moldable.

She might be the key to the next big step of growth now that we'd gathered all the coffee-bar types.

"I won't keep you. I just wanted to say what a great job you did. We're blessed to have you."

"I'd love to chat, but I've got to meet my mother around back. Sorry."

"No problem. Well, Merry Christmas."

"Same to you."

She walked down the hallway, her blonde hair picking up the beams of the recessed lighting. Halfway to the door, amid kids in costumes running up either side of her, lots of chatter and relieved sighs, she turned. She hurried back to me. "I don't know why I'm asking this, because I'm sure you're busy, but if you aren't doing anything tomorrow evening, my mom and I are having a little get-together. Just deli trays and meatballs, the best red velvet cake you'll ever eat, shrimp spread, that sort of thing. You're welcome to come, although like I said, I know you probably have plans."

I smiled. "I'll keep it in mind."

"Great. Take care."

I drove back to my apartment afterwards, heated up some soup, and slid in a DVD of The Port of Peace Hour. After the New Year I would begin my role as "dorky young guy on the couch." I wanted to get to know the Hopewells's on-air personalities, how I could springboard off of them to create my own persona. I certainly didn't want to be oil to their water. I prided myself on being able to get along with everyone.

Christmas morning came, I called my father. He was due at Senator Randall's at one o'clock. I suspected him to be doing exactly as I was, making a turkey sandwich and watching some football games or that old movie.

I could've refused Daisy's invitation and gone camping. But she was too valuable and completely worth a solitary Christmas day in my apartment.

It was a lonely life, yes. But I saw myself as a man on a mission. You can fool yourself about your needs for a long time, about what you can give up, what it takes to be successful. Whatever your definition of success happens to be.

I showed up at Daisy's house at seven p.m. She let me in with a smile and a blush that told me, no doubt, she was interested in me. She sang at the piano while her mother played, and everybody joined in on the caroling. A few people begged her to sing a few songs alone and she kept declining, until finally I said, "Please, Daisy. Sing us a song." I *wanted to see how magical she really was—if I'd been wrong the night before.*

She sang us a song. Intimate, without a mic. And it was even more beautiful. Everyone in the room sat breathless, waiting for the next note, and the next.

Yes, we would make a great combination. She was definitely what the church needed.

I pulled Trician aside and asked about her daughter's singing. Was it a career? What had she done previously? Oh, pageants and talent shows, contests and state fairs. That sort of thing. Daisy was first runner-up for Junior Miss in the state competition.

Trician nodded like a weed in the wind. "I've led her every step of the way. We're going to the top. We just need to figure out how to do that, but I know we can."

"She'll go far with that voice."

"It's the best voice you've ever heard, don't you think?" she asked.

"Yes. Other than opera." I had to keep her in her place.

"Well, yes. But that's a different ball game altogether."

Yes, it was.

It was the start of Drew and Daisy—with a little Jesus thrown in for good measure.

But if that had been the case, I wouldn't be sitting here with this bald scabby head and all these cigarette burns on my arms and legs now, would I?

Speaking of cigarette burns.

This time, I slather on the Neosporin.

Hermy's research said cigarette burns can get infected if left untreated. So. Thanks for that, man.

Hermy knocks on my door. "Hey, Drew. It's almost midnight. You done writing?"

"Sure, come on in."

He holds up a half-gallon carton of eggnog with both hands. "So, how 'bout a little sharing of the nog?"

"What are you doing tomorrow?"

"Nothin', man."

"Got any statistics on eggs?"

"Naw, not tonight. Just a little Christmas spirit. For some reason you can forget your troubles on Christmas Eve. Feel holy in a way."

"Did you know that in wars, on Christmas Eve and Christmas Day there'd be a ceasefire?" I take the carton and pull down my mug and my glass.

"Sure did. Except for George Washington. He desecrated it during the Revolutionary War."

"Really?"

"Yeah."

Figures. We were mixing the wrong things from the beginning. My father would approve.

"It's still the holiest night of the year though. God coming down and all," he says.

"So why didn't Christ's birth make more of a difference? Why didn't His death, Hermy? Do you believe in that stuff?"

"Oh yeah. Suckled on it from day one."

"Do you have any of the answers?"

"Naw, man. I just know this stuff in my heart. You can't prove any of it beyond a shadow of a doubt. I've seen all the statistics. You just gotta know it, like you know the way your nails are shaped or how far your heels stick out behind your foot. You don't got to know why, just that it is."

"Maybe it's like that for you." I pour the eggnog into the glasses.

"Maybe. But if it isn't for you, too, if *you* don't find faith, find Jesus around the place, then maybe I'm wrong; maybe He's really not here. Do you believe He's really not here, Drew?"

I hand him the mug. "I don't know, Hermy. I don't know about it anymore, I guess."

He raises his arm in a toast. "Can we agree it's a holy night? A night of stars and stables and shepherds?"

"Yeah. We can."

But then, Hermy's not really all there, is he? I mean, that was a pretty corny speech he just gave there.

"You want to walk down to midnight mass?" I ask after downing the eggnog.

"Sure."

Hermy's game for pretty much anything.

We head to the corner of Baltimore Avenue and Talbot Street toward St. Mary's. A handbell choir is playing "Silent Night" as we enter. Very nice.

Everyone sits in their pew. It's quiet.

"Catholics sure know how to do reverence," Hermy whispers.

You can feel it.

And I just let myself ooze into it. I don't sing the songs. I don't sit and stand, sit and stand. I just sit in the very back corner and watch Father Brian do his thing.

Or the church's thing. Or whatever it is.

What I do know is that he doesn't expect any more or any less than what he's doing right now. I think he's fine with that. A year ago I would have pitied him.

Now I'm not so sure.

SIX

◆◆◆◆◆

Valentine: 2008

Augustine has shown up every day since Thanksgiving, drinking coffee, sitting with Lella and me to watch a movie. While Lella sits in her stroller and directs, he helps me string lights in all the shrubbery and along the rooflines, cover the front door with gold wrapping paper, hang the ugliest wreath in town, and figure out how to get the molded plastic nativity set Rick found at a flea market from blowing over in the wind.

"Thanks for the help. Last year it was a mess." I hand him a cup of hot chocolate as we rest on the porch. "Who wants to keep running outside to rescue the holy family every time an errant gust of wind rolls down the street? Lella nearly choked last year when she saw Mary and Joseph scattered across the lawn."

"Oh truly, Val! It seemed so sacrilegious! A little shameful, don't you think?"

"It's bad enough to make a plastic baby Jesus in the first place, but to allow him to be blown on his face a good twenty feet from his manger feels downright sinful. I'm not the most religious person in the world, but even I know this isn't right."

"Well, it won't happen this year, friends." Augustine had hauled over some weights from his bench and affixed them to the bottom of the figures with electrical tape.

◆◆ 75 ◆◆

"You work out?" I ask as he raises Joseph to his feet.

"Yeah. Some. I don't obsess about it. Just like to work out extra angst."

That night I talk about it with Lella. "He seems kinda strong, doesn't he?"

"He surely does."

"But he's still a little chubby; nothing major, just not the kind of guy you're dying to see in swim trunks. Notice I didn't say a Speedo. Those should be outlawed, all remaining pieces gathered up and thrown into a big Speedo bonfire in front of which a million thankful women dance in happiness and relief that they'll never again have to wonder if 'that guy' will be around when they step onto the beach."

"Oh, Valentine, you always make me laugh."

"It's what makes it all bearable."

"Surely. That and other things too."

"Thanks for helping, Augustine."

He cuts up bread for my sausage stuffing. He's pulled his gray dreads back into a blue rubber band, the kind that holds broccoli stalks together at the grocery store.

"So you know your way around a kitchen, Val. How'd that happen?"

"Before I went on the road, I was a cook at an elementary school in Lynchburg. I learned to make things tasty there, I suppose."

"Obviously you're not scared of cooking for a crowd."

"You kidding me? It's easier cooking for a crowd."

He scoops up some bread cubes in both of his hands and

deposits them in a big aluminum bowl. Five silver rings encircle his fingers. Blaze told me he has a Harley he hardly ever uses.

"So these walks you take at night. You and Lella ever want company?"

"Not really. I mean, we go at midnight, Augustine. That should clue you in on things."

"True. True."

I set a saucepan on the range to heat up the chicken broth, into which I'll melt two sticks of butter. On the back burner five pounds of sausage browns in Blaze's prehistoric cast-iron skillet. "Love the smell of sausage frying."

"So would you mind if I came along sometime?"

Man, this guy is persistent. "Why do you even want to?" He deposits more cubes in the bowl. "Right. That's enough bread. Go ahead and dice up some onion. Really little pieces. I'll brown those in some more butter. I'm not shy about butter."

"As far as I'm concerned, butter is the true lubricant of life."

"You're obviously smarter than you seem."

"Back to your question, Val. I'd like to come just 'cause I'd like to come."

"You're still not trying to 'reach out' to me, are you? Because I swear I'm just fine."

He lays his knife on the table. "Do you find yourself that unworthy of other people's time? I mean, can't I just want to be with you two? I like you. You're both independent women in your own way."

"Lizard Woman and Lella the Human Cocoon." I can't help it, I laugh out loud.

"Don't laugh. There's more to offer people than good skin and arms and legs. I mean, how many times do you make a friend based on their skin, or if they have arms and legs?"

"You're a trip." He deserves a bone. "Hey, we're working a benefit show tomorrow night for the local theater's fund-raising gala." I stir the sausage. Getting nice and crispy. "The dinner's by invitation only, but you could come for the show. That would be no problem."

"Sure I'll come. Thanks for asking. Where is it?"

"Elysian Heights Educational Center."

He raises his brows. "Really? That's weird."

I roll my eyes. "I heard they're doing more stuff for the community. Letting the place out on off nights. Maybe they're not trying to hog everything for themselves like they used to."

Augustine winces. "That's a little harsh, isn't it?"

I shrug. "Honestly?"

"Okay, they deserved that, I guess."

"Especially during the Drew Parrish days. I hated that guy."

"He was a little plastic."

"A little? It was worse than a sideshow, that show. And that poor Daisy woman!" I lean forward. "I've been on the freak show circuit for five seasons now, Augustine, and I've seen what they call Skeleton People. You know what I'm talking about?"

He shakes his head.

"Isaac Sprague, The Living Skeleton, was probably the most famous of these guys. He lived in the eighteen hundreds, was five feet, four inches tall, and weighed forty-eight pounds."

"Did he have an eating disorder?"

"Nah, he had a good appetite. He worked as a cobbler, then a grocer, but despite seeing doctors and all, he continued to lose weight. And so"—I spread my arms wide—"the sideshow took him in. Because we're the place for folks who don't have a chance in the real world."

I stir the sausage again.

"Sounds like my kind of people."

"And you know what? That church, that guy, weren't they supposed to be like the sideshow too? Accepting and all? And yet, even that woman, Daisy, she wasn't accepted for who she was. She changed and changed and changed. And then, when she was finally formed into some freakish image, guess what? She disappears!"

"How do you know so much about her?"

"I like to read about sideshows, circuses, and television preachers."

He sets down his knife. "Well, it doesn't take a genius to see the connection."

"And anyway, you're not that kind of minister so that's a mark in your favor."

"There are some good people at that church, Val."

"Well, they're not beating down my door, that's for sure."

We finish up the dressing, spoon it into gallon bags, and store it in the freezer to be used in a week's time for Christmas dinner.

"You know, Valentine, you don't have to wear that scarf in front of me if you don't want to."

"Thanks. I'll keep that in mind."

Roland's Wayfaring Marvels and Oddities isn't the greatest show on earth. Not by a long shot. We don't even begin to compete with The Brothers Grim. Now they've got it going on with The Enigma and Pumkin Head. And Zamora the Man of Torture, real name Tim, can shove all sorts of sharp things, needles and skewers and such, through his arms and legs. Even down under his tongue to come out of the bottom of his neck. I literally threw up when I saw him the first time. I—Lizard Woman—went running out of the tent with my hand clapped over my mouth, cheeks flared under the promise of the inevitable. Thank goodness we were at the edge of a wooded area.

I haven't watched him since.

I can't say anybody's thrown up upon seeing me, and I am glad for it.

Our show may be smaller than Grim, but we demolish them in the sparkle factor. We're a little classier if you want to know the truth. Seems crazy to say, like saying Melanie Griffith is classier than Madonna, but there you go.

Lella sits on Blaze's easy chair as I prepare our costumes for tonight's benefit show, the hand steamer burbling nearby.

I pull out my gown covered with sequins of various greens laid out in a reptilian, scaly pattern.

"These are works of art, Valentine," Lella says. "I just adore those gloves."

Full-length green satin evening gloves. "On anybody but Lizard Woman they'd be sexy."

"Oh, now, hush."

I turn the dress inside out and run the steamer head over the fabric. Next, Lella's suit based on Starry Night.

"I think that one's my favorite," she says.

Lella's suits, sort of swimsuit affairs, are sequined too, and I get really creative on those. One is a rather cubic, geometric number, another winsome and floral. It all depends on my mood when I sit down with my needle and thread. I always design the neckline with great attention to detail in the needle-work, a frame for her beauty. And they're always in pale, neutral shades—ivory, beige, ecru—to go along with the cocoon theme.

"Starry Night in neutrals. Only you could get away with that, Lella."

She smiles, her dark eyes glittering as I steam her costume and hang it next to mine.

Rick's new stretch suit is tasteful in black and brown with cream-colored striping down the outside of his arms and legs. It really shows off his configurations.

"You did a fine job with that one, Valentine."

"I didn't want him looking like a girly male figure skater."

"Oh, surely not! Some of those get-ups are downright embarrassing to watch a grown man skate around the ice in."

"Who do they think they are, Freddie Mercury?"

"What are the twins wearing tonight?"

"The twins are on their own."

I wouldn't risk venturing near enough to take measurements. Especially after last week when they made Lella cry. I've started taking their dinner up to their room so they don't have to distribute their misery amongst the rest of us.

Lella and I get ready along with the other women in one of the side rooms in the Education Center, which doubles as a school during the week. Judging by the age level of the toys and the height of the tables and chairs, it's a toddler room.

I'm ready to perform tonight. Of course I don't use makeup, other than false eyelashes—green false eyelashes and glittery green eye shadow.

I apply the final touches of Lella's makeup, a few stick-on sparkles. "My goodness, Valentine, your hair looks especially beautiful tonight. So lovely and thick. And dark. Did you put a rinse on it?"

"Nah. I just tried a new shampoo Rick brought in."

"It's even more gorgeous than usual."

"Well, when you're a giant Drano burn, you have to accentuate the positives."

"It reminds me of my Aunt Dahlia when she was young. She'd pile her hair up on her head in those big soup can curls."

"That's what I was going for. If Chubby Checkers starting singing *The Twist*, my hair would dance right along and with all the right moves."

"Oh Val, you're exactly right. Aunt Dahlia called me this afternoon while you were working on your jewelry. She's visiting soon! Isn't that delightful news?"

"Delightful."

I adjust my gloves and turn away.

"I was looking at house kits online this afternoon," I say over my shoulder as I lift her earrings from their box.

"Oh yes?"

"Uh-huh." I turn back around. "What kind of house style do you like, Lell?"

"Surely it doesn't matter what I think. Any place is fine with me."

"Because we could go modern." I thread the heavy Zirconia dangles through the holes in her lobes.

"That might be a little stark now that you mention it."

"Or cottage. A little seaside cottage?"

"Perhaps with a Victorian spindled front porch?"

"Exactly. Like that."

She smiles into my eyes. "You pick, Valentine. I know you well enough to know it will be homey and good."

I turn away and mumble, "I wish I could get the money together before Dahlia comes."

"What, Val?"

"You must be excited about Dahlia coming."

"Oh yes, I surely am."

I slide my feet into bright green, high-heeled satin pumps. Sexy shoes.

Who am I trying to kid? Just who am I trying to kid?

Some sideshow acts perform their oddities and wonders: fire eaters, glass eaters, people with piercings galore from which they suspend great weights or worse, have themselves suspended. There aren't as many people like Lella and me on display anymore. We remind the populace that not everything is a choice. When Johnny Eck was asked by a reporter whether or not he was being exploited, he replied, "No. They pay to see me. You're the exploiter. You're not giving me a dime for this interview."

I lift Lella onto her platform.

We normally line a stage approaching the tent. Me, Lella, and sometimes a woman named Cyndi Hayes who weighs six hundred pounds and can fire off the greatest insults you've ever heard. People walk by and try to put her down, and she cuts them to size in five seconds. It's her schtick and everybody loves it. Her outfits are a challenge. We go for the Little Lotta look. Bloomers, puffed sleeves, a baby cap. Not original, but practical.

Inside, the performers do their acts. Rick does his contortionist moves; Clifford does his blockhead stuff; RayAnne Foley, who I have yet to mention, walks on glass and eats light bulbs. She calls herself Impermeable Me. But she's more ticklish than a toddler. She winters down in Alabama with her parents who run a photo development company.

Lella and I are the only displayable human oddities on tonight. Rick's twisting and turning near the drink table. We sit upon our displays at the back of the gymnasium. Mine, well, I hate to brag, but it's beautiful, a shimmering jungle scene, lush, with stunning hoards of flowers that seem to advance from the backdrop and around my seat. I made it myself three years ago with Rick's help and improve it a little bit every winter. The only thing not beautiful about my display is me. I remain silent the entire time, taking stock in that old phrase, "A picture paints a thousand words."

Lella's display, all angel hair and twinkle lights, further locks in the cocoon idea. She says nice things to all the passersby. "What a lovely little girl!" or "Oh my, that sweater is gorgeous." Or "Now you, sir, you must be a judge, you look so distinguished." Or "Madame, I'll wager people approach you all the time and ask you to be in television commercials, don't they?" They blush at first, extremely uncomfortable at the sight of her, two velvet pillows supporting her head. I'm so careful to lay her down just so and arrange her hair like a cloud around her. She turns her head to the side, eyes sparkling, expression friendly and open. At some shows a group will form around Lella, because a true optimist, someone who only sees the good in people, is more rare than a Human Cocoon.

Tonight holds no exception in my MO. I remain frozen, staring with haughty eyes as people pass silently by, too polite to gawk for long, a line like a slithery snake sliding on past. Every once in a while I'll bestow a wink to the kids. Okay, most of the kids get a wink. But only when their parents aren't looking.

One woman looks right at me. "That's the most beautiful gown I've ever seen. Did you make it?"

I nod a queenly nod and she smiles at me, moving on.

Augustine stops in front of me. Looking almost as out of place as us freaks, he holds up a hand. "Now, now, I noticed you don't talk to the people going by and that's okay. I want no special privileges. But I just gotta say, Valentine, you look wonderful."

Okay, so I laugh.

"I mean it. That dress is beautiful, and your arms and legs are really shapely. Do you exercise regularly?" He says it so matter-of-fact I have to laugh. Besides, the man is b-*lind!*

Lella overhears. "I'd surely take them in a heartbeat."

I laugh again and I can't help myself. "This is not the way it's all supposed to go, Augustine."

He winks. I wink back. He leans forward, whispers, "I'm glad you took off that scarf," and sidles on by to talk with Lella, who says right away, "I must say you have the prettiest tattoos I've ever seen."

Augustine turns to me. "You could learn a thing or two from Lella, Valentine."

Beautiful, sweet Lella.

Like I could ever be like Lella.

I curl my hands into fists. "And you need to mind your own business."

He zones for a sec.

"D'you hear me? I don't need some crazy preacher telling me what to do. You got that?"

"Yeah, I heard you. Sorry."

"Move along, bub. You've seen all there is to see."

"Valentine, I didn't mean—"

"Get moving. You're ruining my act."

The man actually mists over and says, "Oh. Okay, Valentine. That's fine."

He hurries over to the drinks table.

"You were awful to him, Valentine."

"I know it, Lella. But where does he get off telling me what to do?"

Lella's already speaking to the next customer.

After another round of apologies, Augustine helps me carry the costumes to my camper. I open the back and he climbs in after me. "Nice digs!" He looks around him. "Okay, I get it. The traveling around, place to place, there must be something to say for it. Especially in this sweet little deal."

"It's nice, isn't it? My dad bought it for me when I told him I wanted to go on the road."

"He must be pretty understanding."

"He's a good guy. So what did you think of the whole show?"

"Most people seemed a little uncomfortable tonight."

"Yeah. To be expected. Although you must be used to that, being a pastor and all."

"Yeah, I guess it's kinda like a non-Christian walking into a worship service or a healing service or something. That must be pretty freaky to them."

"I see your point. Have a seat." I turn on the heater. "I love my little home. Can I get you a cup of coffee or something?"

"Sure! This place is fully equipped?"

"Yep. Everything I need right here."

"And you sleep in that loft? Does the mattress have enough support?"

My heart warms. "Yeah. Yeah it does, Augustine."

I grab the coffee and a bottle of water from the cupboard and set a pan of water on the stove. And then the plastic filter holder that sits right on top of the cup.

"Hey, that's nifty."

"I don't need a coffeemaker with this little thing. Space is at a premium, obviously."

"No kidding. I can imagine. So how did it go for you tonight? They filed past pretty quickly."

"It's okay. These people weren't our usual sideshow aficionados. They don't want to offend us. I can definitely understand it, but this is how we make our living, Augustine." I lean against the counter and cross my arms. "We need the curious in order to make ends meet, to keep us in our sheltered community, to save up their willingly paid fees so that in the winter I can sew costumes, make jewelry, read comic books, take Lella for walks, and research other freaks. And religious nuts." I pretend I'm shooting a gun at him.

He pretends he's shot. "Point taken."

"So tell me, what's it like for a guy like you to be in a church like Elysian Heights? It seems like you and that type of Christianity are miles apart."

He shrugs. "It's a little uncomfortable. Of course I look around at all the facilities—a pool?—and think how the pool at the Y is plenty good enough, not to mention it would actually get people out into their community, and how much good that money could have done for people who are desperate."

"I thought the same thing."

"But then I feel bad for being so judgmental."

"I didn't."

"No, Val, you wouldn't, would you?"

The water now boiling, I pour it through the grinds and into his cup. "I checked out that church, before I was burned."

He leans forward. "When was that?"

"During the Drew Parrish days."

"What did you think?" He clears his throat and crosses his arms across his chest.

I add some more water. "They were friendly enough, at least some of them, enough of them. But that preacher"—I shudder— "I couldn't stand him."

"Why is that?"

"You could tell from a mile away he was just trying to prove something to himself."

"Really? He was pretty popular. How could you tell?"

I hand him his cup and start on my own. "Some people see inside people better than others."

"I'll have to admit you're right there. I figured he was about power, pure and simple."

"Maybe."

We sit in the camper at the Elysian Heights parking lot and talk for a long time about, well, not much really, sideshows and ministries and the like.

Rick steps into the kitchen two mornings later. "You gotta see this. Come out front."

We step out onto the porch and down the front walk. "Look."

"Oh my goodness!"

Plastic Mary's arms and legs are cut off and Joseph's face is destroyed, eaten away by battery acid or something, I don't know what. Spray-painted on the gift wrap on the front door in neon orange: Merry Christmas FREAKS.

"This has never happened before in Mount Oak," Rick says.

"At least they left the Baby Jesus alone."

"Should I call the police, Val?"

"No. Let's just clean it up."

"Yeah, that's probably best."

"We never hurt anybody."

"No. We never did. Maybe we touched a nerve at that show. You know some people just don't like to be uncomfortable."

"Let's not tell Lella."

"I'm with you there."

He unplugs the holy family. I tear down the gift wrap, my heart crushed.

"Val?"

I look up.

"Are you crying?"

"No, Rick. It's just the cold wind."

Lella calls for me. "Merry Christmas, Valentine!"

I click the play button on my iTunes. "Embraceable You," this time by Tony Bennett. Love Tony. Love his crinkly eyes, his curly hair, his hooked nose, his slanted smile. Love the way he just loves singing and will sing with pretty much anybody and never feels the need to steal the show.

"Merry Christmas! Be right there, Lell!" I throw back the covers and grab her present, wrapped in tissue paper even though I'll have to unwrap it for her.

"Oh, Valentine!" She nods, her way of pointing, in the direction of the gift. "You're so kind!"

I slip off the hot pink paper and hold up the sweater I embellished with beads and sequins. Saint Augustine found the plain, black, almost-cashmere sweater for me at the Goodwill.

"It's divine!"

"Divine? You're priceless, Lell."

"And you kept the arms on for the prosthetics. You knew I'd want to wear prosthetics for a sweater like this!" She's always so surprised at how well I know her.

I ready my friend for the day and we head down to the kitchen. Around my neck a new necklace, a sparkly little green Christmas tree on a silver chain, tells me Lella loves me too.

Need to get the turkey in the oven soon. Blaze declared the Thanksgiving dinner such a success, she enlisted me to knock myself out for today's meal.

Lella keeps me company in the warm kitchen, the smell of coffee brightening the air, reading off the measures in the recipes so I don't have to keep looking back and forth. "This makes everything go so much quicker, Lell."

"Oh, dear, surely I wish I could do more."

"Lella, you completely undervalue your contribution to the world."

We listen to one of those *LIFE* compilation CDs. Not a pop singer in the bunch grunts out peace on earth, good will toward men.

Augustine and several people from his mission thingy arrive for dinner. Poppy Fraser's dinner to the street people went well and everybody loved my stuffing and mashed potato casserole, he said. Having already engaged the scarf, I sit at the table Blaze set with poinsettia-themed paper products and coordinating plastic cutlery. The ugliest old Santa centerpiece imaginable sits in the middle, looking a little demonic with white winged eyebrows.

"Christ is born!" Augustine spreads wide his arms. He sounds like a hoarse John the Baptist and looks like John the Tattoo Artist. But his unapologetic proclamation surprises me.

"He really lives and breathes this stuff, doesn't he, Lell?" I whisper.

"Oh, surely he does."

Blaze points everyone to the table. The scuffle begins amid the aroma of turkey, sage, and potatoes. The table filled, one person is left without a seat.

"Rick. Doggone it, it's Rick," I whisper to Lella.

"It's always Rick in situations like this because he's so nice and unassuming," she whispers back.

I get up. "Here, Rick. Sit here."

"No way, Val. You cooked this meal."

"And I tasted everything at least ten times. I couldn't eat even one bite of this stuff." I hold the corner of my scarf down to keep it from puffing out with each word. "I'm really insisting here."

Augustine stands to his feet and I point to him with a bold index finger. "Don't even think about it. I'm so serious it isn't even funny."

Blaze unfolds her napkin. "Don't cross Val, Gus. Believe me, she doesn't ask for much in this life, so when she does you'd just better listen."

"Nice, Blaze. Very nice."

"Do You Hear What I Hear?" ekes from the kitchen.

Augustine sits back down. "I've never been one to argue with strong women."

I snort. "I'll be back in a minute. Augustine, why don't you say grace? You're the minister here."

Lella helps me out. "Oh, please, Gus. That would be so lovely."

He stands to his feet, removes his bandana, and bows his head. His words of love to Jesus are all I need to send me packing, and I make my escape without a sound.

Embrace me, my sweet embraceable you.

This time, as I settle on my bed, it's Nat King Cole. That man. That wonderful man. Speaking of Nat, who died from lung cancer, and this version was recorded when he was older and raspier, I feel like a smoke. I don't think Blaze will kill me if I lean out my window just this once, considering I'm missing Christmas dinner and all.

I pull my scarf down, and as I throw up the sash an ocean of air—filled with the aroma of cooking spices and roasting meat—rushes in with a snowflake or two. Holding my lighter up, guarding it with curled palm and fingers, I breathe in through the filter.

Halfway through the cigarette, Nat ends his smoothness and believe it or not, Ethel Merman starts belting out the song.

"Man! That's the worst version of that song I've ever heard in my life."

I whip around.

Augustine stands in the doorway, trying to completely push open the door with a booted foot while maintaining two filled plates in his hands. I throw the cigarette onto the lawn and rush over, grabbing a plate.

"You're right. It proves even the beautiful can be made ugly and people will pay good money to see it. I have a lot in common with the woman that way."

"I'm not going to argue." He hands me my plate. "I learned better than to do something like that ever again."

"I guess I was a little harsh the other night." I set the plate on the bed then shut the window and tie on my scarf. "It's cold enough upstairs in this drafty house without my help."

"We keep it cold at our place too. Fuel's expensive."

"You didn't have to do this."

"Lella told me which foods were acceptable."

My plate overflows with stuffing, mashed potato casserole, broccoli cheese casserole, cranberry sauce, and turkey, shredded up impossibly small and held together with gravy. I point to it. "You did that?"

He shrugs. "You really know how to cook, Valentine. I've been practically starving at Shalom."

"Oh. Shalom. Is that your church? Very granola Jesus."

"Yeah, I know. I like it though. You know what shalom actually means, I guess?"

"Peace. Right?"

"Actually, shalom happens when everyone is living up to their responsibilities."

"In other words, Mr. X isn't lording power over Ms. Y, who isn't lazing around while everybody else does the work?" I snicker.

He flinches. "Yeah, sort of. There's a little more to it than that. Are you one of those people wounded by church?"

I turn away and fork a bite of potato into my mouth and shrug.

"I'm a pretty strong guy, Val. I can take it."

"If I tell you will it shut you up?"

"Probably not."

"Whatever. After I was burned I was pretty much thoroughly rejected. Nobody wanted to be reminded of the fact that God lets really, really bad stuff happen to people."

"Sorry."

"So you know how they twisted their way around it so they could still feel safe and secure? They said I probably wasn't 'saved' in the first place. Ha!"

"I'm sorry, Valentine."

I fork up some dressing. "Save it. Really. After a while you just got to put people like that behind you or they take over your mind." I lay my fork back down. "And I think they were right. I hardly feel saved or anything else anymore. Don't know if I want all that spiritual stress anyway. I can't bear another salvation speech, as if faith is this sudden decision, like should I have pie or cake? And once having had the pie, does life stay relatively like it was, only I have pie inside of me? No thanks. I want more than pie. In fact, I tried the pie a long time ago and I still ended up like this."

"Sorry, Valentine."

"Save it. Really. And take the hint, Saint Augustine. I'm not going to tell you any more about anything else today, okay? So. What's this shalom thing about?"

"You'll probably laugh."

"Probably."

He barks out a laugh. "Okay."

I eat my dressing while he tells about his "missional community." This is one weird tale, one strange dude.

"So basically you're saying you and a couple of friends from Philadelphia decided to start a monastery. A *monastery*? Like chants and hoods and whacking yourself on the forehead with a two-by-four, monastery?"

"Uh, well, a little less stringent, now that you mention that. And not at all Monty Python."

"Got it. So you Catholic or something? You don't look Catholic."

"No. We've made up our own monastic rules."

I spoon up some turkey and gravy. "Are you allowed to do that sort of thing? Are there monastery police out there who go around and check to see if all the monks are following the rules?"

"No monastic police that I know of. We have marks we follow. Some new monastic communities are stricter than others. Ours is pretty strict. We go with poverty, chastity, and obedience. Relocating to forgotten places and ministering to forgotten people. Hospitality to the stranger."

"Chastity. So you don't have sex. Figures."

"Do you?"

"Well no, but it's not like I took a vow or anything. So is this chastity vow for a lifetime?"

"Mine is. Not everyone's is. Celibacy within marriage is fine too."

"No wonder there aren't many of you over there." I set my plate on the nightstand. "So you're never going to get married?"

"I can't."

"That doesn't sound really holy if you ask me. You sound like you're escaping reality. I know another freak when I see one. You're doing what I'm doing. You're just acting all holy about it."

"I'm not holy, Valentine. Have I ever acted like I think I'm holy?"

"I guess not. You got me. Most of these religious types you can blanketly accuse and they'll accept it on behalf of all the morons who actually act that way. Maybe there's something to be said for that, come to think of it, or maybe it's just stupid."

"Maybe they're just scared. And there's something noble about sticking together, Val, in believing that all our victories and all our defeats belong to all of us. I mean, we think we can dissect the Body of Christ, but we can't do that any more than we can dissect our own. So all bad things done in the name of Christ are mine to bear. And all the good things."

Augustine wears too many dreads and chunks of stainless steel in his flesh to be talking like he actually thinks about things.

"Anyway." I open the window. I'd rather smoke than eat right now. I really wasn't lying when I said I'd eaten a lot when I was cooking. "So I still think you're taking these vows to keep you from doing something you'll regret later on."

This blanches the ruddy skin of his face. "Some people need more heroics to keep them from sinning like I'm capable of. Me being the primary example. It's best for me to stay away from women altogether."

"Oh, you were one of those."

"It's different than you could ever imagine."

"Try me."

"You can pretty yourself up with flower tattoos and still know a monster lies in wait beneath the foliage. And that's all you'll get from me today."

I light my cigarette. "Oh, so I share and you stay mum on your past. That's typical. Want to hear all my gore but refuse to bare your own."

"Gore is a good way to describe it. Take comfort in the fact that I don't trust a word you said anyway, Val. You've been lying about your burns."

I hand him my pack of smokes, the creep.

"No thanks, Val. It took me years to quit. But you go ahead."

"I guess I'm lucky to wear my faults right on the surface."

His blue eyes appear earnest. "You may not believe this, Valentine, but you're exactly right."

"People feel sorry for me. But the one advantage I have over normal folks—and I used to be one, so I know—makes me happy. My face is the greatest filter imaginable. I screen out the superficial, the easily sickened, and the self-proclaimed superior. I screen out the weak, the selfish, and the perfectionists. Usually what remains are people who see themselves the way I do, burned and deformed and able to admit it right up front. Like you." I drag in deeply on my cigarette. "I have no time for anybody else. I'm an acquired taste for the select few. And believe me when I tell you, I'm okay with that."

"I believe you, Valentine. But will it be enough in ten or so years?"

"Shut up, Augustine."

"Okay."

SEVEN

DREW: 2002

I meet Father Brian for lunch out at The Crepe and Omelet Place. His choice. Having ordered, we sit drinking coffee in the atrium-style restaurant, surrounded by plants and pink table linens.

"Tell me how you became a priest, Father Brian. What made a young guy like you want to give up your entire life? You aren't gay, are you?"

He shakes his head. "You know, I wish you'd just call me Brian. I'm not your priest. I'm new to this stuff, and right now I think God's just calling me to be your friend. It's a little lonely down here anyway. And no, I'm not gay. When I left high school behind, I left a very angry girlfriend too."

"Where are you from?"

"Ann Arbor."

"So were you Catholic all your life?"

"Yep. Cradle and all."

"I think you have to be to swallow all of it."

If he's offended, which he probably should be, he doesn't show it. "You'd be surprised at all our adult converts. But that's neither here nor there. You were asking about a calling." He sips his coffee. "Did you have one?"

I shake my head. "No. I've never admitted that to a soul. I just thought it made sense for me."

"I've always loved the church, Drew. And God and Christ. Even the saints. You know, one of the biggest criticisms I hear from protestants is that Catholics don't know their Bible, or even what they really say they believe."

"That's true across the board."

"I think so. But I was always interested. And one day at school—I went to Catholic school—they had a special assembly where one of the local priests got up, and one of the sisters, and they talked about a vocational religious calling. It was like I had a personal Pentecost that day. I just knew I'd been called out by the Holy Spirit."

"Just like that?"

"Basically."

"So then what?"

"Went to college, Xavier in Cinci, for my undergrad. Then Mount St. Mary's for seminary. You go to seminary?"

The waitress delivers our food. Cheese omelet for me, bacon and cheese for Father Brian. You know, it just feels odd to see a priest eating real food. Why do they seem so unreal?

"I went to Duke, majored in theology, and then went to Trinity."

"Which one?"

"Does it matter?"

"That's okay. You don't have to tell me everything."

"What did you mean by a personal Pentecost? I've never heard that term."

"Well, you know what happened at Pentecost, right? The Holy Spirit descends and people speak in tongues and the world is set aflame, the gospel spreads, faith increases."

"Sure."

"Much like that. Only inside of you. And I felt the love of God consume me. You know what I mean?"

I shake my head. No, Father Brian. Brian. Whoever you are. I really don't.

We eat, I ask him about his family. Six older brothers and sisters, "Rhythm method, you know," twelve nieces and nephews, parents run a dry cleaner in Ann Arbor, angry high school sweetheart now married with two kids and uses him as an easy source of confession when he's home, likes to watch World Cup soccer and NASCAR.

NASCAR?

He tells me to keep writing and refuses to let me help with the tab.

After the Christmas concert I scheduled Daisy for a special song every Sunday, telling my congregation, "Friends, I'm your Senior Pastor. Daisy is your Pastor of Praise."

Pastor of Praise. What a great ring.

They didn't balk. Something trusting mingled with Daisy's confidence as if she said, "Just point me in the direction you want me to go and I'll take off."

After my intro, she stepped onto the platform and drew them in.

"Thanks, Drew. Thank you fellow Elysian Heights members. I can only pray God blesses us all." She took hold of that microphone and something mystical happened. She truly ministered to people. Even now I don't doubt that for a second. Daisy had a calling on her. You could see that from anywhere you stood. I don't know if it was a personal Pentecost or just a person doing what God made them to do. Encouraging notes began to fill her box in the church mailroom. Nobody minded seeing her week after week. Attendance grew. I had been right about it all.

The board sung my praises because giving was up and people felt blessed. A part of me still felt good about that, I'd like to believe. About people being blessed, I mean.

Saying all this to a priest makes me feel a little silly. I can hear you in my head: "You protestants, always trying to reinvent the wheel." And yet, we do have a certain freshness, an appreciation of creativity that's undeniable. I guess it's all in how you use it and why.

Harlan and Charmaine Hopewell pretty much held the patent for Southern gospel music in Mount Oak, so Daisy and I centered her ministry on contemporary music. Smooth, adult contemporary, classy and . . . smooth.

Trician grabbed me after church and asked if I agreed that Daisy just needed to lose a few pounds and become a little more sculpted-looking to fit the music itself. A willow tree. "You know as well as I do, Drew, that looks matter in the long run. If we can get her a recording contract, think about what it'll do for the ministry. You'll have more people than you know what to do with."

Yes, yes. Man looks on the outward appearance and God looks on the heart. I'd read that verse. But God wasn't just zapping money into our treasury was He? We had to work for it. And when we decided to break ground on the activities center and school building, my work was cut out for me. Father, I don't know if you can understand that kind of pressure.

I'd heard of plenty of churches in Nashville that grew exponentially because of the famous singers and such that attended. People are attracted to fame. Trician may have been a little overconfident, but she wasn't completely off the mark.

"See what you can do, Trician. I'm sure Daisy'll want to succeed."

The people adored her, loved her endearing smile, invited her to come along and sing on small group retreats. Some women's groups even asked her to speak; though, to my way of thinking at the time, Daisy had nothing important to say. She'd never been to seminary or even Bible college.

She lost weight slowly but steadily, and Trician was trying to make some Nashville "ins," but that was slow going as anybody can imagine. Charmaine made a few introductions but nothing was coming easily on that front. Daisy was new, untried, no sales numbers, no large platform from which to sell a lot of albums. They were after the sure thing—the bottom line being the god of their bank accounts. It had to be if the people they were giving contracts to instead of Daisy was any indication. Daisy could sing them all down the road and back without breaking a sweat.

I played a good part on The Port of Peace Hour *as well. Charmaine and I bantered easily and the guests had a good time. It was fun.*

The church continued to grow, bringing in a hundred new members a month. And the more they came, the more room we needed. The more space we had, the more members we needed to support it all. The vicious cycle became a cyclone. I could blame the board for their pressure, but at the end of the day I loved it.

A few months ago my father even noticed.

"I just saw your church listed as one of the top one hundred in America by Time *magazine. Interesting. Good job, Son."*

Talk about an eye opener.

Elysian Heights is now at twelve thousand members.

I reach for my smokes. Twelve thousand members. Twelve thousand people I left behind due to a busted water pipe in my apartment building. At least it wasn't a fire. That would have been overkill on God's part in the metaphor department.

I realized the extent of my popularity on The Port of Peace Hour *the Thursday before Easter. Harlan Hopewell called me on my cell phone as I worked out at the gym near the mall.*

"Drew, Charmaine and I got the greatest idea." He paused.

"Well, okay, Charmaine got the greatest idea, and we want to tell you about it in person. Can you come on over to the house this afternoon? Charmaine's making an icebox cake. She makes the best icebox cake you've ever tasted. And she got a pound of hazelnut coffee from Java Jane's too."

Elysian Heights basically shut down from the Wednesday before Easter until Easter Sunday, upon which our celebration blew the doors off of Mount Oak. Yes, I can hear you sigh, Father Brian. Well, Good Friday is such a downer, isn't it?

For the previous two years, our sunrise service was the most well-attended service in the entire state.

"I can make it, sure, Harlan. Right now?"

"That would be great. Charmaine!" he called, right into the receiver. I held it away from my ear. "He can come right now! Okay, good, Drew."

He clicked off.

The phone rang two seconds later. "Didn't mean to cut you off. I mistakenly hit a wrong button with my chin. I hate these cordless phones."

"No problem."

That was Harlan for you.

"Well, good. See you soon then, Drew."

I showered, changed, and hurried over in my Civic.

Pulling onto their blacktop driveway, I had to wonder about the Hopewells. Charmaine made a lot of money from her gospel music career. She toured in a big silver bus every summer, headlined at Gospelganza each July in Greenville, and was always winning Dove awards. Granted, all the money that didn't go to pay for the show's expenses went to counseling ministries and homes for addicts and unwed mothers and such, but certainly Harlan drew a good salary from a congregation that size. It was the largest church in Mount Oak at that time, and I knew how well Elysian Heights paid me.

Yeah, no vow of poverty for us.

And yet, their house looked like the digs of a small branch bank loan officer, or the manager of a radio station, typical middle-middle class. Nothing fancy but not a hovel either—the red brick rancher sat on a dead-end street amid other ranchers alarmingly like it. New landscaping had been planted, judging by the tender shrubs still resting arm's length from one another. But other than fresh paint around the window frames and on the green door, maybe on the shutters, the house didn't seem to have been added to since it was built.

I remember wondering at the time how they could be content there like that. They had to have been raking in the donations.

But they'd been caught up in those televangelist scandals back in the eighties, not so much for excess but for Harlan's antipsychology message. They were playing it safe and who could blame them? They should have been more careful back then. Covered their backsides more thoroughly.

Seeing their home still made me feel good about my small apartment over Java Jane's. The Hopewells had the right idea if they were as committed as I was to traveling light.

"Could it be they were just content?" you might ask. Perhaps yes, but that thought wouldn't have crossed my mind that day.

Harlan greeted me at the door and ushered me through the living room, furnished with antiques and a couch with doilies, and into a kitchen decorated in shades of red and yellow. Two older women stood side-by-side at the kitchen counter, quite possibly explaining the antiques. Charmaine didn't seem like an antiques kind of lady, more of a Wal-Mart gal.

I was horrible. I am horrible. I realize this, all my posturing and judging. But believe me, it's pretty uncomfortable for a jackass like me to admit I had feet of clay clear up to my thighs. A man people looked up to, asking him to show them the way to God.

Show them the way to God? As if I knew!

Oh sure, I knew about salvation and Jesus's death on the cross, but knowing God, walking in the cool of the evening in the garden with Him? I couldn't have gotten them closer to their Creator any more than I could have set their feet on Saturn.

I was liar and a phony. Lying about who God is and speaking of Wal-Mart. That's what I was. A sprawling old big-box store stealing customers from the mom-and-pop shops. God have mercy. We actually ran our church on a "business model," as if efficiency and the bottom line would usher in the Kingdom of God.

The parish system is looking better and better.

Of course the Hopewells welcomed me into their home like I was a long lost relative, their favorite nephew come home from a three-year stint around the world.

"Grandma Min, this here is Drew Parrish. Drew, Minerva Whitehead."

"Hello, Drew. Just call me Min." Her smile stretched to its limits beneath light blue eyes and white hair shorn close to her head.

"And this is her daughter, Charmaine's mother, Isla Whitehead."

Isla didn't say anything. She turned her head, lovely eyes staring in blankness. Overweight, she must have once been a beautiful woman. It was easy to see.

Harlan offered no explanation just then.

Grandma Min tucked her arm through her daughter's. "We'll just take a little walk out by the daffodils, Isla."

I looked out the sliding glass doors visible from the kitchen. Yellow blooms popped up in all the wrong places.

Harlan explained. "When we moved here, the previous owner had planted bulbs all over the yard. It's the craziest thing you've ever seen. But Charmaine won't get rid of them. Her mother, Isla, well, you've got to have noticed she's not quite all there. Schizophrenia. She's catatonic without her meds. But heaven help us, she loves the flowers."

"You have a schizophrenic living with you?"

This was news to me.

"Oh sure. On her meds she's a lamb. Doesn't say much, but Min takes good care of her."

"Both of them live here?"

"Yep. Got a regular intergenerational something going around here. Four generations of Whiteheads. Well, if you count our own children as Whiteheads, which they half are. Although our oldest, Grace, is adopted. She's away at college. Charmaine!" he hollered.

"Be right there!" Her voice came from one of the bedrooms down the hallway. "Just mash the button on the coffeemaker, if you please, Harlan."

"All right, shug!"

He put some reading glasses on his nose and searched for the button. Finding it, he pressed it down. "Have a seat at the table, Son. We're glad you could come and hated putting you out, but we wanted to strike while the iron was hot, as they say."

Charmaine bustled into the room, a tomato pincushion fastened to her wrist. "I've just got to finish the kids' Easter outfits. I'm so behind. Make the news quick, Harlan, so I can get back to my machine."

"You make your kids clothes?" I asked.

"Mine too."

"She's a whiz on that machine, Drew. I tell you what."

"I would never have guessed."

Charmaine laughed. "I like to sew, Drew. It relaxes me. Do you have a hobby?"

Hmm. "Does reading church growth books count?"

Harlan slapped his hand on the table. "It does to me."

"Oh, Harlan." Charmaine slid into the seat opposite me. "Well, get on. I want to see the look on his face."

"All right, then. Here it is. You've become so popular on The Port of Peace Hour, I think we need to do something about it."

I nodded my head. "And that would be?"

"A spin-off!" Charmaine sort of hopped in her seat.

"A spin-off?"

"Your own show!" Charmaine practically shouted it.

"From my church?"

"Well, not yet." Harlan scratched his cheek. "We don't have the financing to get that kind of operation going. We were thinking something more intimate, like a talk show."

"A talk show?" I was stunned. Charmaine filled in the silence.

"Oh, not the Phil Donahue type, but the Johnny Carson type— without the audience." Charmaine stood up and crossed to the cupboard. "Harlan wanted the Phil, but I reminded him about the cost of a studio audience, not to mention a studio." She laughed, pulling down three mugs as the coffeemaker gargled and spat the last of the water in its pipes.

"Where would we tape it?"

"We'll take the Sunday school room closest to the sanctuary and make a set."

"It sounds like it could work," I said.

"Now, it'll be up to you to find guests, incorporate regular features," Harlan said. "We'd like this to not just be about spiritual matters but current events, human interest, subjects across-the-board."

"How about Daisy?" Charmaine lifted the coffeepot. "Wouldn't it be great to have her sing each week?"

"Oh, shug, that's a fine idea! I tell you, Drew, the woman's a whiz."

"Sounds good to me."

And I began to dream, picturing myself sitting on the couch with famous people. Oh, my father would be a great resource. We'd have Christian ministry leaders due to his connections, politicians too. Charmaine could help us with the celebrities. I'd be more popular than The Port of Peace Hour—you could bank on that. Harlan was a good preacher, but that kind of show was on its last legs.

I called my father on the way home and told him the news.

"Your own show from right there in little Mount Oak," he said.

"It'll go all across the country."

"On cable I presume?"

That day I drove fifteen miles from town to a small gas station and bought a pack of Marlboro Lights. I pressed the burning tip of the cigarette into my flesh right there in the car. And I felt such release. I'd been cutting myself for years before that. Not much. Just every once in a while to relieve the pressure. I was sixteen when it started. The same year my father told me my mother committed suicide. A friend in school did it and said it helped him cope. He was right.

Another sin, surely. But then again, Father, your people mortified the flesh. Is that what I'm doing now?

I haven't burned myself for three days. The first notebook is full and I've given it to Father Brian. This one's cover sports an extreme, bulbous close-up of a Jack Russell terrier. I write as Hermy sits at the end of the bed reading *Animal Farm*, with *1984* lying next to him.

The phone rings.

"Drew Parrish?"

"Yes."

"The truth will set you free. Thus saith the Lord."

"Who are you?"

"I can't say."

"Why?"

"Because . . . I love you, Drew."

And she hangs up after gulping down a sob.

My face burns as realization fills me, bringing with it more questions than I knew could be asked.

"Who was it?" Hermy asks.

"It was my mother."

"Isn't she . . . ?" He draws an index finger across his neck.

"I guess not." My veins catch fire.

"Crazy."

"Tell me about it. Hey, I gotta go." I grab my beach chair and head out to the sand. I smoke every last cigarette in a brand new pack, a new theory erupting with each one, none making any sense whatsoever.

◆◆◆

I place a phone call to my father before he leaves for work the next day. "So where's Mom these days?"

He huffs his condescending laugh, but I hear the fear around the edges. "Have you gone a little crazy, son? You know as well as I do that your mother is dead."

As well-versed as he is in political maneuverings, I hear all the earmarks of keeping something under wraps: accuse the accuser, and employ the "everybody knows that" defense.

"Then dead people make phone calls."

"You're going to have to be more specific."

I tell him about the series of calls.

"Oh, Drew. It's just some crazy. You're on the air now. It could have been anybody."

So he hasn't noticed they've only been showing reruns since I disappeared.

"It was her voice."

"You were twelve when she died. How can you be so sure? Look, I'll meet you in Chapel Hill. I'll take you to her grave."

"I know where her grave is, Dad!" Anger elevates my voice. "I went there every day for three years."

"Don't raise your voice. I brought you up to be more self-controlled."

"Okay. Right."

I hang up the phone remembering how it went down. I pick up the phone again.

Father Brian answers on the first ring.

"Can I come over? There's been a bit of a monkey wrench in my life."

"I'll meet you at the church in an hour."

True to his promise, he is waiting in his office, his dark hair an unruly mess. "I just made some coffee. I was up all night. Couldn't sleep."

"Thanks."

"Sometimes it all feels a little overwhelming."

"I know what you mean."

He points to a small sofa across from his desk. "Have a seat. And feel free to just jump right in with whatever's bothering you."

Okay. "It's about my mother. She died after she created one of the biggest scandals to ever hit presidential electoral politics."

"I'm sorry to hear that. What was she like, Drew?"

"Nobody looked more polished and classy, more beautiful than Monica Parrish."

"Much prettier than Daisy, I assume."

So he read the notebook already. "Much. My mother was classically beautiful and very sophisticated. Daisy was more *Star Search,* if you know what I mean."

"Got it."

"That night she embarrassed my father for the last time. Mom looked like a Greek goddess in a white dress, and she moved with the grace of a ballerina."

"I pretty much remember my mother stirring soup or running us around but I can't remember what she wore. But I shouldn't be inserting myself into this conversation. I'm sorry."

"No, Brian. This is friend-to-friend anyway, right?"

"True. Do you have a picture of her?"

I pull out my wallet. "I've been carrying this around since I was ten and I got my first wallet."

I slip the picture from the clear plastic sleeve and hand it over.

Brian takes it, examines it, and nods. "Very beautiful. Not too many women could compare to her."

"But she was kind too. I didn't mention that."

"No. You didn't."

So I tell him the tale about the party, a schmoozing who's-who in DC. The primaries were over and Richard Marten, the party's candidate, was throwing the party to say thank you in a most posh manner. I watched my mother apply the final touches of makeup and finally the fur wrap my father gave her for their tenth anniversary. She kissed my cheek, walked to the car where my dad was already waiting, neither of us knowing the course of our lives would change that night. I'm sure, if she could have looked into the future, she would have stayed home. We would have played Scrabble and watched an old movie, and we would probably have continued to do so for years.

Of course I heard all about what happened because of the argument that ensued that night after they returned. My father parked the car and hurried up the steps to our small townhouse in Alexandria. He never stomped, but his anger still somehow made it into his footfalls.

Mom was about to head upstairs.

"Why did you say that to Richard, Monica?"

"It was true." She walked up the steps.

"How could you know that?" He followed at her heels, into the bedroom.

"I just did."

"I'm tired of your prophesying or whatever it is you call it."

"He's cheating on his wife with two other women, Charles."

"He's the presidential candidate."

"So much the more important then."

"Didn't you see Bill Morris standing there?"

"No."

Bill who? I wondered.

I found out later. Bill was a journalist for the *Washington Post*. Mother went right up to Richard Marten upon hearing the voice of the Spirit (as she called it) and confronted him about his sin within earshot of a reporter.

"It's going to take a fortune to keep this hush-hush," my father said.

"I'm sorry."

"No, Monica. You're not."

"You're right. I'm not. Lying is a sin. Forgive me."

I heard her clink her jewelry down on her dresser.

❖❖❖

I sit back into the couch cushions.

"I can see where she would have aggravated your dad," Father Brian says. "Prophets are never exactly appreciated in their hometown."

"Tell me about it."

"What happened after that?"

"Two weeks later my father told me she was dead."

"Suicide, you said."

"That's what I was told."

"You have reason to doubt that?"

"She called me on the phone where I'm staying."

"Are you sure?" He leans forward.

"Positive. You don't forget your mother's voice. I don't care how long it's been."

"No. My goodness. This is strange, Drew."

"The question is, why would she walk away from me willingly until now? What would make her give me up so easily?"

"Maybe you need to go see your father, Drew."

"Yeah. It's the last thing I want to do, though."

"Then maybe it's why you should. I remember when Richard Marten stepped down. My mom followed politics closely. Of course none of us really knew the unseen story."

"All because of my mother. Prophets can be such a pain, can't they, Brian?"

"It's their job."

"I'd better go, then. I'll leave for DC tomorrow."

"Keep me posted."

"Pray for me."

"I will. That's *my* job. Of course you know how that goes."

"Not really." I was too busy to do much praying.

So I shave my head again and Hermy and I jump in my car and head toward DC, a two-and-a-half hour ride from Ocean City. I tell him about my father as we sit in a truck stop off of Route 50.

"You're gonna confront your old man? That's cold."

"Why? She's my mother."

"But shoot, it sounds like there's a lot of cover up and craziness. I mean, you sure you want to get involved with all of that? Politics is nasty business. The true insiders eat preachers for lunch after they've used them up."

Hermy's right. I'm glad I didn't fall completely into politics like some of those guys. It must have been God's mercy in knowing I didn't need all that on my account as well. Who knows who I would have used to climb that ladder?

I pay for the meal, just a couple of grilled cheese sandwiches and iced teas, and we slip back onto the highway.

"The Lord is calling you," my mother had said.

Those words keep ringing in my head like that nagging church bell at five o'clock in the morning. But if she's right, what kind of a calling could she mean? Then again, Dad may be right. She may be crazy. Or maybe it really wasn't her.

No. I'm right about this. I've come to doubt almost everything else about my life, but this one thing I know for sure.

"So you really think that's her? I mean what if you're wrong?" Hermy asks an hour later at a rest stop on Kent Island—too many iced teas on both our parts back at the truck stop.

"I'm not wrong. And I've got to get the truth from my father." I turn on the tap to wash my hands.

He slides some coins into the soda machine in the lobby. "Do you trust anything the man says?"

"No. I still have to try. It's my mother we're talking about."

Hermy's probably thinking how sad that is, but he doesn't say so.

I go for a pack of gum. "It didn't matter what I thought or said when I was growing up. It was either not quite good enough or completely wrong. Why I kept trying I don't know."

"Kids are crazy like that, Drew."

But heading up to DC with Hermy feels right, like maybe this time a change is coming and I'll stick with it. See, I've stood on my feet before, challenging my father's ways, his sly barbs, his chilly, wordless dressing downs. Somehow I always backed down, ended up apologizing. This time it's not going to happen.

"What's he going to think of you, Drew? I mean, look at you."

"I'm not seeking his approval anymore. Just the truth."

Hermy heads back outside. "Hopefully the truth will set you free."

I follow him. "That seems like a little too much to ask."

Just shy of the car, Hermy starts flirting with a couple of college girls.

I get in the vehicle, pull out my Jack Russell notebook and settle into my seat.

After the big announcement from the Hopewells, I started jotting down plans. The guest list would need to be as first-rate as we could

make it. Daisy would also be a huge part of the draw once people heard her voice for the first time.

But I needed help and I knew who would give it to me. Who would work her fingers to nubs to see her daughter succeed?

I met Trician for lunch at Josef's, our only gourmet restaurant.

We ordered no wine—I was on the clock. Trician dutifully pushed aside the bleu cheese on her salad. "So. The show."

"Yes. Informal and talkative, friendly and laid back. But I believe much of what will separate us is Daisy's voice and her natural way with the audience."

"She's not very photogenic, Drew."

"I'm surprised you'd say that. She's no beauty, but I find her face extremely accessible and friendly."

"It's why we've always chosen live venues for Daisy. Pageants, musical theater, and now what she's doing at church. It all fits together with her ability to grab people. She's never been great on camera—but I guess it's worth trying, isn't it?"

"Of course." I wiped my mouth and set my napkin back in my lap. "What's so bad about her?"

Trician leaned forward, pressing her breasts atop the table, just behind her plate.

Her gesture annoyed me.

"Her nose. She had it fixed when she was seventeen, just before the state Junior Miss pageant. But it's not quite right. It was rather large beforehand. The surgeon said it might take two surgeries. But she's done fine enough without the second one. We could make another investment in her career, I guess."

I smiled that smile.

She continued. "This show could go so far. It could give her the necessary platform for a recording contract, and her close proximity to Charmaine Hopewell will be such a boon. We'd need some help with the surgery, of course. We can't afford anything like that."

"Are you sure plastic surgery is necessary, Trician?"

"It's one of the reasons I'm having a hard time in Nashville with her, Drew. They hear the demo and love her, but the headshot always stops them."

She was using me. But I'd retain the upper hand.

"Well, I don't know. It's a lot of money to throw around."

Trician grabbed my hand. "Drew, I need to explain something. I come from nothing. My family was trash, the laziest, meanest, worst kind of trash. I'm doing all I can to break that. Daisy deserves better."

Oh brother. What an amateur manipulator. Charles Parrish would have eaten her cry for pity in a midmorning coffee break.

Never, never show your weakness.

Never.

What's next? Tears?

She took out a hankie. "Daisy and I are just going to have to work a little harder, climb more obstacles than those born to privilege. You'll never find a better sidekick. She ministers. You know it. You'd be a fool to throw that away."

"I'll help you with it, then." Why, oh why, did the Daisy package include Trician?

"You won't regret it."

"There's something else I'll need from you, Trician. I'll need you to help me schedule guests. Can you do that? Pursue the more sought-after people?"

"I'm like a bulldog when I want something."

Aha.

"Let me break the news to Daisy," I said, and she agreed.

I don't know why, but as we drive down the streets of DC toward Foggy Bottom where my father lives, I feel the need to tell Hermy I used to be a minister.

"Just can't picture it, man. Sorry. Were you at one of those big Death Star churches?"

I almost crash the car. "*Death* Star?"

"Sure. You see those massive things. Big windows. Big gym buildings, glass lobbies, and all. Looks like you expect to see Darth Vader walking around in there giving orders, wreaking havoc on the galaxy. Why did churches stop looking like churches anyway?"

"It's less expensive to build simpler buildings."

"I guess there's that, although—well, I dunno. Whatever. Were you at a Death Star?"

"Yeah."

"You always at a big church?"

"Pretty much," I tell him. "I started out as a youth pastor at a megachurch my father had connections to in Dallas. Loved the kids, but got a little scared they'd hold me back from my goals, not to mention I got into a little trouble with one of the kids' moms. Divorced from her husband for several years, lonely, and ripe for the picking. She came after me and I told her no thanks."

"You don't like sex?" Hermy asks.

"It wasn't that, Hermy, sheesh. Can't a guy have morals every once in a while? She was persistent and I'll be honest, we made out a few times, got pretty hot and heavy, but I always cut it off just before we had sex."

"Aw man. You have no idea what you're missing. You ever try it?"

"We were talking about how I became a pastor."

"Oh yeah, right."

"So I rebuffed her for good one night when she started pressuring me to bring us public. I said no. She got mad and said she'd tell the board I'd made 'untoward passes' at her—"

"She said that? 'Untoward passes'?"

"Yeah. Direct quote. So unless I resigned, she'd lie to the board. I was getting tired of it there anyway. The pastor wasn't going anywhere, the people loved him as well they should have, and I'd learned a lot. I didn't want to call in any favors from my father. I applied for a position at Elysian and moved up from there."

"You know that woman could've been a little more original. Plagiarizing Genesis. That's lame."

"Anyway, it put me on my guard. I wasn't going to make that mistake again."

I pull up in front of my father's brick townhouse.

Hermy whistles. "Nice."

"He got this from, well, you've heard of riverboat gambling, haven't you?"

"Sure."

"Do the math."

Hermy whistles, louder and longer this time. "So he gets it any way he can."

"Preachers on the one hand, casinos on the other. Don't even try to figure that out."

"I don't think I can."

"No kidding. Let's get a room. I can't do this yet."

"No prob."

I drove Daisy out to Lake Coventry, to the Cunninghams' pier. The Cunninghams owned a vacation rental home out there and they let me use it when I needed to get away to write my sermon in the quiet. When I told her about the show, to be called Faith Street, and asked her to be the permanent musical guest as well as a cohost, you know, be the interviewer on "sensitive women's issues," she wound her arms around my neck and squealed. Her breasts flattened against my chest and I couldn't gauge whether she was being forward or oblivious. I chose oblivious because it suited me. But she felt good against me. I couldn't deny that.

I pulled myself away and we walked around the lake, laying down big, big plans.

EIGHT

Valentine: 2008–2009

I look up from my work. During the week between Christmas and New Year's Eve, I made thirty bracelets, ten necklaces, and twenty pairs of earrings. I hear fireworks popping somewhere across town.

"New Year's Eve depresses me more than any other holiday," I say to Lella who's lying on my bed. We just finished watching *An Affair to Remember*.

"I surely know what you mean. Thanksgiving and Christmas we can somewhat re-create that family feeling with the group here at Blaze's. But New Year's Eve is for people who can dance and go out in public."

"And next year is just going to be the same as last anyway."

"Oh, but surely not! We'll save up more money and look at more house plans. And I was thinking, Valentine, maybe we could travel a little bit, just you and I, next fall after the season closes down and pick out a spot we'd like to live. Maybe even start paying on a lot somewhere."

"Great idea. I can start researching on that now."

She sighs. "Valentine, long ago you surely had dreams other than settling down with a legless-armless woman. Before you were burned?"

"A century ago I wanted the typical life. A good man who loved me for me. Actually, I was quite pretty pre-Drano, Lell. I wanted kids to love and care for, to help with their homework, and bake cookies for school parties. I wanted to just be there for them."

"I'm truly sorry your mother wasn't like mine."

"My mother had a lot of issues. Why did your parents put you on display, Lell?"

"They were poor, uneducated, and hopeless."

"But surely—"

"No, Valentine. There was no way out for them but me. Please trust me on this."

"Sorry."

She softens. "As am I. Some things are too painful to talk about."

"I know exactly what you mean." I reach for the Martinelli's and pour us each a cup. "Did you ever have a dollhouse, Lell? I always wanted one."

She nods, comets of delight speeding across the surface of her eyes. "Mother would bring it down off the shelf of our trailer and set it in front of me. She'd place everything just so, exactly as I'd ask her to. After we'd arranged the house she'd tell me the most delightful stories of the imaginary inhabitants."

"My camper's kind of like a dollhouse you live in."

"It surely is."

"I'm ready to get back on the road, I think."

"You always say that on New Year's Eve, but you never mean it on New Year's Day."

Charlie Parker's version of "Embraceable You," live at Carnegie Hall in 1949, mellows me with its sugar-crystal trumpet as the clock continues to tick toward a new year. Only four more hours left until I can kiss this one good-bye. "This rendition is a little cheesy."

"Sometimes we all need a bit of cheese, Valentine."

A light tapping rattles the door. "Valentine?"

"It's Augustine," Lella whispers, eyes shooting off those comets again.

Oh, Lella! You like him?

"Come on in!" I adjust Lella's collar just so and grab my scarf.

The door inches open. He peers around it first. "Okay to come in?"

"I just said so, right?" I pointed to a space heater on the floor. "But hurry up and shut the door, okay? We've got bootleg warmth going in here."

"What?"

I sit on the desk and push the chair out with my foot. "Have a seat. In case you didn't notice, the house is freezing. Blaze keeps the heat at, I don't know, fifty-five degrees?"

"It's sixty, I believe," Lella corrects.

"Yeah. Sixty. And so Lella has a hard time with the cold. On our walk last night, someone put this heater out by the curb to be picked up."

Lella nods. "I said, 'Valentine, why not take that back with us and give it a go? Maybe they're just wasteful folk who simply don't need it anymore.'"

"So we plugged it in and suddenly we're in sunny Florida."

"Is it too hot in here?" Lella asks.

"No way. This is a treat."

"You seem like the conservationist type."

"I am. But if you two don't deserve a little warmth, I don't know who does."

I move to the bed, cross my legs Indian-style, place a pillow on my lap, and settle Lella's head on the softness to give her a better view of Augustine. It's easy to see why she likes him. There's something cute about his face, even though not much of it shows with that beard he wears.

His T-shirt tells me *God is not a Republican or a Democrat.* I point to it. "Does anybody really think either of those things?"

"You'd be surprised."

"So what's up?" I ask. "You all having a New Year's Eve party at Shalom?"

"Nah. Jessica and Rachel are going down to the square to watch the fireworks, and that just leaves Justin, who's in bed by seven every night."

"Are they all monks?" I ask.

"Well, they've taken the vows."

Lella lifts up her head. "What vows?"

Augustine explains, going so far as to tell about the whole eternal chastity business.

She lays her head back down on my lap and listens. "I've never heard of this sort of thing, Augustine. Is it binding?"

I smile. He smiles. "Of course. I promised God."

"But does He hold you to these promises if, well, if other opportunities come along?"

Augustine's no dummy. He reaches out and touches Lella's cheek with the tips of his fingers. "Lella."

She closes her eyes. A tear slips from the corner and slides down the ledge of her nose. "I'm sorry," she whispers. "I don't know what I was thinking."

Augustine kneels in front of her. "No need."

"I wish—"

"That your eyes didn't display your heart?" he asks.

"Oh, yes." Her eyes remain closed. I look down upon her. *Oh, Lella. Oh, Lell.*

"There are other ways to love." He lays a hand of blessing on her head and he looks at me. "You know that. Many ways. Look at the love between you and Valentine."

I nod, yes, that's right. Lella nods. She opens her eyes. "Do you love us, Augustine? It seems as if you do."

"Yes. God's stamped you on my heart. And when I see the both of you, something rings, a sort of song."

"I could never be much good to you or Shalom," she says.

Confusion stitches a line from brow to brow. "You two have no idea how precious you are, do you?"

We stare at him.

"I wish I could hug you, Augustine. I've never given anyone a hug in my entire life."

Augustine lifts her into his arms and holds her against his chest. "I'm sorry, Lella. But pretend you're hugging me, all right, and I'll feel it in my heart."

She closes her eyes, screws up her face.

Augustine blesses the top of her head with a kiss. "Yep. I felt the love!"

Lella smiles. "I did too. You can put me down, if you please."

"She hates to be held like a baby, Augustine."

"Oh! Sorry." He lays her back on the bed then sits back down, rests his palms on his knees.

I shake my head. "Don't mind me for saying so, but that was a little, well, TV movie-of-the week."

"I'm not very original, I guess."

"It was a lovely gesture." Lella.

"Why don't you tell us why you're here, Augustine?"

He taps his fingers in succession. "I came over with an invitation for tonight. Blaze told me yesterday you all had no plans for New Year's Eve."

"Oh, dear me, no!" Lella almost gasps. "It's the most depressing night of the year as far as I'm concerned."

"We were just talking about that," I say.

He rubs the tops of his legs with the palms of his hands. "Remember Poppy Fraser?"

"Of course," I say.

"She's part of a group of ladies who get together for prayer every week, along with Charmaine and a few others. So they're having a little feast over at Charmaine's to ring in the New Year."

"Ring in or pray in?" I ask.

"Ring. Wanna come? I've borrowed Rachel's truck. Room enough for all three of us."

"How can we, Augustine?"

"Oh, but, Val!" Lella screws her head around, eyes teeming with excitement. "Wouldn't it be fun?"

"I'm sorry. I just can't. You should have known better, Augustine." I lift Lella's head with the pillow and slide out from under her. "I've got to go to the bathroom. Maybe you should see yourself out now."

I close the bathroom door behind me and lean against it, feeling the indentations of the panel along the back of my ribcage. With about as much emotion as a refrigerator, Judy Garland, recorded years ago in *Girl Crazy*, sings my favorite song.

My bedroom door clicks shut. Augustine must be gone.

"He tries too hard," I say loudly enough for Lella to hear.

She doesn't answer. She's probably a little miffed at me for turning down the invite for the both of us.

After slapping some cold water on my face and combing my hair back into a neater ponytail, I step back into the bedroom. Lella's gone.

Lella's gone!

He took her with him? That rat!

I rush down the steps and yank open the coat closet door, the coat I made her nowhere in sight. The stroller is gone. Shoving my feet into my boots, I grab my parka, my scarves, and run out the door into the coldest night of the year. Nine o'clock, the hall clock begins to chime. Nobody loiters about. No pedestrians traverse the sidewalk.

And there are the tire tracks. I am not going to Charmaine's. But I'm not going to sit alone with the space heater either.

Zipping up my coat, winding one scarf from ear to ear and the other to circle around my face, I head off under the stars toward Lake Coventry. I walk by the hot spots on the town square and beyond. Hotel Oak is thumping with a live band, Java Jane's has a guitarist and a singer in the back corner. Nobody looks my way. Just another soul bundled up against the soon-coming January.

On the road to the lake I pass Josef's. A party's going on there too.

What in the world are these people so excited about? Don't they remember they failed almost every resolution last year and that life is still a big old pile of quiet desperation? What in the world is the matter with them?

I haven't come here yet this season. To my dock on Lake Coventry. Its stumpy legs disappear into the shining waters of the lake, a full moon lighting the expanse sitting calm in no wind at all as if nature proclaims it just another night, not even worthy of the breeze. I wonder if Charmaine will show up.

She's been meeting me here for three off-seasons now.

Probably not.

Maybe I shouldn't be so hard on the world. Maybe they know something I don't. Maybe I could take a lesson on this night when people decide to pull back a little or take chances, when hope for change ripens fully yellow, begging to be plucked and bitten down to the seeds.

But it's at night when I feel with a desolate song that we are allowed only a few drastic chances, and Daisy, as she rubbed the Drano into my skin, used up almost all of them.

I was pretty. I was just one of those fresh pretty girls you see on the street with swinging hair and a little bounce to her breasts.

A board creaks behind me. I turn.

"I knew you'd be here. When Gus came carrying Lella, and you not in sight, I just said to myself, 'Charmaine, now get on over to that dock, 'cause sure as rain in spring that girl's going to be there.'"

"Hey Charmaine, come on over."

She sits down next to me. "I'm not going to ask why you didn't come. I already know."

"Yeah. So how come you left the party?"

She reaches into her pocket and pulls out a knit cap. "Oh, I don't know." She shoves the cap over all that hair. "I figured it would be so much better out here in the freezing cold night than sitting by our warm fire with a cup of tea and a plate of home-made cinnamon rolls. Call me crazy."

Charmaine just makes me laugh.

"Why don't you come on over, Valentine? Poppy made crab cakes and she's from Maryland. They're really good."

"Nah. I really don't want to. Plus, you'll have to say you found me, and I don't want everybody coming down feeling sorry for me and acting all sad. I mean, pity's okay, but not when it pulls people away from a party. And then they'll realize we're closer friends than anybody knows."

"Except Harlan. He knows everything."

"I don't want everybody in Mount Oak thinking they can be my friend just because you are."

She sighs, puts on some gloves, and leans back on her hands. "Sometimes it's nice to keep something or somebody mostly to yourself. I like that about us. So you'll never guess what I did."

"What?"

"I actually volunteered to cook dinner next week at Shalom."

"Oh no, Charmaine. Why would you ever do a thing like that?"

"It's Augustine. He could talk a fish onto dry land. He said he needed a couple of big pots of stew or soup or something for

Wednesday night. There's some group coming into town, The Psalters. They're a band of Jesus-minstrel types or something like that. Augustine had a hard time pinning down their style."

"Jesus-minstrel types?"

"That's what he said. Kinda gypsyish too." She waves a hand. "Don't ask me, Valentine. And there'll be some of the street people. When they hear there's a meal at Shalom, a few always show up. Folks from the neighborhood too. You need to help me cook. I'm terrible in the kitchen." She waves a hand. "Oh, I try and Harlan's so nice about it, always complimenting the meal no matter how horrible it tastes, but cooking for a crowd? You know how to do that in your sleep."

I lay a hand on her leg. "Charmaine, think about it. I don't want to go to a party tonight *or* share you with anyone. So why would I help you out in public?"

"Because I need help. Augustine went on and on about moving outside our money and busyness so we can see God in fresh new ways." Her eyes deepen like the waters. "I need to see God in fresh new ways, Valentine. And so do you. *You.*"

Her hot steel gaze slices through my frozen soul. She knows. She knows who I really am down underneath this crust of skin and scar.

Looking up at the crystal stars, I say, "Can we cook in the middle of the night and maybe you can heat it up the next day?"

Charmaine hugs me. "Of course you silly."

"I was just totally manipulated, wasn't I?"

"Not a bit, Val. You talked yourself into it all on your own."

"I must be slipping."

The next Tuesday, Charmaine drifts into the driveway at midnight, lights off, engine off.

I jump down off the porch. I open the passenger door to her plain white sedan. "Well, we don't have to be quite this clandestine."

She waves a hand. "I just thought it'd be more fun this way."

"You're right, it is."

"I got bags and bags of groceries in the backseat."

I look in the back as I hop in. Seven paper sacks line the bench seat. "IGA?"

"Only game in town far as I'm concerned. I got everything on your list." She starts up the engine. "I tried that new Safeway out near the mini-mall right when it opened. Too big and fancy. My lands, I don't need to buy Chinese take-out where I get my Captain Crunch. Honestly, how we're going to support a big Safeway is beyond me." Charmaine turns onto Mortimer Street. "So I got in the checkout line and you should have seen the magazines at eye level! My lands, talk about body parts. More body parts than I want to see!"

"You crack me up."

"It's not that I'm all against body parts, in the right circumstances. Fine. God made all the bodies and all the parts. I just don't want to see your body parts when I'm buying milk and eggs." She quick turns her head in my direction. "Well, no personal offense meant."

"None taken. I'd rather keep my body parts to myself anyway."

"Me too. But bras are pretty good these days. For a while, back in the eighties there were those underwire things with the flimsy fabric. Now me, I like a little padding."

"Me too. Not too much, but enough for no topographical show-through."

"That's exactly right!"

"Don't you just love girl talk?"

Charmaine's the only person in the world who talks to me like I'm just another woman. "You don't know how much."

"Glad I can supply the need. Did you forget your scarf on purpose?"

Oh no. "No. Shoot. Do you think anybody's going to be awake?"

"Nope. We've made sure of that!"

"Well, if you don't mind."

"Of course I don't, Valentine."

She turns down Oakly Road, probably one of the most forlorn, forgotten lanes in town. It's only a few blocks from our house, but it seems miles away.

"Shalom is on Oakly?"

"Uh-huh." She leans toward me while still keeping her eyes on the road, lined on either side with shotgun shacks, crumbling frame houses and one or two heroic little homes with fresh paint that seem to be saying, "We're doing the best we can with what we've been given."

She gestures up and down the street. "He moved down here with those other people. And one of the homeless guys said to him, 'You movin' onto Oakly? Dag, but I'd never live there!'"

We laugh.

"He's a unique piece of work," I say.

"Oh, don't I know it. When I look at him, I see what maybe Jesus might look like if He came back to do it all over again, but in Mount Oak, not Jerusalem."

"Does he ever get in trouble?"

"All the time."

"What's he do that's so controversial?"

She leans over again. "He tells people they can't serve God and money."

I shake my head. "Exact opposite of that guy that used to have that show with you and Harlan. Do you know what happened to him?"

"Nope. Nobody knows. His show did real well for a time, but then his cockiness started to show through." Her voice turns even more down-home than usual. "If there's one thing I've learned after all these years on the air and on the road, it's that people don't like arrogant. They don't like that at all. It's a shame, though. There was a good man underneath there."

I just grate out a *hmpf* and then add a little snort for good measure.

"I know, I know, I see the good in everybody. Harlan says it's a good thing I'm not a Calvinist because that whole total depravity thing would be lost on me!" She laughs as she pulls up to the building at the end of the road. Low-slung, it's held in closely by the edges of the narrow lot outlined by a rusty chain-link fence, its surface a pebbly concrete that makes you want to stand there and pick out all the stones.

"What did this building used to be?"

"An old laundromat. You can see in the big front room there's a lot of water damage on the tiles. Where there are tiles."

She fumbles with her key ring, locates one in particular, then shoves it in the lock of the front door, a glass door with a push bar anchored from side to side.

"I'm a nuisance for making you come out so late, Charmaine. It's a good thing you don't mind that."

"Are you serious? I'm just thankful you're here at all. Let's just get back through to the kitchen. Don't cut on the lights or somebody might see us!" she whispers. "Oh, isn't this so fun?"

I follow her to the back of the room, past two card tables, then two old couches facing each other with a coffee table in-between. Somebody made the coffee table from four cinder-blocks and two lengths of evenly cut board. On its surface several votive candles sputter amid Bibles, prayer books, and incense cones on brass plates. "What is this? Some eastern religion stuff?"

Charmaine waves her hand. "They pick and choose from church practices throughout the ages. I don't begin to understand it, but it really means a lot to Gus. And it's all Jesus, so no worry there. At least there's that."

"Like I care."

"There was incense in the temple, you know," she says.

"Like I care about that too."

"Oh, Valentine, you care more than you'd like to admit."

She ushers me through a doorway into a small kitchen. An old 1970s gas range in that dark gold color with a tea kettle on one of the burners, a porcelain sink, and a worktable, probably an old folding table from the laundromat, seems to be the sum and substance of the food preparation operation. "At least it's a gas stove," I say.

"The fridge is on the porch."

"I'll start bringing in bags."

"No, no. Let me do that while you get cooking." She points to an old armoire. "Pots and stuff are in there. My lands, you can tell this place is run by unmarrieds. There's just some spoons, a couple of knives, and a few pots, but somehow they make it work."

"Then we will too. I'm not going to let these monks have anything on us."

"Good for you, honey."

Over the stove an icon of Jesus and the twelve disciples blesses the food. "These people sure are strange," I whisper to the disciples. They look at me like they agree.

A calendar still on August hangs over the sink and time gels into something solid and unbending, something you live inside of, not run away from.

A grating cough exudes from beneath a door off the main room. Sounds like rusty bed springs. Only one other time did I hear a cough like that—when my father was sick. And I swear, I thought he was going to die when he coughed.

I open the cupboard door and pull out two big stockpots. All that's there practically. Two big stockpots and two frying pans.

After setting them on the stove, I turn on the gas burners to heat them up. Charmaine bustles in with three paper bags squeezed between her arms. She sets them on the table.

"Thanks. I'll get the oil heating in the pans."

"I hope I got the right bags first."

I peer inside. "Yep. There's the oil. And the onions and garlic."

"Oh, that's good." She blows out some relief and heads back out to the car.

No cutting board. I fold an empty grocery sack and lay it on the table. First the onions, then the garlic, and soon the two will sweat together in the olive oil. One pot is destined for a vegetarian white bean chili, the other beef stew.

Charmaine returns with more bags, holding ten loaves of Italian bread, butter, tin foil, more cans, and six boxes of brownie mix which she says she can take care of. Charmaine knows how to do box mixes.

"Charmaine, can you start opening up cans? And will you pour some flour into a bowl?"

"Of course. I'm so glad you're doing this for me."

"The aroma alone is worth it."

The bedspring cough returns.

Charmaine freezes above the bag of canned goods. "Was that a cough?"

"Horrible, isn't it?"

"Oh, my lands!" She runs toward the door. "Gus? You in there?"

His reply is so muffled I can't hear what he's saying.

"Is it just you in there?" She looks at me. "Are you decent?"

Poor Augustine. Alone and sick. That doesn't seem right.

She opens the door and disappears inside. I search the bags for the chuck roasts.

"Valentine! Come on in," she hollers.

I lay down my knife, turn down the burners, and walk into the back room.

Plainly, it was once a storage room, shelves lining one wall. Four military cots bump up against the rest of the walls, each bed empty except for Augustine's. "He's burning up." Charmaine kneels on the floor.

I feel his forehead. "Wow. Let me get a cool rag."

"No, I'll do that. You keep cooking."

Augustine tries to lift his head. Man, he looks old lying there like that. Kinda sun-dried and grizzled. "You cooking for The Psalters?" His already *sotto voce* tones are practically gone. I strain to hear him.

"Yep."

He lays his head back. "Nice. Thanks, Val."

"Go on, Valentine. I'll take care of Gus for now."

Back at the folding table, I cube five pounds of chuck roast, dredge the meat in flour, and brown it in the heated oil. Simply have to brown the beef if you want stew to turn out just right. Browning is the key. That slap into the hot oil, the sizzle, the pop. When I add the beef to the onions and garlic, the smell that rises up makes you know something very, very good is on its way.

Forty-five minutes, a nicked forefinger, and four more cool washcloths later, the white chili and the stew are simmering on low heat.

Augustine tries to smile when I check on him. "Smells great, even to this nauseous person."

"Quite the compliment." I turn to Charmaine. "You okay?"

"Sure am. Want me to take you home?"

"Nah. Still needs to cook awhile. Then I'll put it in the fridge. We've got at least another hour to an hour-and-a-half to go. Why don't you go on home? I'll watch over Augustine tonight and walk home really early in the morning."

Augustine tries to raise his head. "Oh, but Valen—"

"Good idea." Charmaine gets up and pats the seat of a chair she'd found earlier. "Gus, what can I bring you in the morning?"

"Some kind of cold medicine?"

After kissing his forehead, she flies out of the room, clicking on her high-heeled boots. "I'll get some right away."

"You gotta love that woman, don't you?" I say.

"Really do."

I leave to stir the stews, turn down the flames once more. The smell of garlic and onions alone should heal the crazy monk.

That cough scours the air again.

Lord, have mercy.

Maybe the fridge on the porch holds something promising for Augustine. I step out into the cold and throw open the door. There's almost nothing in there.

Back in the bedroom. "How long has it been since you've eaten a decent meal?"

"I've been sick for three days. Had the last can of soup."

He spasms in a fit of coughing, but it doesn't stop, the cot springs bounce up and down again and again, until finally, he vomits. All over the side of the bed. All over my jeans.

"Oh, no. Oh, man." Sweat pours off of him. "I'm so sorry."

"It's okay."

In the kitchen I dig up some rags.

"Let me clean you up."

I'm so used to wiping Lella and cleaning her, the smell doesn't bother me at all. It's easy to see he hasn't eaten for a while. It's that kind of vomit.

"Sorry."

"Stop apologizing, Augustine. It's really okay." I touch his forehead after throwing the nasty rag into the bathroom sink. "You're absolutely burning up."

"Got some ibuprofen in the medicine cabinet. Forgot to mention it to Charmaine."

Talk about head in the clouds.

In the bathroom, I shake a few tablets into the palm of my

hand. A water glass rests on the edge of the sink. Lifting it, I hold it against the light. Probably all sorts of sick germs congregating there.

In the kitchen I fill a clean cup with cold water.

"Here." I sit beside Augustine, lift his head like I've done a thousand times with Lella, and give him the medicine. "Drink the rest of the water. You're probably so dehydrated it isn't funny."

"I just feel so—"

And he vomits again. This time I jump clear.

I root through the kitchen cupboard for a bowl and return to his side. I clean him up again. "I won't leave you tonight."

"Thanks, Valentine."

"Why are you alone?"

"The others . . . in Thailand. Left on the second."

"I'm here."

Thirty minutes later, the pots simmering on low, a cup of tea and a piece of dry toast inside of him, Augustine sleeps. I lay down on one of the cots, looking around me in the darkness where only a candle burns on an old table in the corner.

What a crappy old place.

An hour goes by. The stew and chili cooked through, I heft the pots into the fridge on the porch. The disciples above the stove look down on me. "This guy's pretty much a lunatic if he thinks this is bringing people to Jesus," I tell them.

They don't say anything.

At five a.m. I lead him into the shower. He's only wearing a pair of athletic shorts and a T-shirt that says, "Obey Gravity: It's the Law."

"Where are the towels?"

"Mine's hanging behind the door."

"One towel?"

"Do you really need two?" He coughs again.

I grab the thin towel. "If you've got hair like mine you do."

"Ah."

"Then again, those dreads must hold a lot of water."

Faucet now running into the tub, I wave my hand beneath the stream of water. Perfect.

"Okay, call me if you need me. You look awful. But you smell even worse."

"I still feel pretty bad. But the ibuprofen's helped a little."

"I'm heading to the IGA for some chicken broth and noodles."

"But aren't you worried about your face?"

"I think your troubles trump mine."

The bathroom begins to steam up.

I leave him to take his shower, hoping he won't faint while I'm gone.

I chicken out on the IGA, remembering what somebody did to our holy family. So I get some soup from Blaze's larder. She's already up.

"Where were you?"

"Augustine's really sick. Can you heat up some of this soup and take it over to him?"

"Sure thing."

"It's chicken soup." How fitting.

"What were you doing at Shalom?"

"Wouldn't you like to know?" I hurry on up to bed.

NINE

◆◆◆◆◆

DREW: 2003

No matter how bad you think your childhood is, there's always somebody who had it way worse. Hermy reminds me of this. It's pretty hard to wallow in your frustration at having the ice king as your father, when the guy sitting next to you landed in the hospital seven times because of his abusive mom. She sounds like a horror, but Hermy's matter-of-fact about it.

"I dunno, Drew. I mean, at least my mom pretty much let me do what I wanted when I wasn't around the house. She couldn't have cared less what my grades were as long as I didn't get in her hair or mess up the house. After a while, I just learned to stay gone."

It's the next evening, nine o'clock, and we're headed to my father's house. I wanted to make sure he'd be home.

"Shoot, Drew, it sounds like you couldn't do anything right. And you didn't even have your mother around to take some of the steam. We need those kinds of people. I had an aunt like that."

We pull up in front of the house and walk up the sidewalk, our boots compressing the deicing salt with small pops and crackles.

I knock on the door and Dad's housekeeper, Malena, answers. Her eyes widen. "Hola, Señor Drew."

"Hi, Malena."

She swings the door and sweeps us in.

Malena, a very proper woman in sensible pumps, a tweed skirt, and a pale yellow blouse, shuts the door. "Please sit in the living room while I call your father."

Despite the verbal formality, her eyes drip with friendliness. While I wouldn't say Malena loves me like her own, she's a kind woman who keeps her private life private, values her position as head of my father's household, and holds his privacy in high regard.

When I was younger, sometimes her maternal instincts got the better of her. She'd stow away chocolate in my lunch sack, or hide my college grades until Dad reached the right frame of mind to view them without shaming me for my 3.75 average. Nothing ever went wrong on her watch.

The formal living room walls are shaded a blood red. Yellow silk upholstery in striped and floral patterns cover chairs arranged in conversation groups. Fine artwork glows under the perfect lighting, and beautiful bowls and vases from China rest on mahogany (I think) surfaces. Not one speck of dust sullies the wood floors, and even the fringes on the oriental rugs are combed perfectly.

With my toe, I mess up an edge.

"I hate this house."

"You grow up here?"

"No. We moved here when I was sixteen. We always lived down south before Mom died, or disappeared, or what have you. My father was a lobbyist for the tobacco industry in those days, so he planted his family in North Carolina. He was gone a lot. His longer and longer stays in DC troubled her, but she never said why."

"He was cheating on her, I bet."

"I don't know. That would presuppose he could feel something for somebody."

"Not necessarily, man."

"True. I never thought he was about an affair, though. I still don't. She just wasn't the right wife for a man like him. Then again, I don't know who would be."

Malena reappears. "He's on the phone. Just give him five minutes. Would you like a drink?"

"No, thanks. Why don't you visit with me?"

She shakes her head and walks out of the room. She hesitates at the door but continues on.

"In some ways I couldn't blame my dad. Imagine being married to a woman who called sin *sin* and knew when somebody was in a major state of it. I don't know if she was a prophet or just crazy."

"Was she ever right about any of the other things she said?"

"Spot on. I just figured, 'That's Mom for you' like kids seem to do without realizing how odd their childhood actually is. Hopefully she's calmed down a little."

"I wouldn't bet on that."

I approach the small writing desk, spring the latch in the middle cubby, and open the false front of the hidden compartment. A fat four-by-six manila envelope is wedged between the sidewalls. I could slip it into my jacket pocket.

But that would give me one more thing to confess to Father Brian.

I shut the compartment.

Hermy whistles. "Man, this reminds me too much of my house. Bad stuff. Bad stuff."

Finally, my father walks into the living room. Charles Parrish exudes power not only from his personality but from his physical dimensions. He's forced to dip his head slightly when he walks through a conventional doorway. Tailors fashion his clothing. Shoemakers construct shoes for his feet alone.

He's a beast. Perfectly made for what he does.

But even this beast can't hide his shock at my appearance. Who was this young man with the bald, nicked pate? This skinny urchin-like youth who once plied the airwaves?

"Drew. A surprise. You've lost weight."

"Yes, Dad. I'm taking a road trip. This is Hermy."

"I see." Dad shakes Hermy's hand, sizing him up. Hermy's found wanting, for Dad turns right to me without saying anything.

"What are you doing here?"

"I came to get Mom's address."

"This is nonsensical. Your mother's dead." He crosses his arms across his chest. "Don't keep at this ridiculousness."

"She called me. I know it was her."

"I told you this is crazy."

"She's alive."

He spreads his feet.

His already dark eyes deepen to the blackness of ink. "You'd do well to stop all this, Son."

But I've got nothing left to lose.

"So you say. But despite your veiled threat, I'll push this to the end, whatever or wherever that is. I did learn a thing or two from you."

Man, I hope that feeds his ego. Please, God.

He relaxes. "Are you going a little crazy, Son? You know, your mother was a bit touched. We think that's why she crashed the car."

And this is the moment I've been waiting for. The man has blood on his hands and crap on his shoes. What he's done is a mystery, *why* isn't so hard to guess. But I venture forward, surfacing a resentment that undergirds me.

I square my chest. "All I'm asking is to see my mother. You give me that address and I am out of your life forever. I won't drag you through the mud; I won't even breathe your air. You'll never have to call me on Sundays or put a little extra into my bank account. I will disappear from you like—" And here I take an enormous chance, shrugging with a knowing look on my face. At least I hope it's knowing. I mean, people disappear from Washington every so often.

"Like who?"

Who, not what.

"Like mail workers at the five o'clock whistle."

"Wait just a minute." He walks toward the doorway, then turns. "She needed to be put away, Son. I only did it to protect you. You and a lot of other people. It was better if you thought she was dead." He leaves the room.

It's funny how easily you can spot an act when you're so good at giving one yourself.

Hermy looks up. "He's one cold man."

Malena clicks back into the room and hands me a sheet of paper. "Your father had another call come in. Here's the address you requested, 'as per your agreement,' he said. I'll see you to the door now." She ushers us into the foyer and pulls an envelope from the waistband of her sweater.

Grabbing my hand and placing the parcel into my palm, she whispers, "God protect you, Drew. If you know what is best, you'll never come back here." She crosses herself.

"Is this address a mental institution?"

"I'm not saying anything."

"Malena, why did she disappear?"

"It wasn't her choice. Your mother, she loved you."

"Was she really crazy?"

Malena crosses her arms and rubs them with her hands. "Go on now. Go!"

In the chill of a DC night, Hermy and I drive away.

As per your agreement, Malena said.

We ride by the memorials, Lincoln and Jefferson. The illumined Washington Monument points into the darkened sky from which a light, icy rain begins to descend and the dome of the capital seems to light up the city blocks around it.

I will never come back here again.

Out of the city, off of Route 66, I pull into a Shell station. "I gotta make a call."

Hermy decides to get some beef jerky. "Want a soda, man?"

"Sure."

I dial St. Mary's rectory and Father Brian answers.

"I did it. I confronted my father."

"What happened?"

"He gave me the address for my mother."

"How was he?"

"The same. I told him I'd never see him again if he'd give me the address."

"And he took you up on that?"

"In so many words."

"Looks like you've only got one place left to go."

"A year ago I thought I had a full life and a really bright future. And now all I've got is my friend Hermy and an address."

"Well, at least you can only go up from here."

For some reason this strikes me as humorous. "Oh, I don't know. I imagine there's always a bigger bag of tricks."

I watch Hermy climb back into the car. I'd better end this call.

"I should go, Brian."

"Did you leave your church voluntarily?"

"Yes."

"Why?"

"I finally began to see myself in a real mirror, the way I really looked."

"Did you have good intentions, though?"

"Does that actually matter when you're leading people astray?"

"Hard to say."

"I'll get back in touch after I meet her."

"I'm still praying."

Sure you are, Father Brian. You're good at what you do.

◆◆◆

Hermy and I decide to camp for the night. We drive on I-70 an hour out of DC, pull off a small exit, and set ourselves up in a grove of trees at the side of the road, just outside a farmer's fence. We'll be out of here early.

Inside the tent I reexamine the address, flashlight highlighting the words Slade, Kentucky.

Hermy sets up the lantern. "You ever been there?"

"No. Have you?" He looks light purple, a little eerie in the battery powered light,

"Yeah. It's near Natural Bridge. Was into rock climbing in college. Great place."

Hermy in college? "How far away?"

"Eight or so hours."

He nabs a book out of his rucksack. I fold up the paper and shove it back into my pocket.

"So what did your old man do that was so bad?" He unrolls his sleeping bag.

I follow suit, untying the laces that hold the bedroll together. "I have no idea what he did."

Hermy's face splits apart and out charges a stampede of laughter like I've never heard before. I swear, if I didn't think the guy was nuts before this, I'd think it now. "You got the stuff, man."

"Thanks."

He slips into his bag as I venture into my own backpack and pull out a small book of Shakespeare's sonnets.

Hermy looks over. "Ah, the bard hisself."

I didn't realize people actually called him "the bard." Huh.

"A friend gave it to me for Christmas one year. She's disappeared. I guess I keep in touch with her this way."

Hermy lays his book facedown on his chest. "Did you love her?"

"Somewhat. Yes and no."

"That's not a hard question. You either do or you don't."

"I don't have an answer for you."

"Do you love her now?"

"In a way."

"Did she love you?"

"Yeah. Yeah she did. Big-time." I grab my notebook then slide into my sleeping bag. "But that seems like years and years ago now."

"So, you squandered a good thing?"

"Yeah, Hermy."

"Maybe the best thing that ever happened to you?"

"Yeah, Hermy. Sheesh."

"Sorry, man."

I examine the title of his book. *Paradise Found* by Barbara Cartland. "Never heard of her."

"Historical fiction. Heavy stuff."

"Oh. Cool. A takeoff of Milton, I assume."

Hermy doesn't answer.

I read my previous entries. Poor Father Brian. Having to read all this glurge. I feel sorry for the guy.

"You know, I traded my mother in, in my mind, when I was about seven," Hermy says.

"What?"

"I watched reruns all the time. Whenever I could, which was a lot with cable, 'cause I just needed to stay out of her hair, right? I'd watch *Andy Griffith, Father Knows Best, Bewitched, Ozzie and Harriet.* I chose Samantha Stevens as Replacement Mom. Man, she was the best."

"I can't believe I'm admitting this. After my mom left, I had Aunt Bee fantasies."

"Oh, yeah?"

I shake my head. "I wanted her to come stay with us. She could have called me Andeeee! Just like she did her nephew."

"Cool."

"But I haven't watched any of those shows in years."

"Naw man. After a while . . . well, you know."

"Yeah. Yeah, Hermy, I know."

◆◆◆

When they removed Daisy's bandages, she squealed with delight. "Even swollen it looks better." She set the mirror next to her on the bed. "What do you think, Drew?"

"Good. When the swelling goes down we'll be able to tell more."

Her eyes widened. "Do I need more done?"

Trician took a good look. She crossed her arms, the bangles on her arms clanging, spicy perfume puffing out with her movements like always. "Hmm." She tilted her head to the side. "Hard to say. But I think it will be fine. That's the thing with all this, it may take some fine-tuning. Some tweaking, if you will."

The doctor frowned. "Don't judge it yet. I think you'll be pleased. With the bruising it's impossible to see the reality of it."

The reality of it. Even now I remember those words. I wasn't so far gone at the time not to catch the irony, Father Brian, believe me.

I laid my hand over Daisy's. She had the softest skin I'd ever felt on an adult. "I say we get you home and we'll celebrate. In two weeks we tape our first show. You're going to look great, we've got some great guests lined up, it's all going along as planned."

Daisy grew quiet. She'd gone through so much already. Even just having Trician as a mother. I knew she was in pain as she recovered and that the outcome didn't seem good enough must have added another layer of discomfort. Not that she showed it. Why I couldn't just say, "Hey, Daisy, you look great!" I don't know.

Maybe I should have esteemed her better than myself, right Father? If we could all get a handle on that, we wouldn't need to confess much, now would we?

After we got Daisy settled into bed at home, Trician pulled me aside. "Have you encouraged her about the diet yet?"

For some reason, she'd decided to make me the enforcer. She said Daisy had taken a shine to me and that she'd listen to me. She kept dangling that Nashville carrot in front of me. "No, I haven't."

She nodded. *"Daisy has a somewhat slow metabolism. But we're going to see a diet specialist on Monday. Also, I've employed a trainer at the gym. A real dictator from what I've heard. He'll get her into shape."*

"In two weeks?"

"Oh no! It'll take months, but she'll be fine. Her voice will carry her on Faith Street *until then. But I need you to encourage her, Drew."*

"Trician, she's a grown woman."

She acted like she didn't hear me. "And you can get the director to fill the cameramen in on what angles not to focus on." Just like that, she laughed at her daughter. That didn't sit well, even then.

Daisy slept. Trician and I planned. She'd already made contact with three of the people on my guest list and wanted to know if she could call my father. Of course, I said, of course.

Dad fell in line, happy to supply names and numbers.

It was easy to see why Trician was so gung-ho. She wanted to be rich, successful, and able to leave her husband in style. But she had no talent herself.

"Daisy's your ticket, isn't she, Trician?" I asked her once as we sat going over the lists of guests for the coming months.

"You know she is." She hated me in that moment because she realized I held all the cards at that point. I knew she'd work even harder on getting Daisy a recording contract, which would benefit me.

I encouraged Daisy as much as I could with her newfound nose and her slimming body. Looking back now, it must have seemed like immense pressure to be perfect. The fact that she wanted to please me, to get me to love her, worked into it well. It would keep her around once the Nashville contract hit. And I was pretty sure it would one day.

◆◆◆

I can't believe how much I used her for that half-baked little show. But it was a stepping stone to greater things. I told myself that every day. People were going to hear my message and they'd buy my books and I'd be on *Larry King Live* apologizing all over the place if he asked any hard questions about the gospel. More and more people would come to Elysian and the money would really start to flow.

And that wouldn't be such a bad thing, would it? It would sure make it seem like my gospel was working for me. Why wouldn't it work like that for everybody else as well?

TEN

◆◆◆◆

VALENTINE: 2009

Lella points her head in the direction of my comic book sitting on the nightstand. *Betty and Veronica*. "Why them most of all, Valentine? Why not the superhero types? *X-Men* and all of that?"

I gather her hair and begin to brush it back. "Well, Lell, I don't know. I just don't relate to all that other stuff. *Betty and Veronica* just have everyday high school stuff going on. I can't handle a whole lot of conflict where the outcome might destroy the world."

Lella laughs. "I surely don't blame you. I was lying on my bed the other day thinking about comics and how one centering on human oddities would be so interesting, don't you think?"

"Sure. It's like that old movie *Freaks*."

"I truly love that movie!" She turns her head and looks at me. "Do you know I met Johnny Eck the Half Man once?"

"No way." I'm impressed. Johnny Eck literally was half a man. His twin brother was born perfectly normal, but Johnny Eck was nonexistent from the bottom of his ribcage on down. "When?"

"Oh, when I was little. He was old then, painting screens in Baltimore where my family hails from. My parents took me to see him and he was lovely, so encouraging, and I knew that if he

◆◆ 146 ◆◆

survived and had a good life, I could too. Had a twinkle in his eye. It made all the difference in the world."

Her hair now gathered tightly, I reach for an elastic band and begin looping her heavy locks through the ever-tightening circle. "Did you figure out how he went to the bathroom?"

"Valentine!"

"Well, don't you wonder?"

"People must wonder the same thing about me."

"Not at all, you just don't have legs. Big difference than not having half of your torso."

"That's true."

"But you're right. It would be a good comic book. Freaks as heroes. That would be good."

"Although there is the discomfort factor to consider."

"That's true."

Blaze enters the room. "Augustine's still feeling under the weather, but he's good enough to go to the concert tonight. He wants to know if you're coming."

"Yeah. I'm curious about this group." I pick up the hot curling iron. "I'm coming in right before they start and I'll stand at the back."

"Suit yourself." She shuts the door behind her.

"I'm glad to hear Augustine's feeling a little better!" Lella.

"Me too." She still likes him. Poor Lell.

"I heard from Aunt Dahlia today. She'll be here in a couple of days. Isn't that good news?"

"Do you want me to curl your ponytail?"

"Oh, no. I don't want to be too much trouble."

"It's no trouble."

I curl her hair anyway, apply her makeup, take her down to lunch, and practically scratch Bindy's eyes out when she says, "Hey, Lella. All the makeup and hair in the world won't begin to disguise the fact you've got no appendages."

"If you two didn't share a heart or a liver or whatever it is, I'd separate you right now," I say. "The hard part would be figuring out which one deserved to live. And what are you doing at the table this afternoon anyway? I thought you were banished."

Rick laughs and nods. "You tell 'em, Val." He sits down. "You having lunch too? Blaze made her special soup."

Ten cans of Campbell's Chicken Noodle plus two Cream of Mushroom and a Cream of Celery. "Uh, no thanks. Not hungry."

Clifford the Human Blockhead, also the big attention hog, sits down. He's normal looking with short brown hair and wide cheekbones. He doesn't really wear a costume when he performs, just a business suit and tie. For some reason, that makes the whole act even more ludicrous, more stunning. He's back from Florida and his winter visit with his kids, Cliff Jr. and Lexy. His ex-wife, Melody, is a piece of work. I ask him about his trip.

"Well, the kids are doing fine. Melody did all she could to horn in on our activities. But I stood firm on the whole. Great kids."

"That's wonderful, Clifford!" Lella nods effusively.

"She's still mad because Cliff Jr. tried to put a nail up his nose and had a nosebleed. I told her, 'But hey, there are a lot of jobs guys do that kids shouldn't.' She didn't want to hear it."

"Well, glad you're back safe and sound." I turn to Rick. "You going to the concert?"

"Sure thing." Rick rakes his fingers through his heavy blond hair. He really is a nice-looking guy. "I'll walk over with you. If you don't mind."

"Why would I mind?"

"I think it would be safer, that time of night."

He doesn't say, "With the holy family and all," but it's what he means.

"At least it gets dark early now." I hand him a napkin.

"Thanks."

Back up in my room I turn on my computer and look up Johnny Eck, probably my favorite freak, and then Mary Ann Bevan, the sideshow performer who billed herself as *The World's Ugliest Woman*.

Well, she's dead so I don't have to beg to differ.

Mary Ann had four kids when she came down with a giantitis condition that elongated her face. After her husband died, she didn't know what she'd do to support herself and her children. Then she got the bright idea of billing herself as *The World's Ugliest Woman*. She went from England all the way to Coney Island.

"Ugly will take you places you never thought you'd go," I say, thinking about that icon of the disciples even though they're stuck in Augustine's kitchen.

I'm standing at the back of the Shalom Laundromat. I know this is supposed to be some community house/monastery, but a Laundromat's a Laundromat.

The Psalters are quite possibly the loudest band that bows the head to Jesus I've ever heard in my entire life. They have this gypsy, eastern European sound, that hollering kind of yelly singing that goes well with the accordion, the banjo, the fiddle, and the percussion that accompanies it.

During a break between songs I lean over to Charmaine. "The main singer's a hottie. I just have to say it."

"Don't I know it!"

Wild, feral almost, his intense black eyes would pull your soul from your body if you let them.

"He makes you want to get up and do something, doesn't he?" Charmaine asks. "Like life is some glorious, whirling gift."

"I heard he liked the white bean chili."

"Oh, Valentine. Someday you're going to have to admit these things affect you like they do everybody else."

"And the stew was a big hit."

Augustine weaves his way through the ragtag group gathered for the show, stopping to say a word to Charmaine who looks as out of place as Gene Simmons in full makeup at a Red Hat luncheon. But she's jumping up and down, praising her Jesus, even though this music sounds nothing like her own. Lella's sitting on her donut on a chair at the front, having been strolled here by Rick and me. The sound must be crackling her eardrums like tissue paper.

"Hey, Val!" Augustine sidles over.

Rick stands closer to me.

"Looks like Lella's having a good time," Augustine says right in my ear.

I lean into his ear too. "She'll be accepted by these people, that's for sure. They're nice-looking young people, but they're misfits like we are."

"I guess you could say that."

"How's the cough?" My face touches his. I pull back.

"Much better. You're an angel. You know that?"

Oh, brother. He pats my shoulder and moves back through the crowd.

The Psalters version of "Holy, Holy, Holy" holds a compelling melody, and on the second go-round I sing along. Rick presses closer still.

Charmaine whips around, looks right at me, and says, "I knew it."

Knew what?

That night Rick knocks on my door and peers around as I lean out the window smoking a cigarette.

He shakes his head. "You shouldn't smoke with a voice like yours. How come you don't sing?"

"I haven't sung since that Daisy woman destroyed my face. But I just couldn't help myself tonight."

"So that was her name, then? Daisy?"

"Yep. Don't ask another thing."

"Okay. You know, I play the violin. We should do something together sometime."

"For who, Rick?"

"I dunno. Just a thought, Val. Sorry."

I throw the burning cigarette out the window, hoping it doesn't land on some tuft of dry grass and end up burning down the house. That would stink. I pull down the sash. "Some things about people should just be left behind forever. You know?"

He puffs air out between his lips. "Boy do I."

"Not you, surely."

"You know, Val"—he shoves his hands in his pockets—"there are a lot of really stretchy people in the world just like me. But not many of us run away to the circus."

"So—why are you here, then?"

"Oh, you'd like to know. But I'm not saying a thing."

"Suit yourself. Hey, I made some chocolate truffles earlier today. They're in the fridge if you want one."

He smiles, realizes it's a dismissal, and pushes off against the door frame. "Sounds good." Turning to leave, he pauses. "Hey, you don't like that Augustine guy, do you?"

"Oh gosh, no!"

"Really?"

"He's really great, but he doesn't have a lot of sex appeal, if you know what I mean."

"Well, no, I mean it's not like I would notice something like that."

"Go get a truffle, Rick. It's late."

No walks for Lella and me tonight. The concert wore her out. As for me, I just ordered a catalogue from Big Sky Log Homes and I'm going to look over every single model. Aunt Dahlia's visit tomorrow doesn't scare me.

◆◆◆

Augustine pulls up to the front of Blaze's on his motorcycle. A two-seater. A man in tatters clings to him from the backseat.

"Beautiful day, Val!" Gus yells.

He's right. The trees might just be budding on a day like today, the bare branches fooled by the warm breeze coming up the Gulf Stream. Lella and I have been sitting on the front porch all afternoon. "January. Go figure."

"I'd take you for a ride but I've got to get Leon up to the health department. Wanna go out later?"

I laugh and laugh.

He zooms away with a friendly wave of his hand, a throaty rumble of Harley engine, and a puff of blue smoke from the tailpipe.

"What do you think of that?" I ask Lella. "Sometimes he seems so exuberant. Like too much. I think it's an act."

"Oh, surely I don't. He merely seems thankful for the blessings he's been given."

I pull back and look at her. "You really think that? I mean, he's living in a rundown Laundromat for goodness sake."

"I really do, Valentine." She scratches her chin by rubbing it on her collarbone.

"Well, if anybody should know, it would be you, the eternal optimist. How much longer 'til your aunt gets here, Lell?"

"Any second."

The woman's got an internal clock like you wouldn't believe.

In between my fingers I arrange the folds of the vest I'm embroidering for Rick and get back to work. I jab the needle so deep into the fabric I impale my own finger underneath.

"Crap!" I mutter. I suck on my index finger.

"Oh dear, Valentine. You poor th—look, there's Aunt Dahlia!"

A bossy, yellow vehicle with no business here shoulders in like it somehow pays the rent. The occupant leans forward and hands the fare over the backseat.

"So what's she like, Lell?"

"Very, very sweet. Just like my mother was."

Dahlia starts to yank what looks like a heavy suitcase out of the backseat. I jump off the porch. "Hang on a sec, I'll get that!"

My stupid face scarf flutters against my neck.

She looks up and smiles with full, bright orange lips, baring large, snaggled teeth. "You must be Valentine."

"Right. Let me get that."

She pats her hair—a cellophane shade of bottle brown, cut into a short pageboy like you see on drawings of medieval guys.

Lella wiggles on her chair as I set the bags on the porch.

Dahlia climbs the steps on four-inch stripper shoes with ankle straps.

"Aunt Dahlia! Why, look at you! I wouldn't have recognized you out in public."

"I'm a free woman, Lella Denise!" She holds her arms out, swaddled in a bright orange velvetlike sweater with lots of fringe, and twirls in a circle.

I reach out and circle a hand around her waist as she almost topples off her high heels.

Lella laughs. She'd clap her hands if she had them. Instead, she shoots off those eye sparkles as her aunt leans down and folds her into a bright orange hug.

Dahlia leans over to me. "Joe was such a mean old coot. And tighter than my grandmother's girdle, honey. Oh, my! The minute the coroner told me he was gone, I went off on a shopping spree." She elbows me lightly in the ribs. "Bet you can't guess what my favorite color is!"

Darn it, but I have to laugh.

"And Joe hated orange. I even bought an orange brassiere!"

The noise of squealing tires pulls me away from Dahlia. Augustine hops off his bike. "I need to use the phone. Pronto!"

"Go on back to the kitchen."

I follow him in.

He dials 9-1-1. "Hey, it's Augustine from over at Shalom. We need an ambulance over on Montgomery Street near the Primitive Baptist Church. Guy's been stabbed. Was left naked in the street. Yeah, I moved him and ran in to call. I'll get right out there."

He hangs up. "I know they'll tell me to stay on the line, but I can't leave him there. I need a blanket."

In the living room I grab one of Blaze's afghans. "Let's go."

We rush across the porch. "I'll be back, Lell!"

I hop on the back of the bike and we ride a couple of blocks. The guy lies on the grass by the road, Augustine's leather jacket over his nether regions.

"Here." Augustine lays the blanket over him. "Help's on the way."

"Oh no, man. I can't go in." Longish brown hair lays in limp strands over his forehead and cheeks. His sharp, shiny nose catches the sun.

"You've been stabbed." Augustine turns to me as he reaches under the blanket with his bandana, applying direct pressure to the stab wound. "I swear, Valentine, I was riding along and I thought it was this bedsheet in the road and I almost ran over it, but I swerved at the last minute and it was this guy, this naked white guy."

"How does a guy end up naked in the street? In Mount Oak?"

"It's our local gang. One of their trademarks. After they stab a guy, they strip him and throw him in the street. He's pretty lucky to even be alive."

The guy groans again.

Yeah, some luck.

But Augustine is on fire with grace. He glows.

The man groans. "Naw, man. Not the hospital."

Augustine, sitting on the ground next to him now, still applies pressure. "You're gonna die if we don't get you there."

"I'm gonna die anyway."

"No, you're not. And you can take that as a promise. What's your name?"

"Garth."

I sit down, stealing looks at the grizzled, gray, gracious man named Augustine, a naked, bleeding man between us. I take Garth's hand in my own.

Augustine nods at me. "It doesn't take much, does it, Val?"

I lean out my bedroom window picturing the disciples at the Laundromat. "You know," I say in my mind, "sometimes acid is thrown in your face. And sometimes it's grace. Both leave you changed somehow. Don't ask me how it works. If I analyze it, it might go away."

The disciples still don't say anything back, even in my mind.

The apostle John looks sympathetic.

He'd understand Augustine's vows. Poverty, chastity, and obedience.

Doesn't that just figure? Thomas must be thinking.

I hold back a laugh. Yeah, it all just figures.

So what are you going to do with all this? James would ask if he could speak.

I feel a bit different now, I admit. Like I want to be with him. Oh, not in *that* way, but you know what I mean. Maybe I shouldn't keep him at arm's length like I've been doing. Maybe he's right. Maybe there's more than just romantic love.

Peter looks like he thinks that's a good thing.

That's it. I'm ordering my own icon.

I jump online and find one with Jesus and all twelve disciples, only it's not the Last Supper like Augustine's. Jesus is washing their feet.

Aunt Dahlia brought in ribs from Love's Rib Room. She minced up a rib and mixed it into the mashed potato side dish. Augustine's the only other person who's done that sort of thing for me. Lella told her right up front that I feed her, and Dahlia didn't try to shoulder into the job.

I enjoyed the ribs.

I figure a walk to the dock will do me good. Lella and Dahlia are already asleep after sitting down in the living room with Rick for a rerun of *CSI*. I sit with my legs dangling over the water.

The edges of the lake catch the rays of moonlight, outlining the far shore in silver. Someone's chopping wood across there. In the middle of the night. Funny what people do when they can't sleep.

It turned cold again this evening.

The stillness around me, no breeze tonight, coupled with the staccato chop of the woodcutter connects me to the world.

"Valentine?"

A hand rests on my shoulder.

"Hey, Charmaine."

"Two a.m. again."

"Yep."

Bundled up in down jackets, scarves, hats, and gloves, we could be twins.

"You okay?" she asks.

"Better than ever, I think. Or at least better than in a long time." I lean into her. "Nope, I think better than ever."

"That's good, honey."

"Why are you awake?"

"Oh, Mama was walkin' around and when I finally got her settled back in bed, I just didn't feel like sleeping. I was hoping I'd find you sitting here, so I took a chance."

"How come?"

"Well, it's like this. We all need to be known for who we really are."

Uh-oh.

Thank goodness she continues to stare out over the lake, as do I. I'm not the type to endure that eye-to-eye intense look-at-me conversation.

"I agree, Charmaine."

"I heard you singing the other night at the concert and my suspicions were confirmed."

"Okay. So?"

"I know who you really are, Valentine. Or rather who you were. And I do mean were."

"At least you realize the truth of that."

I remain silent, gaze locked on the new night, a night of fierce, sparkling calm.

"You're going to make me come out and say it, aren't you, Daisy?"

"I'm not Daisy."

"Not Daisy, or not Daisy anymore?"

"Never again Daisy. Daisy's gone. She was destroyed and there's no hope of a resurrection."

Charmaine grabs my hand. "What happened, Valentine? Who did this to you? Who burned you?"

"I don't want to talk about it, Charmaine. You know who I was. I loved you back then when I was Daisy. You were the only person who made sense, who lived just like she spoke. I still love you. You have to know I love you more than you could bear if you just knew."

Charmaine begins to cry. I've never seen Charmaine cry. She's just not a crier. "I won't make you tell me, Valentine."

"I may never want to. In fact, I can pretty much guarantee that."

"It's okay." She pulls a handkerchief out of her pocket and wipes her eyes and nose. "I'm just sorry you've had to go through all of this. I'm glad we're back together now though. Those years must have been tough. All alone and all."

"I made it through."

"Well, we all make it through, Valentine. It doesn't mean it was good."

"That sure is the truth."

We sit in the chilled night air. Charmaine reaches into her pocket and takes out two pieces of chocolate wrapped in foil. "Here."

I chew mine up fast. She savors hers as the moon barely moves across the sky.

"So what now?" she asks later.

"What do you mean, what now? Just because you know, Charmaine, doesn't mean I'm suddenly going to come out of the closet."

She barks out a laugh. "Fair enough. Well, maybe it's just enough that you know I know."

"I figured you were onto me a long time before this."

"You were right."

"When did you get an inkling?"

She waves her hand. "Oh, I thought you might be Daisy the first night on the dock."

"Really?! What gave me away?"

"Your speaking voice. Even with the bitter edge you've got

now, and the change in pronunciation because of your lips, Valentine, you can't change the tone. I'm a singer. I notice these things."

"Bitter edge?" I stare at her and begin to laugh. She joins in.

"I guess this is all okay," I say. "I know you can keep a secret."

"That's for sure. I'm the queen of that."

ELEVEN

◆◆◆◆◆

DREW: 2003

The sun climbs onto the saddle of the valley's horizon, illuminating the strata of rock in front of us as we stand outside the visitors' center at Sideling Hill. A massive cut opened up this ridge in 1983 to make room for I-68.

Layers of rock in a U-shaped semicircular pattern speak of 350 million years of formation according to one of the displays inside. My brethren at the seminary I attended would have had the proverbial field day with that kind of dating. Some people spend their whole lives trying to prove otherwise. Me, well I don't know and I never did really care. But I learned to keep my mouth shut about that.

Hermy's gleeful. "That dark stratum near the top is coal and shale." And he proceeds to point out shale, sandstone, igneous, and combinations thereof. He's disappointed when I suggest we hit the road.

I don't doubt God made all this. I never have. And it stands to reason I never will. I just wish He could control His people like He does the great earth. Particularly me.

The wind slices through our clothing as we climb once again into the car.

We pull into the coffee shop at the Best Western in Cumberland for a quick breakfast and a hop onto the Internet. I map the journey, we eat eggs and home fries, jerk back some coffee, and head back into the Allegheny Mountains.

I let Hermy drive. The car devours I-68 and 79, though Hermy rarely exceeds the speed limit by more than five miles an hour. God bless West Virginia's seventy miles an hour. You can say whatever you want about the state, but it doesn't micromanage its populace, and face it, at the end of the line, people are going to do what they're going to do.

I'm living proof of that, which is saying something. A lot of people are dead proof of the very same adage.

It's afternoon now, we've managed I-64 and have entered Kentucky. According to Hermy we're in the Daniel Boone National Forest.

"Thirty-four hundred miles of cliff-line around here, man. Pretty amazing. You could rock climb practically your whole life and never have to repeat. But you'd want to. Some of the places are that good."

"Good camping then, I'll bet."

"Sure. You like just heading out with your tent?"

"Yeah. I do." No church growth books this time, though.

It's almost time to see her. I'll be there in ten minutes and twenty-one years. We pull into one of Natural Bridge State Park's parking lots and use the bathroom at yet another visitor center.

The room smells barren, of old leaves left for spring cleaning.

"I'm going for a quick hike," Hermy says. "That okay with you?"

"Take your time."

I breathe in, grasping the slip of paper with my mother's address. I pull my notebook out of my rucksack, sit on the john, and start to write again.

◆◆◆

Well, Father Brian, I thought I'd give you a little more info on my mother. Maybe it'll make the rest of this glurge easier to understand. My twelfth birthday, it all began.

My father refused to speak to my mother for almost two weeks after the debacle at the party. He'd flown out of town the night before my birthday, leaving a small gift-wrapped box on my nightstand.

"Don't open it until tomorrow. You'll be a man soon, Drew. And a man needs something to be accountable to."

The next day, I opened it up. A gold wristwatch.

So it was time I was accountable to, not God like my mother always said. Well, well. My mother took me down past Charlotte to an amusement park. That day we rode every roller coaster at least three times. We ate corn dogs and funnel cake for birthday cake and our skin burned to the red of a hard smack. We loved every minute, laughing and running from attraction to attraction. She gave me a skateboard and the Bible I used to preach from until I left Elysian Heights.

Three days after that, my father, having returned from his trip, pulled me out of chess camp and told me of the accident. The car over-turned down a steep incline. According to him an oncoming vehicle swerved over the line and my mother jerked the wheel to miss the car. And down she went, flipping over and over, the car igniting.

Closed casket. No viewings.

Hey, but at least I had that watch.

On my sixteenth birthday he took me out to dinner in DC where we lived permanently by then and told me they actually believed her death to be a suicide. Yeah, he was that calculating. I'd started asking questions about her death, why I couldn't find anything about it in the papers from that time period, why it seemed like it almost didn't happen. He said he'd been trying to protect her reputation. She'd actually run her car into a tree. He made me assure him I wouldn't say anything to anybody. And of course I didn't. I loved my mother.

◆◆◆

I look down on my wrist and check the time from a simple Seiko. My gold watch was damaged in the flood and I didn't care to get it fixed.

Hermy's going to be a while, I guess. At least I hope so. I don't know if I'm ready for this.

◆◆◆

Back to the real story, then.

Daisy showed up to tape the first episode of Faith Street *with a garment bag protecting a purple suit. She pulled it out. "Isn't it great?"*

"Oh, Daisy." I held it up by the hanger. "Purple's Charmaine's signature color. This will never do."

She reddened. Then smiled. "Mother's idea."

Behind her, Trician shook her head, but didn't say anything. I believed Daisy.

Daisy faced her mother. "What should we do?"

"I'll be right back. I saw a gorgeous mustard-colored dress in the window of Ivy and Rose. Hopefully it won't be too small."

Trician hurried off on her high-heeled, pointy pumps. Her toes must have looked like electrical wire all twisted together. Honestly, there wasn't one thing about that woman that didn't turn my stomach. At least my father never micromanaged me like she did Daisy.

I honestly kept looking for a bright spot, something that wasn't so grasping. Daisy told me her story was true. Trician grew up with nothing, alcoholic mother, distant father who spent all his time at the factory, then at the bar in the evening. Daisy said she looked it up and she figured Trician had some disorder where a person can't connect emotionally to people. It seemed pretty right on.

"You look nice." Daisy snaked her hand through my arm. "Nice haircut."

"You think?" We looked at my reflection in the window leading into the office of Port of Peace Assemblies of God.

"Please, you're gorgeous, Drew."

I knew she was overdoing it. I was not gorgeous. I could have listed at least a dozen imperfections to my outward person. But the hair sat right. A little longer on top, short on the sides and in the back, like some intelligent Oxford student. No red-haired Howdy Doody on this show. I felt a softening toward her, but I shoved it down. The show was the thing. We had to retain our focus.

"Just finish up your makeup, Daisy, until Trician gets back."

Her lips pursed. Of course she thought her makeup was finished. She hurried off.

The day had been horrible to begin with. This show had to be a hit. We had broken ground on the new building at church and we needed more money. Add to that one of the elder's wives spent an hour in my office complaining we weren't getting enough meat at Elysian. My father pressured me in his previous Sunday call. "Cast aside this little ministry venture you've got going, Drew, and come to DC and play with your guests for real. I've got just the position for you. You'd be a much better lobbyist than you are a preacher."

Working with my father every day? If there's a better definition of hell, I'd like to hear it. Although I'm sure you have one, Father Brian.

Unfortunately, he was right. I would have made a better lobbyist.

Daisy came out of the women's restroom looking like a clown. Thank heavens Charmaine Hopewell, Faith Street's first guest, stood with me receiving instructions from the director.

After a quick chat introducing the show, she'd sit along with our state's US Senator, Jack Tyne, a devout Catholic crusading against abortion. Jack was the real deal. He saw people like my father and those radio personalities as caricatures, in it for the power, the money, and . . . the power.

I knew this because it took me weeks to talk him into coming on the show, using every rationale I could drum up short of coming out and saying, "I'm nothing like Charles Parrish."

And you know what? Back then, I honestly didn't think I was.

Charmaine turned to Daisy. "Oh, honey! Look at you, you pretty thing! Now I know you're used to making yourself up for stage, but TV is a little different. A little more subtle. Let me help you. Would you mind?"

"Not a bit. I had made my—"

"You're a lifesaver, Mrs. Hopewell." I turned my back on the women. Especially Daisy. I did feel a twinge of remorse. I'm not a sociopath.

◆◆◆

I look down on my wrist and check the time once more.

The park's deserted this time of year and the wind runnels through the gorge, shaving off microscopic bits of sandstone, carving up nature in bits and pieces. That's what Hermy the Encyclopedia told me on the way down.

Sitting at a nearby picnic table, I pull out my pack of smokes, light one, inhale. Ah yes, and press it into my arm. Nobody's around but God and the birds anyway.

◆◆◆

This isn't confessional, but I'm waiting to see my mother, Father Brian. If I write it down, maybe I'll remember it more, remember her more. Maybe my stomach will settle down and I won't feel the need to press cigarette after cigarette into my flesh.

My last real block of memory comes from the summer of my twelfth year, a summer that crawled along in the sordid heat of Chapel Hill, North Carolina. Dad still lobbied for the tobacco industry, and I was shorter than everybody else in my class at The Duke School.

Mom rarely entered Dad's world. She carted me around to school, sports—consisting of fencing, golf, tennis, piano, and chess lessons. Monica always presented a hot, bordering on gourmet, supper for my father when he wasn't taking someone out to dinner or off on some trip with an elected official. Only once or twice a week did Dad sit down at his own table. During such meals both my mother and I found ourselves as grilled as the steaks by the time we arose from our seats. Breathing with relief when he hid away in his den and we cleared the table, our eyes would meet and we never had to say what we were thinking. "It's just you and me in this life. It doesn't matter what he thinks as long as we have each other."

A week before Mom's "car crash," the thick summer seethed, the blacktop burned the soles of my feet, and breathing felt like an easy-listening version of swimming. Mom, from Louisiana stock, preferred the humid blanket of real-time weather to the artificial snap of air-conditioning. When Dad went away, she turned off the cool and we sweated out our days together. I never minded.

We spent our afternoons at the pool, Mom with that golden brown, Southern woman glow that served as a backdrop for her gold jewelry and her yellow and white two-piece. She'd clip along in yellow high-heeled sandals with daisies on the straps, an oversized white shirt that belonged to her deceased father billowing behind her. I figured that because she was easily the prettiest woman at the pool, the other women steered clear.

Now I'm not so sure. Maybe others saw crazy spiraling in her eyes that was invisible to my own. Maybe she was prophesying to them too.

After we came home, showered, and changed into fresh shorts and *shirts, she'd assemble a meal of corn on the cob, sliced cucumbers, and some cold chicken, or maybe a tomato stuffed with tuna salad. We'd sit at the glass-topped table on the screen porch and we'd talk. I could always talk to my mother and she listened to my opinions, sometimes letting what I thought color her own. It wasn't always the other way around with Mom.*

How did my father become such an influence on me? Why does it happen? Why does the aloof parent become the prize, when the attentive one, the deserving one, is taken for granted? Not that I had the chance to take my mother for granted. Maybe never having the opportunity to turn my back on her was a blessing. Maybe Dad was right.

But perhaps I wouldn't have turned my back on her at all. Perhaps I would have ended up just like her. Okay, not crazy in Kentucky, but devoted to the Lord. What does true, all-out devotion really feel like?

Do you even know, Father Brian?

After we cleared and cleaned the dishes, we'd walk down to the pond in our development where she'd spread a blanket and we'd sit until the fireflies came out, or we'd swing in the hammock with our books. Mom loved Clyde Edgerton and T.R. Pearson, Lee Smith and Flannery O'Connor. At twelve, I'd gone through all the Newberry Award winners she thought worthy and was already onto Orwell, Steinbeck, and Hemingway. For fun, I read James Clavell and James Michener. Sometimes we stayed on the screen porch and played hearts or spades.

I'm waiting at the car now, eating a very stale honey bun from the center's vending machine. Hermy finally returns. "What an experience. You can see the whole world from up there."

"Where?"

"Top of Natural Bridge, then on Lover's Leap."

Lover's Leap. Where was that when I needed it?

"I'll have to head up there." I tuck a trail and campsite brochure into my rucksack. "Lots of places to pitch a tent in this area."

"Sure. Ready?" He reaches for the door handle.

I slip inside the car. "Gotta be."

"Turn left up there on Route 715."

I steer the car accordingly. Only two more miles.

I back down to about twenty miles per hour. "Beautiful scenery."

Hermy doesn't say anything. Bare, smoke-brown trees, the leaf-carpeted arboreal floor, blue sky. Nothing like the cliffs we just passed at fifty-five. But now it's close and it's real. Monica's almost around the corner. Will she be surprised? Something tells me no. She'll feel that I'm on the way.

"I sure hope she doesn't mind our just showing up like this," Hermy says. "If she's anything like you say, this could be interesting." We ride by a small brick church, a closed-up flea market. "Hopefully there's a library in Beattyville or Campton."

"As if you don't already know."

He grins.

At least it'll get my statistical friend out of the house during the day.

"Take a right at that Deer Creek sign and then you'll take the next left after that. You know, she could really be crazy, like your dad says."

"Yeah."

"We could find a sanitarium at this address, or maybe some nurse is taking care of her, giving her antipsychotic shots, or tying her down when she goes—"

"Okay, Hermy! Man!"

"Sorry."

It's easy to see why someone would settle down out here for some peace of mind. We've only passed a few cars since getting off the highway. The branches move in the breeze. I'd guess it's about fifty degrees.

I take a left at the next road. Wooden planks set in stone advertise Deer Creek in gold letters. Nice. But even in what I'm guessing is some sort of exile, my mother would be well cared for. My father's pride wouldn't let her weather any sort of physical storm. Maybe he even loved her once. I don't know.

Stopping the car by the sign, I reach into my pocket for my cigarettes. "Sorry, Herm. Gotta have one." I get out.

He joins me. "No prob. Don't blame you." He holds out his hand and I offer the pack, jostling it upwards to exhume a smoke.

"So, I'm not sure what to expect." I drag on the cigarette a moment later, feeling the nicotine seep into my body. Oh, man, how the cells remember.

Hermy shakes his head. "A nice woman like that going crazy all of a sudden and at that party too. I mean, I looked it up; crazy can happen quick. But that doesn't make it any less sad, if you know what I mean."

"Yeah, I know what you mean. I don't trust a word my dad says. I mean, yeah, she ruined it for that candidate, but . . . I don't know, Hermy. Was she certifiably crazy? I don't know."

Finishing up the smoke, I grind the butt with my heel then throw it into the tall winter grass. I bend forward at the waist to give my head an extra helping of blood, straighten up, and stretch my back. "Let's hit it."

The cabin is what I would expect of the woman who made me Coke floats and wore straw hats while reading or gardening in the sunshine. White chinking visible between the squared logs, the structure clings to a ledge. The strata of wind-carved sandstone across the great crevice soaks up the rays of the setting sun, somehow throwing back a golden arc over a mist lying low in the gorge.

Hermy whistles between his teeth.

Low-slung light illumines tree trunks digging their gnarled roots to the sides of the cliffs. The conifers rustle in the wind driving down from the mountains, and I feel the urgent swelling of a million lives being lived right under my gaze.

"Nice little place," Hermy says.

"Uh-huh." I get out of the car. Decking angles from the front around to face the gorge. On either side of a front door holding an intricate window of beveled glasswork, flowerpots of all sizes sit empty. If she's still the same, they'll be cascading with plants by June.

"She still loves flowers, I guess."

The door swings open and she stands there in white pants and a sweater as blue as the sky. "Your father was right. You came right here."

I nod.

"Come in, Drew. And bring your friend."

What could such a reunion be? She let me go. I thought her dead. We found each other, and quickly once again the wheels begin to turn. But Hermy's here. From what I remember, Monica wouldn't get slobbery and emotional in front of a stranger.

We follow her into the cabin, mellow log walls covered with beautiful wall hangings still emitting a pine scent. I smell stew too.

I tower over her.

Monica is small. I never knew. I just never knew.

She turns to Hermy. "Excuse us, will you? Help yourself to some stew. You all must be hungry."

My mother puts her arm through mine and leads me down the hall into a sunroom overlooking the cliffs. She shuts the door, leaving Hermy to his meal.

"I'm sorry and I love you."

I shake my head slightly.

"I've been wanting to say those words for years, Drew. You must know. I love you and I'm sorry. I love you."

She draws me to her. Finally. And leads me to the sofa. We sit and she takes me into her mother arms, and she is sane, and she is good. And I don't know how this all fits together, but for now, I'll rest.

TWELVE

Valentine: 2009

No matter what I say, I can't convince Blaze to turn up the heat. I plead with her when she walks in the door from work.

"Look, I'll pay an extra fifty bucks a week, even."

"No way! Miller Renault down the street, same basic floor plan as our house, put his up to seventy and the bill was almost seven hundred dollars."

"How much are you paying with it at sixty?"

"Almost four hundred a month."

"Oh."

"Is Dahlia still reading those books to Lella?" Blaze puts the kettle on.

Thing is, the contraband heater is pretty much out of my reach because Dahlia—who rented a roll-away bed from ABC Rentals—is staying in with Lella, reading romance novels aloud, rolling her mouth around the smutty parts like pieces of cinnamon candy. After one session, I beat it out of there.

"Yeah, poor Lell. She's so innocent. I don't know what Dahlia's thinking."

"Lella can take care of herself. Want a cup of tea?"

"Thanks. Did you see the latest makeover she did on Lell?"

"No. Was it bad?"

"Awful. I think it should go on the list of deadly sins or something."

"You can't help but like her, though."

"I know. I wish I didn't."

Sitting at the kitchen table the next day, a draft from beneath the door tearing at the fabric of my slippers as if they were tissue paper, I shell some fresh peas Blaze bought at the IGA. Across from me, Rick shreds a brick of Monterey Jack for the scalloped potatoes destined to accompany the ham, resting beneath a glaze of brown sugar, dried mustard, and a dollop of Blaze's raspberry jam and warming in the oven.

Rick slides the creamy block down the box grater. "So, this Dahlia. You like her?"

"Who wouldn't, you know?"

"Seems like a straight-up lady to me."

"Me too."

Rick stops the cheese. "How much longer is she going to be here?"

"Why?"

"Straight up or not, she just makes me uncomfortable the way she dotes on Lella. She treats her like a baby or something. It's just kinda weird."

"She'll only be here a little while longer."

"Lella's probably sick of her by now."

"If she is, she's not letting on."

Rick moves the cheese again. "Well, maybe now's as good a time as any to let her go, Valentine. You're going to have to someday, right?"

I stand, reach over to the coffeemaker on the counter, and turn off the burner. "I don't know who it is that almost empties the pot, leaving just enough to burn to tar, but they should be shot."

"Hey, it wasn't me. And don't avoid the question, Val. You have a way of doing that."

"Why do I have to let her go? I've been helping Lella for over three years now. We've wintered here four times and we'll be back next year after another successful season on the road. I'm picking out house plans for us once this all goes away. This *someday* you're talking about, I just don't buy."

He holds up both hands. "Sorry, Val."

"And why are you always apologizing?"

"Because I'm always getting under your skin, that's why."

I sit back down and pick up another pea pod. "Well, I should be the sorry one. There's been just too much upheaval this winter. This Augustine guy and his weird Laundromat monastery, Charmaine Hopewell coming over all the time—"

"You don't like *her* either?"

"I love her! She just makes me face things about my life I'd rather not think about, that's all. Kinda like you, if I think about it."

I push the bag of potatoes, Yukon gold, the best as far as I'm concerned, in his direction and ask if he'll scrub them. Of course he will. He's Rick, a really nice, really stretchy guy who deserves to have a crush on someone other than me.

After sliding the potatoes, swimming in cheese and cream, into the oven, I hear Lella's voice call down from her room. "Valentine!"

I practically wound myself tripping up the steps, I run so fast.

"Yeah, Lell?"

"Aunt Dahlia went over to the square to get us some Sunday morning donuts."

Lella's hair is teased around her head and I imagine beady eyes opening up, a tail whipping forward, and the whole affair jumping off her head to return to its native woodland setting.

She frowns. "It's awful, isn't it?"

"Yeah."

"Oh, well. Aunt Dahlia makes up for it in so many other ways, doesn't she?"

I just nod and say, "Ham, peas, and scalloped potatoes for dinner after Blaze gets home from the Laundromat."

It sounds pathetic, this little offering of meat with nitrates, peas from who knows where, and potatoes that grew to maturity in common dirt.

"Can you take me to the bathroom, Valentine? I wouldn't ask, but—"

"Sure, I will. Just because Aunt Dahlia's here doesn't mean I don't want to help."

"You still do? Really? I thought you'd be glad for the break."

In response, I lift her into my arms.

Lella thanks me over and over again, more profusely than ever before. Because plainly, it must not really be my job anymore.

I settle her back onto her bed.

She sighs. "I don't know, Valentine. Is this the life we want for good?"

"Oh, Lella, it's the only life I have."

Heading back to my room, I look up at the icon I bought on the Internet.

"And I was so happy that night on the lake," I tell John, or at least who I think is John because he's right next to Jesus and doesn't look evil like the other guy, who must be Judas, right? "But this Aunt Dahlia business is driving me crazy."

I'd hung the picture over my CD player. I push the button only to hear Frank Sinatra croon my song.

Bartholomew would approve.

◆◆◆

Yesterday Bindy and Mindy left, having been hired by a bigger show. We had a going-away cake. After they were driven away. Ha! Ha!

Sitting on my bed, listening to a young Nat King Cole version of "Embraceable You," I love how he rounds his vowels ever so slightly, an almost imperceptible slur on the final consonants of the words. The burbling jazz guitar, electric and warm, trips along beside him, and I follow behind. I somehow feel the blackness in my heart lighten to more of a slate gray. Charmaine sits on the end of the bed drinking a Diet Coke.

"I didn't ask for this shake-up in life any more than I asked to be born to Trician Boyer."

She's proclaimed herself my counselor, having counseled hundreds of people on the phone lines for *Port of Peace*.

"She was a piece of work, wasn't she?" Charmaine.

"I hate my mother, and Drew Parrish taught me how. Before I met him I merely felt deep annoyance paired with a crippled affection. But those two brought out the worst in each other. He couldn't stand her."

"Did you ever love her?"

"In the days before my voice flowered. Well, maybe it wasn't an overwhelming love where I felt safe and pedestaled like you do for your kids, Charmaine. But she fed me, pushed the swing at the park, and never picked me up late from day care. Yeah, I guess I loved her then. But the realization of my talent lit some sort of fire in her and she stepped out of her saleswoman pumps and into those spikier heeled, pointier-toed shoes of a manager of an artist. All in my best interest, of course."

"I doubt that."

"I often wondered if she just liked having good excuses to go shopping."

"Why was she like that, Val? I could never figure her out."

I pontificate. In the course of her lifetime, my mother dealt with disappointment at almost every step. Her parents divorced when she was fifteen. She couldn't afford to go to a top design school so she wound up at the local state university, and even there her design portfolio was rejected after her sophomore year. She ended up graduating with a degree in textile management, accepting a sales position at Fieldcrest. When she met my father, he talked big, big, big—someday he'd be the CFO of a Fortune 500 company. He started doing taxes on the side a year after they married, dreams of power cars and club sandwiches at the country club dancing in circles around Mother's pretty little head. Another H & R Block? Oh, but they could diversify, surely. Perhaps consult. And Dad knew a thing or two about computers. But he ended up hanging out his own CPA shingle, fully planning to "keep it small and manageable."

No wonder he sells beads now.

Undaunted, Mother eagerly signed up for Mary Kay, buying feminine business suits for the day she'd be some kind of regional manager, get off the sales trail because, naturally, she'd sign up so many people beneath her she could become a motivational speaker, encouraging others that with enough vision and courage they, too, could be where she was today.

"Dad literally wailed—which should tell you something—that she was spending twice as much money on clothes and lunches than what she was bringing in."

I put on my Trician Boyer voice. "'You've got to spend money to make money, Wally. You might want to consider bringing in another accountant to make up the difference.'"

Charmaine shakes her head. "I'll be honest. I never liked her.

She was horrible to me behind your back. I just tried to steer as clear as I could. What about your dad, honey?"

"I can't believe I let you talk me into talking about all this stuff! I thought I was quite clear on the dock."

"I have that way about me." She hands me a piece of chocolate and I continue the tale.

"My father, however, wasn't motivated by money. He was motivated by order and balance, and Mother's idea of business had nothing to do with either of those. It simply didn't make sense that he should step up his responsibilities due to her lack of common sense.

"No extra accountant, Trician. You're throwing the monkey-wrench into this situation, not me.

"Well, Mother supposed, it must be the product that kept her from moving forward. Yes, of course. The product."

"Oh, you don't have to say more." Charmaine waves a hand. "If you're around the church long enough, you soon find out there are as many direct-marketing companies as there are views on the end times, once-saved-always-saved, and baptism!"

"Well, Mother sure sampled her fair share. I'm surprised our church didn't kick her out because she tried most of her recruitment on Sunday mornings and Wednesday nights. After Mary Kay she tried Avon, Amway, Bee Alive, and ended up with a 'Lose Weight Now Ask Me How' bumper sticker on the back of her old Buick, a car Dad said he'd be darned he'd replace so she could rack up the mileage on something new and put them further in the hole.

"And then one day in the eighth grade I sang 'Have Yourself a Merry Little Christmas' in the holiday concert at school. I bowed my head after the final note of the soundtrack faded, the auditorium burst into applause, and I was awarded a standing ovation.

"If Trician Boyer couldn't sell cosmetics, cleaning supplies, vitamins, or weight loss products, by gum, she could sell her own daughter.

"She got me into pageants, talent contests, tryouts for regional musical theater and TV commercials, model searches, and special music at churches, weddings, social gatherings, and fairs all over the state. I did it all. I became popular with the locals because I was pretty but still approachable."

"I can't fault you there." Charmaine. "You were the real deal. At least inside."

"Right. Mother never realized this, but I did. I watched the entertainers who endured throughout the years and not only endured but were much-loved and well-respected, and not a one could be called anything but believable. The fact that audiences liked me for me kept me with Mother's program. It was her drive, coupled with my aura, that made for the perfect combination. We would have been just fine if Drew Parrish hadn't entered into the picture."

"Oh, honey. He was hurting like the rest of us."

"You'd say something like that, Charmaine. I think he was a snake. But I can't say he fooled me completely. I realized his ambition, I knew he played to some script he'd bought only heaven knew where. I simply had the misfortune to fall in love with someone who, I realize looking back, hadn't the capacity to fall in love with anyone. Not really."

"I thought you loved him. I could see that a mile away."

"My bad."

"I should have stepped in more than I did. I'm just terrible at confrontation. And then, well, Valentine, I thought you were the driving force behind a lot of it."

"I was the allowing force. I don't know how much of that stuff I would have come up with on my own. Did you ever confront them about it?"

"I confronted Drew, but he blamed Trician. He really could

have cared less about your looks. He just wanted you to get that Nashville contract."

I shrug. "Who knows who was the bigger criminal? Maybe they fed off each other's worst parts."

"Probably. Things were different in my day. It's so much worse today. Girls having so much surgery beforehand just to try and get their foot in the door. It was the final round of surgery when I knew I had done the wrong thing in not stepping in more than I did." She sets down her drink and takes my hand. "Valentine, I'm so sorry." Tears fill her hazel eyes. "I should have said something. I've wanted to ask your forgiveness for years now."

"It wasn't your fault, Charmaine. You were the only one who ever shot straight with me. You were really who you claimed to be."

"I let you down. Please, Daisy."

"I forgive you, Charmaine. I never held anything against you in the first place."

"I love you, Valentine."

"I know." I squeeze her and break the embrace. "Are you sure about Drew? He really wasn't the driving force? Tricia was?"

"I'm almost 100 percent positive."

"Does it matter though? He still let Trician do what she did, all so I'd get a contract and his show would do well."

"As much as I saw the good in that man, that line of reasoning is something I can't fault you on."

After she leaves, I point above my CD player to Andrew, standing there so nicely with his halo. "Curse that Charmaine Hopewell for dragging this all out again. I've carved out my life the way I like it, the only way I can live it without doing something like burning myself with Drano again."

John still looks sorry for me.

When I heard through the grapevine years ago that Drew Parrish disappeared, I began dreaming up possible scenarios. My personal favorite? Polishing floors at night at a big mall somewhere in the Midwest.

John shakes his head.

Rick has conjured up some crazy ideas in his time, like suggesting I "just get some good makeup," but this eclipses them all to such a degree the penumbra almost blinds me with indignation. To be honest, I'm a bit incredulous that Rick could be so, well, stupid really.

I throw my cigarette onto the front lawn and pull my coat around me more tightly. "Absolutely not! I'm not going to stand there and sing while you contort, Rick. Please! Can you imagine it?"

He holds up both hands. "Wait, wait! I'm thinking a sort of cobra angle, coiling myself like a snake and rising up, my back bent at a forty-five degree angle like this." He splays himself on the porch and I watch the move.

"I've got to admit, it's pretty impressive."

He jumps back to his feet. "And you can make me an outfit that mimics a cobra's hood."

I roll my eyes.

"Now, now. So you can keep a beautiful veil over half of your face and it won't be weird because we're supposed to be in India, right? And you can stand there and sing like that! You know, your voice slipping and fluttering and sliding around like that singer in that Sting song."

"'Brand New Day'? This gets weirder and weirder, Rick, not to mention the fact that I don't have that kind of voice. I don't think I can sing that way even if I want to."

"You sure about that?"

"Positive."

"Then how about a duet for Valentine's Day? Gus says they're throwing a Love Feast for the lonely that day. This'll be their third year and it's a big deal at Shalom. With music, it'll be so much more like a real event."

"Did he put you up to this?"

"No way. I swear."

Rick's obviously not as dumb as he seems. Despite his poor theatrics, I fell right into his trap. I'm so good at that.

"All right. Just three songs, though, and one *has* to be 'Embraceable You.'"

"You got it."

He holds open the front door for me as we walk back into the house.

"And you have to worry about accompaniment, arrangements, everything."

"Okay, Val. Got it."

I unwind my scarf. "And don't make it hard. I don't want to have to practice more than a couple of times."

"Sheesh, Val."

"And don't play your violin so loud I have to compete with it."

"I got it, okay?"

"Hey, no reason to get all huffy on me, Rick."

He throws up his hands, screeches, and clogs back to the kitchen to feed his impossible metabolism.

◆◆◆

Okay, John, so be it!

I hold the icon on my lap. If he wants to hear the entire story, so be it. I've been avoiding it for years. Maybe getting it out in the open will do me some good. Lella's downstairs anyway. She won't hear a thing.

John asks me to tell him about the final surgery.

Well, the day of my final unveiling started off pretty much like all my other unveilings. I ate a little box of Total cereal, drank a glass of skim milk, a plastic foil-capped cup of orange juice, and black coffee.

I knew not to expect much with the bruising and the swelling. After two rhinoplasties, liposuction, and a butt lift (oh, sorry, John, don't mean to be crude), my expectations rose right to where they should on the yardstick of such things.

It mystified me that Mother and Drew sat with such expectation, their spines stretched from skull to pelvis like rubber bands, their eyes glazed with hope that I'd finally be perfect, truly beautiful, with a hint of Victoria's Secret gathering just below the surface.

Well, maybe it wasn't Drew so much as I thought. But still. I didn't know that then. And Charmaine could be wrong.

The doctor snipped away the lengths of gauze and removed the cotton strips, then stared at his handiwork, still somewhat in the raw.

He nodded. "When the swelling goes down, I believe you'll be very satisfied with the results. They should be just what you were seeking, Ms. Boyer."

He didn't say I was going to be lovely. Dr. Denlinger didn't believe a woman had to be a cross between Brigitte Nielsen and Pam Anderson to rank among the beautiful people of this world.

He presented the hand mirror and I inspected my face. This had been major work. The implants in my cheeks, giving me sharp cheekbones for the first time in my life, were balanced out by a chin implant to, as Mother said, "remove that birdish quality from your face." Though only twenty-five at the time, I had my heavy upper eyelids given a more defined crease with blepharo-plasty and my brows raised a touch.

Yeah, John, I know what you're thinking. We're way too caught up in the whole youth thing. I hear you, friend. I hear you.

It wasn't that I had deep wrinkles. I'd always had eyebrows that simply rested a little too close to my eyes. I could do much more dramatic eye makeup with greater space in which to work.

So I went home to fully heal.

I called some of my friends from my former sales route and chatted about their lives. They told me how much they loved the show, that had, by this time, been on for almost eighteen months. The viewers were increasing week-by-week such that Charmaine and Harlan were as pleased as they could be.

Drew wanted more than that though, and he'd fallen into such a state of ego that every success rained like gold on his shoulders and every failure sat on mine like Atlas's world.

Oh, Judas was a little like that too? I'm not surprised.

Not only that, a major network had contacted him. They were thinking Drew and Daisy, a chatty morning show on the order of Regis and Whoever. They loved our chemistry. Now that was good.

Okay, okay, we had sex!

But as soon as he realized I wanted commitment, he backed off. I don't know why I expected anything different, to be honest. He never said he loved me. I just thought . . .

Well, I guess I thought what millions of women do when the man of their dreams takes things too far.

Maybe he'll really love me now.

Maybe he'll be a gentleman.

Maybe he'll do the honorable thing.

Oh, brother.

But this opportunity for a network show? I was going to do whatever it took, and if it took another round of surgery, so be it.

Trician could hardly follow us to New York, could she? Honestly, that sealed the deal on the surgery for me.

But the Christmas season was coming up and with my looks honed, the songs picked out, the guests engaged, and the set that Drew found financing for through various companies—their products displayed or their logos emblazoned on our coffee mugs—it all promised to be a major coup in "Podunk programming" as Mother called it. Mother, who was already talking to Nashville, who assured me she had some takers along that route if we could get our numbers up.

I prayed for New York instead.

I know, I know, John. It's a good thing Jesus wasn't all about the numbers here on earth. You're right about that. I mean, how would any more of you fit on that icon, right?

I let my mother move forward, figuring she'd be busy pursuing Nashville and would leave me alone. At least away from gospel entertainment there'd be no pretense that at the end of the day, the show was really the thing after all.

Drew solo-piloted *Faith Street* during my healing, inviting notable guest hosts while I was "on a well-deserved time of rest and restoration."

I received over seven hundred letters during that time, begging me to come back soon. I felt loved. Some folks sent snapshots of themselves or their kids or their pets. It meant a lot to me.

On the Monday after Thanksgiving, we began taping our first Christmas special, our debut show with the completed Daisy, a size zero masterpiece by this time, sculpted and without flaw. Despite what people may say, I didn't have an eating disorder. I realized I was too skinny and looking freakish. But I saw the tabloids every day, and skinny and freakish had become the new normal.

But nothing can be perfect, and those who seek it and display what they perceive to be just that are not reliable. You simply can't trust that kind of artifice.

What's that, Peter? It's the flaws that sometimes give things their beauty?

I see that now. Up to a point. Back then, though, I couldn't wait to hear the feedback once the show aired. As I walked onto the set to tape, my face bearing no bruising, no noticeable swelling, the crew gasped.

Well, sure. I looked a lot better, and quite different. I mean, yes, I saw a difference, but nothing deserving of a gasp, for goodness sake. The camera would love my new angles. They'd see. And I'd be off to Nashville or New York, leaving Trician behind. We taped the special for the next three days.

Catching my reflection in windows, mirrors, and shiny surfaces, I navigated through the snowfall of heavy glares by convincing myself I was finally beautiful. Perfect. But most important, I could leave Mount Oak behind.

That was the goal of it all.

Looking over the footage in the editing suite the next day, Drew looked at my mother, then laid a hand on my shoulder and squeezed. "Now, this may sound improper and I don't mean it to be. But what if your front balanced your back a little bit more?"

"Another boob job?!"

Sorry, disciples.

I slammed myself back in the swivel chair. And something came over me. I reached out and smacked him across the face, as hard as I'd ever smacked anything, including my lips at a perfectly done steak—and boy did Drew make sure I'd never have anything like that again.

"What's the matter with you?" he yelled, laying a hand on his cheek.

"You, Howdy-Doody. You're what's the matter with me."

He winced.

"Stop thinking I don't know what's going on with you. Just stay away from me. I'll do the show. But leave me alone."

Peter would cheer if he wasn't painted in one position. I'm pretty sure of that.

Something snapped in my brain. It's hard to say how a true snapping occurs. I felt something loosen, almost physically, inside my skull, as if a cage door opened and let loose a small, glinty-eyed creature who stared out of my eyes and groped through an almost drunken haze at the same time.

I hurried out of the suite and ran for my car. Drew didn't bother to follow, not surprisingly. The animal in my forehead scratched down to the bone and I longed to scream in frustration. It was easy to know where to go. Since childhood I'd stood before her medicine cabinet in the bathroom off her bedroom—Dad had been down the hall for several years by this time—memorizing her prescriptions, wondering what they were all for.

But now I knew.

Reaching up my hand, I hesitated, wondering which bottle to choose. Maybe I should ask Trician, I remember thinking, suppressing a chuckle. I mean, she knew everything about everything and everybody, everywhere, and everyhow. The woman was a storehouse of smarts and savvy and *stick with her kid and she'll take you places you never dreamed of going.*

And what were my dreams, you ask? Thank you, James the son of Alpheus. Not much, in answer to your question. Just to be rid of Trician in a way she didn't mind, a way that would get her off my back by the sheer affirmation she was right all along about my talent. Other than that, I liked selling comic books. I wasn't naturally high in the ambition department and I was fine with that.

I grabbed two bottles and stared at the face in the mirror, unrecognizable as myself, then tiptoed down the hall to my own bathroom, the walls hung with twenty-two framed comic book covers denoting the issues I made top sales. Each frame displayed little gold plaques with my name and the month they debuted. *Sergeant Hero, Lady Illusion, Lizard Girl,* and my favorite, *Conundra and Indestructibo.*

Grabbing my spit cup, I turned on the water. I filled it up, then counted out two of each prescription. Vicodin and OxyContin. I didn't want to die or anything, I just wanted to sleep, really sleep like I hadn't done since I left Action Packed Comics and worked for Drew. Because after I woke up, I had to come up with a whole new plan for my life, and that was going to be the most difficult thing I'd ever done.

Then I realized there'd be too much noise at my house; I had to get away. And Mother would come barreling in any moment, asking me to explain my behavior with Drew. So I put the pills back in the bottles and hit the road.

By midnight, I found a small motel near Durham. A little strip of a place off the highway, rustic with mullioned windows, it was going for chalet and failing miserably. I paid cash for the room.

The pills went down easily, and I looked at myself once more and began to cry.

I had lost myself. I was so sure I could keep it going, make it somewhere decent enough to leave everyone behind and still keep my self-respect. But it didn't work out that way.

THIRTEEN

◆◆◆

DREW: 2003

The night settles in, blanketing the gorge in silence, the wooden house comforting in the darkness. Monica remarked over and over how much bigger I seemed in person than on TV.

We sit at the rugged dining table and eat stew. Hermy's down for the night, reading in his bedroom, resting assured that yes, Campton has a library that, while not well-stocked as city libraries go, will at least offer some books he's probably not perused.

"So you watched me on TV?"

"I did. I've been watching you since you were on *The Port of Peace Hour*. I even visited your church a few times. You have a gift for communication. It's a shame you were bent on squandering it. I never should have left. I never should have let Charles talk me into it; I should have trusted the Lord more, Drew."

"What happened? You know he told me they thought it was a suicide. When I was sixteen he offered up that bit of information. I was starting to ask too many questions about the accident, I guess."

She holds her hand to her mouth, rounded in horror. "Oh no! No! That wasn't part of our agreement. I would have never left you of my own volition."

"Isn't that exactly what you did?"

◆◆ 189 ◆◆

She rises and collects our bowls. "Let's have some coffee for this talk. I'm going to need it."

I head to the bathroom while she prepares the coffeemaker. I won't burn myself, not here. "Can I smoke in the house?" I call.

"You're a grown man."

"It's your house."

"All right."

I have a feeling I'm going to need this smoke more than any other. But for the first time in years, a sense of gratitude overwhelms me as I light up the cigarette. Monica's alive, she's fine, she's fixing coffee in the kitchen. And I never have to see my father again.

If this had happened five years ago, I would have been all right, my life would have turned out so differently. Daisy would probably be fine. But in the span of life, what's five years? I mean, we now live in a world where the second chance is really the beginning of it all, because we believe we've a right to as many chances as we need with little consequence to pay.

After smoking half of the thing, I throw it in the toilet, flush, and head back out. Monica's arranging store-bought cookies on a plate. Oreos. We always did love those.

"When did you start smoking, Drew?"

"Dabbled in it since college. Started full swing a couple of years ago." Yeah, the viewing audience would have loved that. Right now I smoke more than a ham house.

"What does your father say? Does he feel bad about that, being a former lobbyist for the tobacco industry?"

"I don't answer to him anymore, Mom. And my smoking has nothing to do with his old job."

"Well, at least there's that." She smiles at me. It's still there, her and me against the world. "You have to tell me how you found me."

"First tell me why you started calling me."

She taps her nails on the counter and I notice a tattooed circle around the ring finger of her left hand. "What's that?" I ask.

"I'm married to the Lord now."

"You're a nun?!"

"No! Well, not really. You know, your father and I are technically still married. We never divorced. I'm sure you can imagine why."

"I always wondered why he never dated after you died."

She looks down. "He wasn't much for sex anyway, Drew. Now, I probably shouldn't say that to my son. But the fact that you're here is God's graciousness to me. We lived in an almost sexless state. Just a few times in all those years, and you resulted from one of them." She looks up at the heavens through the ceiling. "You were the exhibition of God's faithfulness, and when I had to give you up—" She gulps down a sob, swallows the years back down to a calmer place inside. "Anyway, you've never married. Are you like he was in that way?"

"No. I almost wish I was."

"Oh, Drew."

"It's not easy being single."

"But the Apostle Paul gave us the perfect out! Now, I've been basically single for twenty years and I'm fine. I go to work, read my books, and I have a cat—you haven't seen her yet—who sits on my lap at night. I still go to church. It's a good life. I don't feel like I've settled in that way."

"I thought I'd be settling if I opted for marriage for marriage's sake. But I made a huge mistake, Mom. I can't talk about it. But there was a time when I used to believe God had something for me."

"Drew, the Lord does have something for you."

"Maybe. I don't know if I want any of it anymore. I can't bear the weight of it all anymore. Me and Hermy, we live a simple life at the Dunesgrass. I will have to get a job soon, though."

Okay, it's a lie. With frugality, I could live for another three or four years, maybe more. But that seems like an awfully long time.

"No. You don't have to get a job soon, Son."

"You're right."

"I always know a lie. Especially from you, Drew. You saved up a lot of money when you pastored that church, didn't you?"

"Yes."

"Drew, do you really know the Lord? You did as a little boy. Sometimes it frightened me, the things you'd say. I wondered if angels visited you."

"So what happened?"

"I left. I thought God would take you through life by another route. Your father . . ."

"Yeah." I run a hand over the stubble on my head. "So why did you leave?"

She lifts up the coffeepot and pours two mugs of black coffee, not bothering to ask me how I take it, which is still with milk. She hands me the drink. "Let's sit on the sofa."

I grab the plate and she smiles. "You were always helpful, Drew. Are you still helpful to the people around you?"

"No. I'm a taker. I take from Hermy and Father Brian these days. I give them almost nothing in return."

"Almost?"

"I suppose the satisfaction of knowing they're helping a messed-up man is something."

"God's giving that to them, not you, Drew."

"I see."

"Do you?" She sits down.

I place the cookies onto the coffee table. "I don't see much really."

"We have so much to talk about. How long can you stay?"

"As long as you'll have me. What about Hermy?"

"He's welcome to stay. God probably brought him here for reasons only He and Hermy know." She leans forward. "Does he eat much?"

I shake my head. "Nah."

She laughs. And heaven knows, I need the levity.

"Look, Drew!" She points outside the sliders to the back deck.

A light shines onto the planking, a golden beam against the darkness of the gorge. Snow falls into the light. "The temperature must have dropped."

"We didn't get much of that down in North Carolina, did we?"

"No, sadly enough." She sips her coffee. "Okay, the whole story. Do you remember the huge debacle when I called that candidate out for his adultering ways?"

Spoken like a true prophet.

"Yes. I heard the conversation you and Dad had. I was listening at the top of the steps."

"I thought as much. Afterwards Charles stewed for days, leaving town to do so. He came back with a verdict. Either I divorced him and he took custody of you, or he'd commit me to a mental institution.

"That wasn't the first time I'd done something like that, Drew. But it was, well, I guess you could say, far larger in its implications. I'd humiliated him for the last time. His career was on the line with this one." She lifts her mug. "I subtracted exceedingly from the equation."

"You were so beautiful on his arm, Mom."

Her face softens. "God blessed me that way. It was my cross to bear. Your father would have never set his sights on me had I been plain. And Daddy . . . my daddy, well . . . he was bowled over by Charles." She shrugs, still lithe and willowy. "Charles was so charming when he sought me. But it wasn't worth it." She lays a sudden hand on my leg. "Except for you, Drew! You made everything worth it." She hands me a blanket. "It's getting chilly."

"I'll start a fire." I set the blanket aside, walk across the room, and begin arranging the wood onto the grate.

"When I refused to divorce him because there were no biblical grounds, he started visiting nearby institutions to cement his threat. But something happened, perhaps his natural wiliness took hold. He thought of another option. Disappearance."

"Ah."

"I balked at that. How could I just leave you? What would that do to you to think your own mother walked out on you, just walked out, never returning? It was my idea to fake my death. I thought it would close doors in your mind, free you from thinking you were the reason."

I close my eyes, remembering the countless moments I'd allowed myself to succumb to my grief in my room, weeping for an hour or more. All those visits to her grave. But she was right, thinking she didn't care would have been worse. My pain was sharp but clean.

I lay on the final log. "Why didn't you just go for the divorce, Mom? We would have seen each other."

"He threatened sole custody based on mental incapacity on my part. And believe me, Drew, he certainly had enough to prove just what he wanted."

"Could you have at least tried?"

She looks down at her hands. "I thought God would reward my faithfulness to His Word."

"And has He?"

She places her palms on her thighs. "We all have things about God we don't understand, don't we, Drew?"

I stuff newspaper in between the logs I've stacked.

When she disappeared, I was too young to even think to investigate. Dad told everyone else it was a drug overdose, a suicide, but that he was keeping the truth from me. There were no articles in the newspapers, nothing. He'd spent a fortune on it all, but there was so much more to be gained.

You've got to spend money to make money, right?

"So where did you go?"

"Even with your grandparents dead, I couldn't go back to Louisiana. I'd have been spotted right away by someone. So I dyed my hair black and traveled the world for the first five years." She laughs. "I spent as much of your father's money as I could."

"Good for you."

"I settled in Maine for a couple of years but couldn't take the winters, so I found this cabin and have been here ever since. It's a good place, seasonal, cold in winter, but not too cold. Hot in the summer, yes, but well, you know I love the heat."

"I remember."

"Do you, Drew?"

"I remember it all, Mom."

"Do you understand I did what I had to do? I had no choice. No matter what I chose, we'd be apart. I tried to do what was best for you."

I shake my head slowly, reaching for the box of matches. "What a monster."

"I'm sorry."

"You did what you had to do. You were going to be gone either way."

"And I watched from afar. He was decent enough to send pictures and updates."

"Really?"

"Yes. Surprising, isn't it?"

"I didn't think he had it in him."

"Drew, your father is the most mysterious person I've ever met."

"Is he really a Christian? I mean, he talks the game to the right people."

"That's not my call to make."

"I guess not. I mean I know about talking the game. I was the chief of sinners, leading people astray with my messages of selfish, spiritual acquisitiveness, as if we can gorge on God and never give anything away."

"I heard the messages. They broke my heart. You were doing what your father did, lobbying for 'blessing upon blessing,' whatever that meant to you, Drew, instead of introducing people to a far greater thing—the Lord Himself."

I strike a long match and hold it to the newspaper. "How could I do that? I don't even know who He is."

"What made you leave Mount Oak?"

I inhale as deeply as I can. "Daisy disappeared and I knew the show was doomed, but I had raised a lot of money. I knew the show wouldn't have been enough eventually, because that's the way it is with power, Mom. You get what you thought you wanted and it isn't enough. So you go to the next thing and that's not enough. It would never be enough."

"God opened your eyes."

"I'm not so sure."

"He's calling you, though. Do you feel that?"

The flame catches, spreading. "It's what you said over the phone."

"The Lord told me to give you that message."

"How did you track me down?"

"I called your church and they said you'd taken a sabbatical and left without a forwarding address. I came to Mount Oak and couldn't find you anywhere. So I took a chance and called our old hotel in Ocean City. And there you were."

The flame continues to eat the newspaper, licking at the dry, peeling bark of the logs.

"Why didn't you just come down?"

"I was planning on it next week."

I stand up. "I needed you sooner than this. Didn't you realize it? Why did you continue to stay away once I was older?"

"You thought I was dead. I was trying to trust God to take care of you."

I blow on the flame then turn to her. "Sometimes, Mom, God wants us to move forward when we see somebody drowning instead of waiting for a sign. Don't you think?"

"I'm sorry."

"You know it's possible to overspiritualize things." I sit back down on the couch.

"Maybe you're right. You have every right to be mad at me. What can I do now, Drew? We're together. What can I do?"

"I need you to help me. Dear Lord, Mom, I need you to save my soul. I've always needed you to do that."

She folds her arms around me, lays my head against her breast, and hums as the coffee cools and the cookies remain uneaten. After a while she leans back and clicks off the lamp, and we watch the snowfall outside, covering the railing, the deck, the picnic table. Falling headlong into the gorge.

I awaken to gleaming sunshine, my head on a pillow, a quilt covering my body. Monica lies curled up on the love seat, still beautiful these twenty years later, her face sweet, serene, and nestled against the cat, a skinny gray tabby, who finally showed herself.

Movement outside catches my gaze. A red cardinal hops about in the snow, the wind ruffling its feathers. It flutters to the bird feeder, pecks at the seeds, and flies away.

I reach over to the coffee table and pick up my notebook.

After a month of taping, Faith Street *had five shows in the can and the Hopewells began teasing their viewers with clips on their own show.*

Another three pounds down and working out like a fiend, Daisy joined me on The Port of Peace Hour *the week before ours was set to air. The show bought time on twenty small religious stations around the south, so relieved to get new programming they were set to air it several times a day. I mean, how many times can a station re-air old segments of* Ever Increasing Faith *and expect to have an ever increasing viewership?*

Harlan introduced us before the crowd at Port of Peace, *conducting a small interview with me, mentioning my father crusading in DC, of course. After that, Daisy and Charmaine sang a duet.*

The flesh on my arms still rises when I remember the way their voices blended. Charmaine's power with Daisy's controlled under-pinnings as they slid their way in and out of the melody and the harmony, neither taking the lead for long. Charmaine sang in that old-school way, smiling at Daisy as she sang, then smiling at the audience, as if she truly enjoyed what she was doing. It wasn't like the young singers today where everything is choreographed down to the dart of the eyes and good Christian girls grunt out praises to Jesus like they're making out behind the bleachers with their boyfriends. Sorry, Father.

After that show, I kissed Daisy on the cheek in great excitement. She flushed like a rose. Pink and soft. Daisy read into that kiss just what I wanted. Enough to keep her with me.

The day our show aired for the first time on a local station, we sat together in her parents' living room. Trician made us punch with diet Sprite, poured some mixed nuts in bowls, and we watched, I still have to admit, an engaging show.

Daisy shone, playing sassy sweet with ease on top of my nerdy every-cloud-has-a-silver-lining angle. You couldn't call us Regis and Kathie Lee but we had a style all our own, a great combination.

When Wally, Daisy's dad, turned off the set and said, "Now that was a real nice show. A real nice show," I wanted to scream. I wanted more than nice.

Daisy walked me to my car. "It was good, wasn't it?"

"Yes, it was."

I opened my car door and began to get in.

"Drew?"

I looked her way.

"You feel something, don't you? Like we've got some little spark? I mean, the way we interacted, the way the senator laughed and said, 'Now you all make a fine couple.' It was good. What he said was true."

What could I say? I didn't want to start a relationship, but I didn't want to lose her once Nashville came through. So I smiled, rubbed my hand down her bare arm, and got into my car.

She tapped my shoulder. "Only ten more pounds until my goal weight."

"Good job."

I drove home to my Spartan apartment. Before I arrived, however, I drove a few miles out of town and bought a pack of Marlboro Lights. I felt more dead inside than ever before, and only one thing made me feel alive. And you can't smoke a knife afterward either.

In the months ahead the show slowly gained in popularity. Daisy grew thinner and thinner, her advances stronger. I held her at arm's length, praying to God He'd keep my feelings from growing. Was that too much to ask?

For the next year she continued to drop more weight, well past her goal, meeting me at the gym where we'd exercise together, me in sweatpants because of the burns on my legs. I didn't start burning my arms until much later. I'd get a handle on it all, the latest round healed up, until everything was pink and new, and then I'd start again. But I remained the same inside.

Was I trying to match up my outer man with my inner man?

I'm not sure. Even now, lying here on the couch, watching my mother sleep, I don't know. Maybe I'm simply a little crazy. Maybe I'm like my mother that way.

The more overt Daisy's advances, the more I tried to shut myself down. Imagine bringing Daisy home to DC, I'd think to myself. Imagine bringing Daisy, however sweet and kind, to a man whose taste ran to the likes of Monica Parrish.

Yet another area where I didn't quite meet his standards. No way. It just wasn't going to happen.

I throw back the covers. All I'm wearing are my boxers and my thermal undershirt. Yes, there are my jeans, folded neatly on the dining table.

199

"It's all right, I saw them." Monica's eyes are open. "I'm guessing there are more on your arms."

I nod. "Yes."

"How long have you been doing this to yourself?"

"Years. On and off. Knives first. On now for a good long time with the cigarettes."

"I'm sorry. I'd like to think this would have been avoided had I been there."

"I don't know, Mom. Who's to say?"

"It's a sin. You know that."

"No."

"Well, it is. But an understandable one."

"Thanks." I stand up and reach for my pants. "I'll make some coffee."

"That would be lovely." She closes her eyes.

"Are you going back to sleep?"

"No. This is my time to pray for you. I do it every morning before I get out of bed."

For a moment, I see a self-righteousness in her I wish I didn't. As if praying was enough when I was in the care of that man.

I have to forgive her. I have to forgive her for praying when she should have been storming the castle walls.

Soon the coffee's spitting from the machine and I stand on the deck smoking a cigarette. Is this a sin too? Or just a bad idea? I've asked myself that a thousand times.

'Cause if this is a sin, so is drinking Coca-Cola and eating Velveeta and Twinkies. I just don't know anything anymore.

"I'm going to take a shower," she calls.

"Mom?" I shut the patio door behind me.

"Yes?"

"Why didn't you just kidnap me? Take me away and we could have hid up in Maine together?"

"I'm not that brave."

"Okay."

"I mean, we all aren't movie heroines, Drew. I'm sorry for that. I wish I had been. I was scared of him."

So she isn't as perfect as I remember.

Maybe it's better that way.

I won't have so much to live up to.

Trician and I scrolled through the footage on the editing machine. "She still looks a little bumpy," she said.

"I don't know, Trician. She's lost a lot of weight."

"Lipo, you think?"

"It's your call, Trician. More precisely, it's Daisy's."

"And clothes look so much better on extremely thin women. She's losing her breasts, though. Maybe we should get some implants. The butt lift looks a bit odd now."

A little bit here; a little bit there.

"We're this close to a contract in Nashville." Trician held her thumb and forefinger parallel, a half inch apart.

"Come on, Trician. This is going a little too far."

"I'll pull her out of the show right now. You've got to convince her."

I sighed. We weren't quite where we needed to be with the numbers. And at the end of the day, Daisy was responsible for herself. She was an adult. If she didn't want to have the surgery, she should speak up and refuse.

Daisy balked at first but a few evenings in my apartment settled it. I'm ashamed to say it went too far, Father Brian. And she suddenly thought we were a real item. I convinced her to keep the "relationship" a secret, claiming it would be a circus if all the church people knew about it.

She came to my apartment a lot, after hours. One night, she took *off her shoes and curled her feet up beneath her on the couch. I showed her a photo album and she said I looked like my mother, that she'd heard of my father but wasn't really into politics.*

I truly loved her at that moment. But I pushed it down. It was a chance at redemption. I know that now, Father. But I cast it aside.

Later she confessed to me she and her mother were having real problems. "I just want to get away from her."

"Why not just leave town? Make your own life?" I don't know why I said it. I wanted to pull the words back as soon as they were out. Mostly because I needed Daisy. She got more fan mail than I did. I think any real love we might have known was simply doomed by the circumstances.

"How many people do you know that really do that, Drew? Honestly. We act like it's an option for everyone, that everybody in the world has it in them to do that. But how many people really do it?"

Wow, does that sound familiar.

"You're right. We can't have sex anymore, Daisy. You know that, don't you?"

"But I love you."

"It's not right."

"I'm sorry."

I prayed she wouldn't ask me if I loved her too. She didn't. She knew the truth.

She made her excuses, a Bible study to attend, and left my apartment. I leaned out the window of my bathroom and smoked a cigarette.

Daisy and Monica. Neither of them brave enough to do a big heroic deed. But then who is? Really?

Monica and I drive into Campton in her minivan. Why she needs a minivan I don't know. She wants to introduce me to her friends at work.

"Where do you work?"

"It's a surprise."

"I see."

"No, actually, you don't. The gang will love you."

"The gang?"

"Just wait."

"So what has happened to your prophesying these days?"

She chuckles. "I just keep it to a more local scale." Reaching over and grabbing my knee, she lets out a squeal of joy. "I can't believe we're together again. You and me, Drew." She sets a pair of sunglasses on her nose and smiles at the road ahead of her, her chin tilted slightly up from her long neck, a polka-dotted scarf tying back her auburn hair, now streaked with white.

We snake along Route 15, passing small farms, a chair store, car repair shops, a woodworking place, until the houses thicken, a church appears, a hardware store, and then a stoplight.

"It's our only stoplight."

"Nice."

"Well, it is what it is, as they say."

She takes a right, drives a short way to the strip shopping center just before a Dairy Queen.

"You work at the Dollar General?"

"No. There." She points to a small storefront to the left. "Mountain Mist Tattoos."

"You work at a tattoo parlor?"

"It's even worse. I own the place."

FOURTEEN

◆◆◆◆

Valentine: 2009

Jessica, a healthy woman with dark curly hair, pulls out a scarf and hands it to me. "For you."

She and the other two "monks" arrived back from Thailand yesterday. We sit at Blaze's kitchen table drinking tea with honey.

"Augustine told us all about you."

"He's pushy."

She laughs freely. "Not really. He just loves people. Pushy and loving are two very different things, don't you think?"

"Maybe."

"So anyway, he told me about your beautiful brown hair and asked me to bring you back something in a dark pink."

"He did?"

"E-mailed me from Java Jane's."

"One thing I don't get about Augustine. He doesn't try to change people. He's never once told me to stop wearing my scarf altogether, although he said it wouldn't bother him if I did. He's never once given me that hokum spiel about loving yourself for who you are."

"No, he wouldn't do that. I mean, look at the guy. He's wearing his own sort of scarf, right? Don't we all?"

"You look pretty wholesome and natural."

"We all walk around with some kind of shame we hide."

I think about that. I'm not telling her what I told the disciples, that's for sure. "Augustine doesn't share his past."

"No. He hasn't with any of us. We respect that."

"It must be a doozy." I refresh our tea.

Dahlia calls me to come get Lella, and I make my excuses, showing Jessica out.

I carry Lella to Dahlia's rental car. Dahlia follows.

"Look, Val. I bought a pair of secondhand legs for Lella. And we've got a wheelchair in the trunk of the car."

The legs are already enclosed in chocolate-brown pants matching a new caramel-colored sweater and shirt she'd bought Lella the day before at The Limited. The Limited!

Lella's eyes glimmer. "Imagine, Valentine. A real pants suit. We're going to the mall to shop for a couple more outfits."

"That'll be fun."

"Oh, yes. And after that we're going to the movies. Aunt Dahlia says they actually have little spots for wheelchairs these days. Right in the theater. Imagine that!"

"You'll have to tell me all about it." Please don't.

"I will."

I set her on the front seat, belt her in, and hurry up the front walk before they drive away.

Why I never thought of legs is beyond me. Lella could have gone all over the place. Of course if she wanted to go out during the day, she'd need someone else to push her, but Rick would have happily volunteered. They could have gone to the movies, sat in the park on nice days, the bloom of the sunshine on Lella's face. Instead, Lella sat in her room day after day with me, reading magazines and comic books, listening to a thousand versions of "Embraceable You," watching me make jewelry and suggesting gemstone combinations.

I'm no good for her.

◆◆◆

Rick pounces an hour later when I come down to get another cup of tea. "That's a great scarf, Val."

"Thanks."

"You know"—he jerks a thumb toward the general direction of the front door—"we should take a lesson from Lell. We should go out too. Show off that scarf."

I place the kettle on the stove and turn up the flame. "You know, Rick, you've said some stupid things in your life, but that's got to be one of the most stupid."

"Come on, Val . . ."

"No, really. Do you think this scarf will make me any less conspicuous? I mean who goes around with a scarf under their eyes? All anybody will do is wonder why I'm wearing it. It'll be a disaster."

"Okay, okay." That rubbery skin on his face turns crimson.

Gosh, why do I do this to him? "Look, Rick, there's no hope for me and you. I just don't like you in that way."

"Is there someone else?"

I grunt for a reply.

"Valentine, your injuries don't matter to me."

"Oh, so it's my sparkling personality?"

"You know, you care a lot more about people than you think."

Now there's where Rick's wrong. I'm perfectly aware that I care about people. More than I should, probably.

"Let's just keep things where they are, okay? I liked it better when you were just my friend."

"I can't help the way I feel about you, Val."

"You're going to have to. Why not Lella? Why don't you love her?"

He shrugs and pulls out a chair at the kitchen table. "I don't know. I just don't. She's beautiful and all that, but . . ."

"Seriously, you should think about going out with her. I mean, she's got these new legs and all."

I lift down a teapot and settle in several tea bags. If I was better at conversation I'd fill the silence, but today is different. Lella has legs and all I got was a new scarf and the same old Rick.

"You want to play a game of Scrabble?" I offer.

"Make it Trivial Pursuit and you're on."

"Great. I stink at Trivial Pursuit."

"That sure is the truth."

"I'm just taking a break from recording," Charmaine says over a phone call. She tells me she's been praying for me like crazy. "You got a lotta pain in there, Val. Maybe it would help to talk about it more."

"Charmaine, it's a gruesome tale. Trust me, you don't wanna know it all."

"I really do. Val, I want to bear your burdens."

"You wanna hear about the burns?"

"I'll be done recording in an hour and then I'll be over."

"I'll meet you at the dock."

"I'll be there."

And she is, because she said she'd be.

"You want some chocolate?" She reaches into her pocket.

"Not today. I just better get this out."

I fill her in on what I told the disciples, then continue.

"The toilet in the motel room was stopped up. I called the front desk and the lady said they'd be right up with some Drano."

"Oh, my heavens," Charmaine whispers.

"The maintenance man, a slippery fellow with long yellow hair, poured some of the stuff into the bowl and said he'd let it set for a little while. He told me to flush in a bit and give him a call if it didn't work.

"His cell phone rang and he hurried out of my room, leaving the Drano on the counter by the sink. I found the Vicodin and the OxyContin, filled the plastic cup half full with water, and they slipped down easily. Three each. I just wanted to slip away for a bit. That amount wouldn't kill me, I supposed."

Charmaine grabs my hand and holds it.

"When I look back now, I realize what happened next was a psychotic episode. Nobody really wants to burn their face off no matter how different it looks, no matter how gruesome a mask it's become."

"I think gruesome is a little harsh, Valentine."

"No, Charmaine. People didn't gasp on the set because I looked different from before. People gasped because I'd become a freak, some sort of Hollywood clown woman, a person who couldn't stop.

"Here's the truth of the matter—though it was Mother's and Drew Parrish's idea, I'm the one who drew the judgment from everyone. I alone was the one to turn away from. As I looked at myself in that gritty medicine cabinet mirror, something snapped in me. There was a lot of snapping going on around that time.

"I started clawing at my skin. *Get this face off of me.* The person inside the reflection was screaming. *Get it off!*

"So I balled up a towel and reached for the Drano, squirting it onto the terry cloth. I slathered it onto my face and massaged it in. I hoped and prayed it would reach those implants in my chin and cheeks and just eat them away."

"Oh, Valentine! You don't have to go on."

"And then, the burn began as the acids in the drain cleaner met living tissue. My breath caught, I reached for another towel, but the world spun and spurted with reds and oranges. I fell. They told me I hit my head against the toilet rim, still open from the maintenance man.

"I woke up in a hospital to the pitying gaze of a young nurse. I didn't remember anything at first. She told me about my injuries.

"Tears soaked into my bandages. The last tears I ever cried. I promised myself that as I picked at my blanket, fiddling with a thread. A white blanket. Loose weave. You know the type?"

She nods. "How did you get to the hospital?"

"I found out later the maintenance man found me when he came back to check on the toilet, to see if the Drano did its job. On the whole, I'd say yes . . . yes, it did."

Charmaine puts her arms around me. Just like I figured she would. "And so you disappeared."

"Yes. The hospital called my father the next day and he came right over. I couldn't talk at that point. So I wrote, 'Tell him not to tell my mother. He must come alone.' All caps, tons of exclamation points after each word. Along with his phone number.

"The pretty nurse nodded. Three hours later my father came into my room. The doctor had informed him of my injuries. He cried, apologizing, telling me he shouldn't have let Trician do this to me. That he tried to step in, but she wouldn't listen."

"I should have tried harder, too, Valentine."

"No. None of this was your fault. Anyway, I forgave him. He was weak. And so was I. We all were. Somehow he realized I'd done this to myself. Nobody broke into my room and slathered Drano on my face. I mean you hear about Drano bandits all the time, right?"

Charmaine smiles.

"I choose to believe he knew because he was my father and I was his child."

Charmaine squeezes my hand. "Oh, he knew all right, honey. I'd bet good money on that."

"Why do you think he never really stepped in until that day, Charmaine?"

"Why we do the things we do is a very complicated matter when you come right down to it. Behind most of our inaction we truly believe it can always get worse. And truthfully, maybe we're just a little lazy. Or scared. Add to that the fact you were an adult . . . I don't know, Valentine. You'll have to ask your father to know for sure. I never knew my father so maybe this isn't a question I can really answer."

"But he showed up at the hospital. And he kept my mother away from me from then on out."

"What happened to your mother?"

"The world she'd created came crumbling down. In a letter I forced her to admit that if the truth of my burning came out, the church and everybody who knew her would secretly blame her. She was the mother after all. She should have known better."

"That's true enough."

"What I do know is that she never really loved me, Charmaine."

"It's the hard truth of the world that some mothers simply don't love their children. I know how that feels, Valentine. Thank goodness she didn't have more than one, just like my mama."

"She packed up her things and drove to New York City, getting together with an old boyfriend who'd kept in touch and often told her if things ever went sour with my dad, he'd be there. And Lionel lived up to his word. They shacked up but she kicked him out once she was on her feet. She'd started a 900 number: Talk to Your Mom. She and her employees said all the right things mothers should say to people whose mothers, I guess, never said it to them."

"That feels wrong."

"Maybe it wasn't phone sex, but it felt creepy all the same, kinda like men that pretend to be babies for kicks. I'm sure those types of guys made up 90 percent of their clientele. Believe me, the irony wasn't lost on my dad and me."

"People sure are strange."

"Truer words were never spoken."

"I'm sorry, Valentine."

"Well, it is what it is now, right?"

"You don't have to be Lizard Woman. You know that, don't you?"

"Who would I be? I'm not rich. I've got to make a living. How else am I going to make a living?"

"Making a living and *living* are two very different things, honey. And don't I know it."

Coming from anybody else, that would make me angry. Charmaine had all her troubles heaped upon her through no fault of her own. She may still be cute, but inside she's as scarred and ragged as my face.

"I guess I'll take that chocolate now."

She reaches into her pocket and pulls one out, the kind with the sayings written inside the foil. "Now, if you took all the advice written on these things, your life would be one big old mess. Harlan and I always laugh at these things."

Mine says, "Do whatever makes you feel good."

Gee, candy people, where have you been up until now? That sage advice is sure to make everything all better.

As I lift Lella from the car, I have to admit that Dahlia's better for Lella than I am. She chatters on in her delightful prattle about all she saw and did, the world big and new and opening up like a pearl-filled oyster. Dahlia backs out of the driveway, headed for the IGA with big plans for chips, dips, and movies later on.

"That's great, Lell," I say, over and over again.

"I kept thinking about you, Valentine, and I said to Aunt Dahlia several times what a shame it is you weren't with us."

"Sorry, Lell. You know it's impossible." I settle her on the bed and gently lift the sweater over her head.

"I know, I know. But it would have been an even lovelier time with you there."

I unstrap the prosthetic arms and lay them aside. "You must need to use the bathroom."

"No. I didn't drink anything at the movie. I'm all set. I truly am."

"Then, there you go."

The Apostle John is sympathetic as always.

I have to let her go, don't I? Dahlia's going to reissue her invitation. I can't hold Lella back. Not if I love her like I say I do.

"How can I let her go, though?" I say out loud.

If Charmaine and I seemed clandestine when cooking for the Psalters, what I'm doing now must be on the order of the Knights Templar or something. At one a.m. I wind my scarves around my head, shrug into my coat, and lift the hood. Rain or not, I'm going to the Laundromat. I look at the disciples. "Let's just see if Augustine is as giving and holy as he seems to think. Let's just see what happens when Lizard Woman turns up in the middle of the night."

Peter agrees.

Bartholemew says, *For goodness sake, Valentine. You know right now he's going to be fine with it. You're not so tough as you think.*

"John, you need to do something about that guy," I tell him.

Lella and Aunt Dahlia asleep in their room, I tiptoe down the hallway, thankful for the rain tapping on the roof.

I walk the streets under the umbrella I grabbed out of the holder on the way out. It's a big sunflower. Yeah, that's inconspicuous. But nobody drives by, nobody walks by, very few lights brighten the night windows, and only a couple of televisions flicker blue behind some front windows. I suppose they can't sleep either.

The cold rain of a southern winter eats at your bones from the inside. I pick up my pace, making it to the end of Oakly Road by one fifteen. Oh, good grief. The lights are still on. Do these monks never sleep? I peer in the glass door. Three people sit on the couch. Candles burn. And with their closed eyes and their respectful posture—two of them with Bibles in their laps—it's easy to see they're praying.

Wonderful.

Well, let's see what happens when their holiness is interrupted. That beats a sleep test any day of the week! Jessica leans forward and sips a glass of water. I've never met the other two: a woman with a dark pixie cut, a man with buzzed blond hair who's reading from a prayer book. I guess. Or a Bible. They have a lot of those inside the Laundromat.

I'd planned on lightly tapping on the glass. Instead, my knuckles impact the door in a full-blown knock.

Three heads turn my way. The man stands to his feet, shoves his hands in his pockets, and approaches the door. He turns the lock and opens it. "Hey. What's up?"

"I'm here to see Augustine."

He swings the door wide. "Come on in. Want me to take your coat?"

"Okay." I unzip my jacket, slink out of the sleeves, and hand it to him. "You're not surprised by a visit?"

"Nope. Actually Augustine attracts people at all hours of the night. How about the scarves?"

"I'll keep them as is."

"No prob."

Jessica stands. "Valentine?"

"Yeah, it's me."

"You want a hot drink? You must be freezing."

"I bundled up good. But I'd like something to drink all the same. I'm sorry to interrupt."

Oh, great. From his spot over the stove, John rebukes my lie. Mr. Holier-Than-Thou. Even if he is.

"I'm Justin," the man says and shakes my hand.

"Good to meet you."

"You too."

"Okay, guys, I'm headed to bed." He disappears down the hallway toward the kitchen and the bunkroom.

Jessica pats the sofa. "Have a seat. We were just praying Vigils and got a little carried away. Our"—she puts quotation marks around her words with her fingers—"'hearts were strangely warmed within.'"

"You're going to have to explain that."

"Wesley. John, not Charles."

"I didn't realize there were two."

"Let me get you that tea."

I sit on the couch. It seems homier in here now that the women have returned from Thailand.

"I'm Rachel," the woman across from me says.

"Valentine."

"Of the pink scarf?"

No. Of the blue scarf. I mean, how many other Valentines are running around Mount Oak? I mind my manners. "Yes. How was Thailand?"

"Sad and good. Lots of tsunami stuff left to be done even after all this time. It was pretty hard."

"Sure."

"Okay, I hear Gus coming. I'm heading to bed. We've got a family of refugees coming into Mount Oak tomorrow for resettlement. They're from Northern Uganda. I've got to get up early to make sure the apartment is ready."

"Refugees. Got it. Good night, then. Nice to meet you."

"Same to you."

Augustine hurries in. "Valentine? What are you doing here?"

"You want me to open up to you, you got it."

"Why?"

"Because at this time of night I've got no place else to go."

He smiles. "Well, that's as good a place as any to be."

"I don't get you."

"No, most people don't."

Jessica sets down a cup of tea. "Here you go. I'll head off to bed. Good night all."

"Thanks for praying tonight, Jess. I don't know what came over me."

"Maybe that phone call?"

"Yeah, could be."

"What phone call?" I ask.

He blows a puff of disgust. "My father. Needless to say, we never really got along."

"Part of your secret past?"

"No kidding."

"What did he want?"

"He's ill. Just thought I should know."

I lean forward and pick up the tea. "What are you going to do?"

"Don't know. Call my mother, I guess. So what brought you out at one thirty in the morning?"

"I feel like crying for the first time in years and I don't know what to do about it."

Augustine sits in silence as I pour out my feelings about Lella. Still, I do not cry—although still, I want to. Finally I am spent. "So what should I do?"

"What can you do? Lella has to make this decision on her own, Val. You know that."

"But where will that leave me?"

"I guess that's the bigger question, isn't it?"

"Is she better off without me?"

He shrugs. "I don't know."

"You don't give good advice, do you know that?"

"Sorry, Val. I'm a loser. I'm better at listening these days. Can I pray with you?"

"Is that part of your act?"

"I guess so." He sighs. "I don't know. It always seems like a good thing to do."

"Go ahead, then, if it makes you feel better."

"I didn't say it made me feel better. Sometimes prayer makes me feel worse."

"Why?"

"Because I'm talking to God, and I don't deserve to, probably."

"I used to go to church, a long time ago. The preacher there told us to come boldly before the throne and claim the promises of God."

"Yeah. I've heard that."

"Well, is that true or not?"

"Maybe for some. For me it's different."

"Aren't those promises real?"

He runs a hand across his forehead. "Yeah, they are. But these days I prefer resting in them instead of demanding them. I used to be quite demanding."

"I can't imagine it."

"Well, then glory be to the Father."

"'And to the Son and to the Holy Ghost,'" I sing, the words forcing themselves out before I can stop them. "Might as well finish it. 'As it was in the beginning, is now, and ever shall be, world without end, Amen. Amen.'" I draw out the last note.

Augustine slams against the back of the sofa as if pushed. His face pales.

"Are you all right?" I rush to his side, grab his hand. "What's the matter? You coming down with something again?"

He shakes his head as if coming back to life. "I'm sorry. I don't know what came over me."

"You'd better get back to bed."

"Yes, I think I should. Do you want me to walk you home?"

"No, I'm fine."

"About that prayer?"

"Skip it. You look like you need it more than I do."

PART TWO

FIFTEEN

◆◆◆◆◆

DREW: 2009

I am Augustine. I suppose you've figured that out by now. The estranged father, the tattoos. The bigger secret is that I was once Drew Parrish. But no longer.

You see, my mother prayed.

Every morning of my life my mother prayed for me. She continues to do so there on her slice of cliff in Slade, Kentucky, and I visit her when I can, which isn't as often as I'd like with all the people in the neighborhood who rely on me in one way or another. But our connection runs deep. I truly forgave her. She's only human. She's weak. Her weakness just manifested itself differently from mine.

Many centuries ago there lived another Augustine who eventually became a saint. Saint Augustine lived raucously before he realized, as all of us do or will someday, that Christ loved him. He wanted to spend his life following Him.

Augustine's mother was named Monica. She prayed for him too. Her prayers are credited for his conversion.

What I should change my name to, when I truly decided that this story of God in which we all play one role or another was for real, was a no-brainer. By that time, a year after I'd found my mother, I'd become a regular at the parlor. It was Monica herself who covered my scars with her artwork.

"I didn't know you were an artist," I said that first day in the shop.

"I didn't either. I think it was a gift God gave me to keep me sane."

"Well, I guess it's the gift that doesn't go away. These people will wear your work for the rest of their lives."

"But they'll go down to dust, Drew. We all do. A lot of people come through this shop. I do what I can for them. People with a lot of tattoos, well, it's about belonging, not the tattoos themselves. They're only symbols of a deeper need, one we all share."

We started with my arms, the flowers, the fish, then my legs which nobody ever sees, because at this time, Monica began to feed me. I became not someone else really, but the person I might have been all along. I returned to something essential by masking the misery of my own mutilation.

My mother and I would walk for hours in the woods, hike the trails. There's something about the dome of heaven, congregations of trees, and the singing of the earth and her inhabitants, coupled with love, both Divine and human, that does something to a soul.

My hair grew longer.

My waistline grew wider.

My heart grew stronger.

I stopped writing. I called Father Brian and asked him if that would be all right if I stopped confessing to him. He said, "Have you other means?"

"I do." To Monica.

"Good."

I sent the notebook to Father Brian, still a good friend, who still listens to my sins over the phone when I need him to. I prayed Daisy and I would cross paths someday, but I waited for God to figure out when that would be. If it would be.

The dorky smile faded and God took away the one thing that enabled me to build that church and the TV show. He took away my voice. Coming home from the tattoo parlor several months after finding my mother, I skidded in a downpour and ran off the road and into a ditch. My airway was blocked, the EMTs did an emergency tracheotomy and damaged my voice box for good. No big sermons anymore. No big plans to announce. Just a guy with a scratchy voice.

We had no further contact with my father.

True to form, Charles Parrish popped up on television from time to time . . . until one day, Monica rose from the couch, opened the screen door, and picked up one end of the TV. "Grab the other side, Drew."

I did as told. We lifted the set, carried it onto the deck, and threw it into the gorge. That night we had a steak dinner at the Natural Bridge Lodge. Neither of us owns a television set these five years later.

That evening, we hiked up to the top of Natural Bridge, which was, true to Hermy's word, like looking out over the whole world.

The sun slid in low, red, and sorry to leave the day behind it, clinging with tenacity to the horizon just for my mother and me, it seemed. I thought of Joshua fighting beneath a paralyzed sun.

"Did you ever feel desolate?" I asked her there on the top of the world.

"I had a rough couple of years when I first settled here. It's lonely. The wind wails at times, the rain pelts the roof, and I've felt as if I was the only soul for miles."

"Did you ever want to kill yourself?"

She shook her head. "Not as long as I knew you were alive. Some things you just live for. Your children are one of them. You've wanted to, though, haven't you?"

"Yes. A little. Never really seriously."

We remained there on the middle of the bridge until the sun set completely and the moon shone, close enough to the edge to rest our ankles and free our feet in the wind, our flip-flops beside us. I put my arm around her and she rested her head on my shoulder. I didn't think about how beautiful she looked sitting there; instead

I thought she had the most beautiful heart I'd ever known. I told her I loved her and she said she knew that; she said it was never in doubt. She said she loved me too.

Hermy stayed with us for a month or two, wooed the long-legged librarian, and they married. They have two kids now, aged two and four. He works in the library too. Some of God's plans seem small. But none are ever insignificant.

I haven't burned myself since that first day in Kentucky. I've wanted to at times. When the yearning gets strong, I'd like to say I pray, but more than likely I head out on my Harley, ride around Lake Coventry, and on out into the country. I've befriended Mildred LaRue, who gave me those ruinous compliments years ago. She always has good food in the cupboard and we watch old movies together.

I became Augustine on August 26, 2003. My mother's pastor rebaptized me, because this time the old man the Apostle Paul wrote about was dying for real. The tears of my repentance mingled with the waters of the Red River. Finally, in the words of Father Brian, my personal Pentecost had ascended.

Was I "saved" before that? I honestly don't know. I don't think it matters. I like to think of myself in the manner the Scriptures say, as one of "those who were being saved." It causes me to remember I serve a Holy God.

I suppose it's easy to figure out what happened when I heard Valentine sing. She was gracious for leaving as easily as she did, not asking too many questions.

I went back to my room, lit a candle to cut the gloom, and listened to Justin snore on his cot. I'd made a life here at Shalom. Putting away those things that were behind me, I pressed toward the mark of the high calling of God in Christ Jesus our Lord. I relate to Paul, serving in singleness of heart, and I am no longer ashamed of that. I'm just trying to serve God now, not myself.

And now as I lay here in the darkness, the candle having sputtered out a few minutes ago—it was just one of Rachel's tea candles anyway—I realize that God doesn't forget a thing. Redemption can be full if we've a heart to let it be. And so I pray for the heart to see this through.

It would be tempting to run away again. Back to Monica.

But I'm committed to this place, these people. And I must wage the final battle to banish Drew Parrish completely.

I don't pray that Valentine will not find me out. I pray that she will. And that somehow, God will be kind to us both. Is that selfish to ask for the Lord's kindness for me as well? I'm not sure. Nevertheless, I pray it, resting in the promise that His mercies are new every morning. And tomorrow morning is coming quickly. I can only pray it takes care of itself.

Her stories of how she got her scars are obviously false. What happened to her?

I awaken later than usual, not surprisingly. Jessica and Rachel have left for their jobs at the refugee ministry. Justin fixes bikes at the local bike shop. Praying Matins, a heaviness descends on me as I remember Daisy once more. It's been several years since I've obsessed about her.

Maybe this deserves a call to Father Brian. He loved the whole name-changing business. Said I should just go all the way and get confirmed in the Catholic church, come back to St. Mary's, and do some good works down in Ocean City. "We've got our share of the poor," he said. But I couldn't have become a priest in the Catholic Church. Too much possible position to rise to. Bishop, then Cardinal, then . . . oh yes, the Pope himself. No, I didn't need that kind of opportunity.

Maybe I should just get out the old notebook.

Uh, no. I'll call.

"Don't tell me you're dragging up Daisy again!" he says. "I thought we worked through that."

"This is different, Brian."

"I'm a little skeptical."

"Just give me a chance." I pour myself a cup of coffee.

"How's Shalom doing?"

"There are a whopping four of us in our fellowship. Nothing like the old days, huh?"

"Your old church seems to be doing fine without you. I was on their Web site."

"They brought in quite a guy from New York. Ex-drug lord, gang warrior type of fellow. Quite a testimony. Keeps them entertained."

"Now, Gus."

"No, I mean it about the pastor. Quite a guy. Have you ever heard of him?"

"Can't say that I have."

"He comes to Shalom every so often to just sit and pray. That's a good thing."

"Yes, it is."

"He's just trying to figure it all out like the rest of us."

"Most likely. NASCAR's about to start."

I tell him about Valentine.

"That's bordering on crazy."

"Tell me about it."

"No wonder you were drawn back to Mount Oak."

"If I'd known I probably would have picked somewhere else."

"I don't think so, Drew. You've wanted this deep down for a long time. But it seems to me I'm not the person to be talking to about this."

"Should I tell her who I am?"

"You have to. She's your sister in Christ. You've got to go to her for forgiveness."

"She hates Drew Parrish. I've heard her talk about him."

"Can you blame her?"

"No. But I'm not Drew anymore."

"Maybe not. But you sure are carrying around the weight of his past, the people he sinned against, aren't you? Anything else would be plain old-fashioned denial. Go on and say what you have to say."

"She's a sideshow attraction now, Brian. Did you know that before Daisy's final surgery we were looked at by a talent scout from one of the networks? I met him in my office and he talked about a morning show, like Regis and whoever he was with at the time. Can't remember if it was Kathie Lee or that bubbly girl.

"He said he liked the chemistry between us. And with a live audience it would be dynamite."

"He actually said 'dynamite'?"

"Yes. I thought then, *What, is there some kind of script going on with you people?*

"The final round of surgery was already scheduled, and you know what happened after that. It was a disaster. After that first post-surgery show aired, the scout called me back and asked me who put the freak on that girl?

"I told him just a little nip and tuck and he said, 'The deal's off. She looks like a freak.'"

"Did Daisy know about the scout?"

"Yes."

"Did you tell her about his callback?"

"No. She'd disappeared by then."

"Well, at least there was that."

"Big deal."

"That's the truth. But it seems to me the Holy Spirit's got some work for you to do."

"I hope so."

"Gus, it's never too late for redemption. The scars never run too deep, so deep that God is not there."

"I should know this. I minister to scarred people everyday. It just feels impossible when the scars are your own, or are those of the person you wronged so fully."

"It feels different when it's you."

"Why is it the good you do seems like a drop in the bucket but the evil spreads for miles and miles?"

"You're a new man, Gus."

"I hope so. But Daisy's in a freak show because of me. It doesn't matter how she was burned. She ran away from me and Trician. And as bad as Trician was, it was my greed and lust for fame and approval that propelled everything."

"And you're sorry."

"Not to mention I was her pastor. She trusted me."

"You've got to tell her the truth."

"Can't I just do penance?"

"I think that will just painfully delay the inevitable. And I don't know why I'm telling *you* this, but you're not Catholic."

A long time ago monks used to wear hair shirts or nails in their shoes to subject the flesh that caused them to transgress, as well as to do penance for their sins. If we did that at Shalom, I'd need glass socks, fiberglass underwear, and a barbed-wire jacket to even begin to pay. My tattoos cover me up, the old me, remind me everyday I'm only a breath away from slipping back.

"Go to your NASCAR."

"Go to Daisy."

"I'll think about it."

He hangs up, promising to visit Mount Oak on his next break.

◆◆◆

I head on over to Blaze's.

Rick answers the door. "Hey, Gus. Come on in. Val and I are just starting up a game of Trivial Pursuit. Wanna join in?"

"Sure."

I follow him up the steps.

"We're holed up in Val's room with the secret space heater. I can't remember a colder February."

"It's been pretty chilly."

You always have to talk about the weather first with Rick. Rick's a simple person. Loves to go walking, fish at the lake, play games, tie himself into a knot. I envy him.

We start up the second flight. "Hey, Rick, you all sang great at the Love Feast. I'm sorry it wasn't better attended."

"Val wasn't."

He opens the door to her bedroom.

"Hi, Augustine," Val says, pulling her scarf up over her nose.

And I hear the voice. It's Daisy's tone all right. How could I have not realized it? The face is so different, and she's so hard now. Not as painfully thin, either. Thin, yes, but healthier looking. Nothing else is the same. Her hair is dark now, presumably she covers her blonde, or the blonde wasn't real in the first place. Even her eyes are hazel.

"Mind if I sit in?"

"Nope. Pull up a chair." Okay, her diction is different because of her damaged lips. Maybe that explains it.

She sits at the head of her bed, Rick at the foot; I pull the desk chair up to the side.

"I'm pink, Rick's green."

"Orange, then."

Rick picks the orange wagon wheel out of the box. "Good choice. Good choice."

I set my wheel on the board. "I'm thinking of getting colored contacts. Any of you ever have them?"

"Yep. Blue. Can't stand that now." Val opens up one of the clue boxes, setting the bottom inside the lid.

Such a simple action. How did she survive it all to get to the point of board games?

"So I'm figuring you didn't come over to play board games." She reaches to a bowl next to her and throws me a Tootsie Roll.

I catch it and unwrap it. "No, just coming by to see how the good folk of Roland's Wayfaring Marvels are doing."

Val rolls the dice. "Six." She hands it to Rick.

He rolls. "Four."

I roll. "One. Val goes first." I pop the candy in my mouth. I don't really like Tootsie Rolls, but I can't refuse this small gift from her.

She rolls again. "Okay. So why did you really come by?" Moves her wagon wheel five spaces.

Rick pulls out a question card. "Who was the first person to play Superman on the silver screen?"

"Kirk Alyn."

"That is completely unfair. Valentine getting a comic book question," I say.

She snaps up her head. "What do you know about that? Have you ever seen my comic books? How did you know?"

"Oh . . . I don't know. Maybe Lella mentioned it or something."

"Probably. When you spirited her off on New Year's Eve, perhaps? And that was pretty slimy."

"I really thought you'd follow."

"Well, you don't know me well, do you?"

That was the problem. I never did know Daisy well. I thought I did. I was such a know-it-all.

Rick rolls. Four again. "Man, I wish I had a dollar for every four I get. I always seem to roll fours."

"He does." Val reaches for a card.

Yellow. As Val reads the clue I zone. Why did I come over? I needed to see her. Be with her knowing she's Daisy. But she's so Val.

"Fidel Castro." Rick.

"No. Che Guevara. Your roll, Augustine."

I throw the dice onto the board. Three. Green. "Okay, let me have it." How can I get to know her again? She must know Augustine better before she recognizes Drew.

I'm still a selfish pig. I'm still making it all about me.

"What year did the Berlin Wall fall?"

"1989." How can I serve you, Valentine? God, help me. Have mercy on us both. Even on me though I don't deserve a drop of it.

"Whoa, big Reagan fan were you?" Rick says.

"Not really. I left politics to the grownups."

"Yeah, me too." Val.

"My dad almost worshipped him." Rick hands Val the dice. "I'm surprised we didn't pray to him. We prayed a lot at my house. It was a good home."

"Family that prays together stays together?" Val.

"I dunno, Val. Just sayin'."

We sure didn't pray together. But maybe it's a thought. I just jump in without thinking, because as the Lord knows, when I start overthinking something I find myself in a whole lot of trouble. "So Val, you came in during Vigils the other night?"

"Yeah. They were just finishing up."

"I was wondering if you'd like to come to Shalom and pray with us regularly. Lent is starting next week and we like to keep all the prayer times consistently." How lame. God, was this what You had in mind?

"Sign me up," Rick says, like I figured he would. Good man.

Val picks up the dice. "How many times a day you all pray over there?"

"Nine, during lent. The traditional amount."

"You got a middle-of-the-night time?"

"Vigils, like you came in on the other night."

"What am I supposed to pray?"

"It's all written out. Scriptures. Responses and all. You don't even have to voice it out loud, Val, unless you want to. Some people chant them."

She barks out a laugh.

Rick snaps his head up. "What?! Val, you sing better than anybody I've ever heard."

"Yes. She's amazing." You're amazing, Daisy. All on your own.

"Okay, okay. I'll do it. But I'm not promising I'll sing. What time do I need to get there?"

"Just sometime in the middle of the night. After one a.m. would be fine."

Lord, I hope she sings those prayers.

We've tried to pare down to the bare necessities at Shalom. Justin would like to be a Luddite, but there's no way I'm taking cold showers and we've got to cook our food somehow. I told him, "Justin, come on, brother. We'll be spending so much time worrying about how little we're taking for ourselves, we'll have nothing left over for the people we're here to serve."

In this place it's a balance. Because once your eyes are opened to justice and mercy, you can't go back. You can't ever look at a pair of sneakers the same way because you know tiny fingers might have stitched them together that should have been playing cat's cradle or catch. You can't eat an apple without thinking about migrant workers and illegal aliens and knowing how much Jesus loves them. And phrases like, "Well at least they have jobs" no longer are an option, because you've met these "lucky" working people and they are enslaved. It wears on the gray matter at times, let me tell you.

We've got to survive and keep our minds free enough to do God's work without walking over the poor to do it. So we grow a lot of our food in a garden in the back and try to buy from the farmers outside of town. There're some great families out that way and sometimes they give us extra to pass out to the neighborhood.

But we're no strangers to the IGA. First time I walked in there looking like this, Crystal, the manager, looked ready to throw me out. Crystal's got the biggest smile now, though. And she'll say, "Now I'm an old Southern Baptist, Gus, but you all got my vote with what you're doing down there." This year we're having an Easter feast for the folks on the street, and Crystal and her husband are providing the hams. Mildred's making up pans of mac 'n cheese and peach cobbler. Val's making broccoli casserole and corn bread—she just doesn't know it yet. She's great at institutional cooking, and why that is, I have no idea. But like anybody serving the poor, we're always ready to take advantage of whatever talents people have to offer. Choosy we are not.

I think that's when trouble starts, when people get picky about other folks' offerings to the Lord. I know that firsthand. I try my best to steer clear of that sort of attitude these days.

Justin meets me in the kitchen the next morning after Matins, bike helmet under his arm. "Gus, you'll never guess what I heard about. About a mile past Mildred LaRue's place on Route 91 there's a, well, almost a Hooverville back down off of Jonathan's Creek."

"In this cold?"

He nods. "I don't know much about it, or even who these people are, but I was thinking of heading over this afternoon. Want to come?"

"Sure thing."

The phone rings. We have no cell phones, just this old black clunker phone we bought at the Salvation Army. The mouthpiece stinks no matter how much we scrub it. I pick it up. "Shalom House."

"Drew."

Not now. "Hi, Dad."

"I was just calling to see how you're doing. How the church is going."

I never answer his questions anymore. He doesn't want to really hear the truth. "How are you feeling?"

"Not too bad."

"Are you in treatment yet?"

"It's inoperable. But slow growing. Or could be. Maybe not. Hard to say."

"I'm sorry."

Why does he want to get his life in order? It's typically selfish. He'll die feeling good about himself, and I'll still be ravaged by his newfound presence in my life.

Yeah, Lord, I know, I know.

"Yes, well, just wanted to call and give you the update. I'll be officially retiring next week."

"No kidding? Uh, Dad. How long do they give you?"

"Six months if I'm lucky."

"Sorry."

"Well, I've made a run of it."

"I'd better go. I've got an appointment."

"Of course. Good-bye, Drew."

I hang up. He's dying. Now do I just forget everything that happened? Everything he did to my mother and me? To who knows how many other people who trusted him?

Well, in my defense, I never trusted him. Not even once.

SIXTEEN

VALENTINE: 2009

Two weeks into Lent and here I sit in the middle of the night, praying out of a prayer book, several candles flickering on the coffee table. I pray the final prayer of the evening, the concluding prayers of the church, humming the Amen.

Two a.m.

As I lean forward to blow out the candles, an older woman pads out from the women's bunkroom just off the kitchen. Her red hair spills down her back. "Hello, Valentine."

Augustine said his mother was coming for a brief visit. I quickly slide up my scarf and she says nothing. "Hi. You must be Monica."

"Yes. I'm just here for a few days."

"Couldn't sleep?"

"Some nights it's hard. Do you have nights like those?"

I join her as she walks into the kitchen. "Frequently."

"Augustine figured that. He said that was the inspiration for your taking on the Vigils."

I nod. "I figured, why not? It's not like I'm doing anything productive in my own room. Just watching movies or reading comic books. I make jewelry too."

"A creative type. I love creative types. Would you like a nice, hot cup of tea?" She grabs the kettle off the stove. "It's colder tonight than it should be."

"I should go."

"Why? Are you tired?"

Okay, so you know those people with laser beams inside their gazes? But they're not mean laser beams, they're just frank. Monica's that type of person, exactly the opposite of Augustine, who has all that sweet Jesusy candlelight coming out of his eyes. Monica probably clears the temple while her son heals the blind and feeds the multitudes. "No, not really. I'm just uncomfortable."

She chuckles. "You know, Valentine, the truth becomes you beautifully."

"Then I guess I'll have that tea."

She fixes it with loads of honey and milk, not asking me how I prefer it, which is with just a little sugar, but okay fine.

"Let's sit back down."

"Why can't you sleep?" I settle back on the couch.

She curls her feet beneath her. Wow, she's a beautiful woman. "Augustine's father's dying and, well, he's trying to get in good with his son before the Grim Reaper comes along."

Her words, frayed and threadbare, are stitched together by weariness.

"Augustine's said you all are divorced."

"Not divorced. Just estranged. Did he say divorced? Really?"

"Maybe not. Maybe he just said you all aren't together anymore and I assumed."

"Well, it would be a good assumption."

"Do you feel bad that he's dying?"

"That's the problem. I don't feel as bad as I should and it's making me realize some things about myself I'd rather not think about. I'm hard-hearted regarding this man, and it's unbecoming to someone who claims to love the Lord."

Well, at least she's as hard on herself as she is on others.

Hard-hearted. That's what I am. I deserve to feel that way, sure. It's understandable. But I'm tired of it.

"These vigil prayers have been the best thing I've done in a long time," I say. "I'm a hard-hearted woman, Monica. This isn't some huge revelation on my part. I've known this for years and have built an identity in it. I'm disfigured, but not lonely. My problem is my heart. But these prayers are showing me I'm capable of forgiveness."

"Who do you have to forgive?"

"Can I not talk about it?"

"Of course. Have you done the forgiving yet?"

"No. But at least I'm thinking about it."

She smiles. "I'm glad the prayers are working for you."

"I'm sure the Laundromat would be glad for you to fill in a prayer slot or two while you're here. Good heavens, I'm recruiting for the place. This is ridiculous."

"My son has that way about him. For good or for ill."

"Monica, how did Augustine come to start a place like this anyway? It's so odd!"

"Isn't that the truth? Well, I have a friend in Baltimore who runs a mission downtown. Sister Jerusha. And we went up there after . . . well, that would take too long to give you the backstory. Suffice it to say, we stayed in Baltimore for a few months and while we were there, Augustine found out about a community like this in Philadelphia. I went back to Kentucky, back to my tattoo parlor, and he went north. Lived there as a novice for a couple of years in this deserted, boarded up church in one of the worst sections of the city. Served the people, saw a lot of heartache and pain. Learned to pray. Learned to forget about himself. Learned to help kids with their homework."

"Makes sense."

"It changed him. And those folk there didn't let him get away with his predilection to wallow in his miseries."

"Augustine wallowing in his miseries? I can't picture that."

"Picture it. After he found me—another long story—he was in horrible shape. Holding God at arm's length, obsessing over a woman he'd wronged—"

"I knew it!" I snapped my fingers.

"What?"

"He alluded to doing something so bad he needed to take the vow of celibacy. It makes sense."

"Well, it's a little more multidimensional than you're guessing at, but suffice it to say, he used a woman terribly and couldn't forgive himself."

"Did she forgive him?"

"He hasn't seen her since."

"Probably better that way. She probably needed to get on with her life."

"Perhaps."

"I mean, if the person who did this"—I point to my face—"to me, suddenly showed up asking for forgiveness, I'd know he was doing it because he wanted to feel better himself. He's just that kind of person. Maybe like your non-husband."

"Maybe he's changed over the years. But even so, you've every right to be angry."

"But I'm getting a little sick of feeling this way."

"I know what you mean." She sighs. "I'm going to have to really forgive Augustine's father. I mean I try. Every day I try. And I do it over and over again. But the feelings just come back."

"Sometimes it takes time. I mean I guess so, right?"

"Thirty years?"

"Good point."

"Don't do what I've done. For your own sake. It's very tiring. Has he asked forgiveness yet?"

"No. But then neither did the people Jesus forgave as He was dying. That's right, isn't it?"

She shakes her head and looks up at the ceiling. "It's the hard truth of it, unfortunately."

I haul myself back home a little while later and point my finger at the apostle John.

I'm praying every night, for heaven's sake, and God wants me to forgive Drew Parrish before he even asks? That's just crazy.

Besides, Drew Parrish is gone. I'm not going to waste my time trying to find that bozo.

◆◆◆

"It's just a little trip, Valentine!" Lella's eyes sparkle like they always do.

Dahlia hands me a new sweatshirt. "I thought you'd like this."

Navy blue, V-neck. "Thanks, Dahlia. It's great."

"I'm sorry I'm spiriting Lella off like this. But my bills will be piling up. I've got some business to take care of with the attorney regarding the will and all. We'll only be six hours away."

"You need help packing up?"

"No. Rick already brought everything down to the rental car."

"Keep in touch, Lell."

"Oh, surely I will do just that."

I hug her and this time I stand on the porch and wave until the car turns the corner, leaving this all behind.

◆◆◆

After making five necklaces, two bracelets, ten pairs of earrings, and watching the sky lighten just a bit, I open up the window by Lella's bed, lean out, and light up a cigarette. The bed is made up neatly. Dahlia did it before she left. And they took all of her clothing, every stitch, except for her costumes.

"She's not coming back, is she?" I whisper to the world outside the window. The breeze answers me, a fresh breeze, tangy with cold and middle-of-the-night lonesomeness.

Lella found legs. Secondhand legs, okay, but legs nonetheless.

Charmaine meets me on the dock the next morning. I hand her a cup of coffee from Java Jane's.

"Did you go in there?" she gasps, pointing to the logo on the cup.

"No! Rick did."

She sighs in relief. "Because if you had, well, I don't know, I'd have felt like I must have missed out on a lot going on in your life."

"Don't worry. I'm still limping along as usual."

She sips her drink. "So what's cookin'?"

"Augustine roped me into cooking for the Easter feast."

"He mentioned he was going to when I was down there."

"What were you doing down there?"

"Tutoring. They help the neighbor kids with their homework. I was a good student in school, believe it or not. Oh, I know I act all fluffy and sweet, but you can't throw much math at me that I can't put in its place."

"I stink at math, but I'm great at geography and spelling and such."

"You should volunteer."

"Right, and scare all the kids away."

"Now, Valentine." She stretches her legs out in front of her. This mellow March day shines on our faces. Well, her face anyway. Across the lake a hammer striking nails alerts us to some preseason repairs going on.

"So why did you want to come out here?" she asks.

"I've been doing a lot of thinking. I can never go back to Daisy."

"Would you want to?"

"No. I never really wanted all that to begin with, not for me anyway. I've got to move forward or backward or something, Charmaine. I can't stay like this much longer." I look out over the water. "I know my face will never be healed. I realize we can destroy ourselves in ways so deep we'll never return to the place we were before we started the destruction."

"I was almost there once. But for Harlan."

"But when I sit and pray at the Laundromat, feeling my prayers join with people a lot more faithful than me, I wonder if somehow I can begin something different. I mean, all those years ago I'd enter into my bedroom, shut the world out, and it was the only place I could ever be true of heart. I felt God loving me there." I turn to Charmaine. "I haven't felt that for a long time. Except recently. You and Augustine show me God's still around."

"Oh, He's more than just around."

"Lella used to show me that, in her way. She let me be God's instrument of mercy. I see that now. But she's gone."

I look down at my drink. Thumb a circle around the top of the lid, dipping the soft pad of skin into the small opening at the front. I set down my cup, pull down my magenta scarf, and stare in full-faced disfigurement at my friend. She doesn't even blink.

"I don't want to be Lizard-Woman anymore, Charmaine."

"Who do you want to be?"

"Just Valentine."

Charmaine leans forward and kisses my cheek, then my forehead. "You know, honey, valentines tell us somebody loves us."

I pull a straw out of my pocket, tear off the paper covering, and thread it through the hole in the top of my coffee cup. I want to say something about sentimentality, but Charmaine is sentimental. And real. It feels nice. Charmaine and I sip together in silence for a good long time as the workmen across the lake continue their improvements.

"Give yourself time to figure it out, honey."

"I don't have much time. We'll be getting on the road come April."

"And you don't want to go back on the road?"

"I just don't want to exhibit myself any longer. I don't know if I can."

Well, here's the Lenten "giving up" list around the Laundromat:

Augustine: all beverages but water

Jessica: meat, dairy, and makeup

Rachel: alcohol, iPod, and the Internet

Justin: any motorized transportation

I kid you not about Justin—it helps he's a great bike rider. I'm not sure where the sacrifice is, other than he's been going over to that encampment of people out of town. It's just a group of the homeless out there, living in tents. Augustine uses Rachel's little pickup truck to deliver propane tanks for their gas grills and propane heaters. It's a new ministry and it's costing the group a fortune, but as Augustine says, "Spring'll be here soon enough."

I blow out the final candle on the coffee table.

Lent, three weeks old, and all these prayers are causing me to remember Christ more than I usually do.

Finally! Bartholomew says from his spot over the stove.

Honestly, who'd think a thing if Jesus suddenly threw up His hands and said, "You know what? They're never going to get it. So I'll just let them bite and devour one another until my return. What's the use of worrying about the *now* when it's all going to come out in the wash eventually?"

For a long time I thought that's exactly what He'd done.

Thomas says, *Me too!*

But too much has happened inside me lately, and as I sit here and pray, the official prayers done for the night, I have to admit, a few minutes ago I felt my heart strangely warmed. I didn't get some vision or a voice or anything, I just felt loved and cared for. Yeah, it was warm.

So I should probably give up something too.

Ugh! Should it be smoking?

Duh, says Bartholomew, who's getting awfully vocal nowadays.

I don't want to give up smoking! I'll get cranky. And that wouldn't be good.

John tells me I can do it.

SEVENTEEN

◆◆◆◆◆

AUGUSTINE: 2009

God's forgiven me much—even more than I thought. Now that I know what became of Daisy—even though I still don't know how she was burned—the loathing I feel for myself comes on afresh.

But years ago, a wise friend told me I was blurring the lines between self-loathing and repentance. He pointed out there was a difference and one doesn't necessarily lead to the other. When I met him, folks called him The Black Jesus, though his name was Chris. Our conversations will always remain with me. Wish he lived around here.

Chris spent most of his days over by the Basilica of the Assumption, on the Charles Street side in the heart of Baltimore. He set Bible verses on cards all around him and played the flute. When people asked if he took donations, he'd say, "Only for the flute playing. The rest is for free."

He played Celtic-style songs which, excuse me for saying, just didn't sound right coming from a black man sporting an afro the diameter of an extra-large pizza.

I sat down next to Chris on his slab of cement, crossed my legs Indian style, and reached into the brown paper sack I'd carried up from the Afghani restaurant down on the next block. The Silk Road.

"Kabob?" I said.

"Most definitely."

We sat eating our meals-on-a-stick, watching some men and women in suits walking to lunch, maybe at Mick O'Sheas or the Thai place, a lady with a double stroller holding twin girls, and Stacy, the local panhandler who's always saying she just needs twenty dollars for a cab to get back to Catonsville. But she'll take less if that's all you've got. Her husband was supposed to pick her up, you see, and never showed, and she's got to get back home because her niece is babysitting and has to go to her AA meeting. Believe it or not, Stacy pulled in thirty bucks a day and the "booze she does choose" was cheap enough.

"Where does she sleep?" I asked Chris.

"She's used up her welcome at the women's shelters. They only give you so much time to get your act together and then"—he snaps his fingers—"if you don't snap to, your bed can be filled by someone who'll put the time to good use. Stacy sleeps on the street except in the winter when Sister Jerusha down at The Hotel opens up the main room. Not a comfortable sleep there, though, is it?"

"Not even close."

We were staying there at the time, Monica and Sister Jerusha pretending it was old home week or month. I can't remember exactly how long we stayed but it was a good while.

The Hotel only has tables and chairs set up in its main room and that's where you sleep if it goes down to thirty-two and you're on the streets. I tried it a couple of nights for the experience. It's uncomfortable, but not as uncomfortable as a freezing parking lot or dumpster.

Chris knew my story. I don't know how he did; he just seemed to know things about people they never told him. Either that or there was a big old gossip network surrounding The Hotel. He said that day, after we'd eaten the kabobs and thrown the bag in a nearby trash can that said, *Keep Baltimore Clean*, "You're just sorry that it all fell apart, angry at your dad, and you see that you failed. And, Drew, you did fail. Did you ever think maybe God took it all away because you were a cancer to the body of Christ? You were just passing along your own greed and discontent."

"Granted."

"Well, it's a new day. God was merciful to you."

"Some kind of mercy."

"Can you think of a better way He could have done it?"

Sure. One not involving Daisy would be a fine start. Why did He drag her into the mess?

Oh, that's right, I did that all on my own.

"And, Chris, I know what I did was wrong. I hate myself for what I did."

That's when he gave me the repentance vs. self-loathing speech. "You see, brother, one of the reasons we need repentance so badly is because we need the forgiveness more. Have you asked God for forgiveness?"

"No. It's complicated."

"No, it isn't. Having been forgiven much, there will be much required of you. You don't like that. None of us do. It's why so many relationships stay in the trash can. Person doesn't want to go say he's sorry 'cause if he does, he's got to stay around and play nice." That must have been funny to him, because he laughed and laughed.

"Not to mention I don't even deserve to ask after what I did. Daisy's just one of the fallouts, Chris. After a particularly thrilling sermon"—my voice fell in sarcasm—"about how God would bless the people of my church if they gave of themselves for the church building fund, one family gave their entire savings—windows of heaven pour out a blessing and such, right?"

"I know the verse." He squinted at me.

"A month later the wife came down with MS, and guess what? They didn't have insurance and no savings either. They're in horrible financial shape now. I don't even know what's happened."

"Brother, if most of those name-it-and-claim-it TV preachers knew, case by case, what havoc they've wreaked across this land, I think they'd never get on the air again."

"Really? I'll bet they do know. I'll bet they get letters all the time, but they've got planes to catch and bills to pay. And they can always blame it on the other person's lack of faith."

"Maybe I'm a little more trusting here on my corner."

"Then count yourself blessed."

"So you've got to repent, Augustine."

"I've confessed, does that count?"

"Are you sorry?"

"Yes."

"Then ask God to forgive you, my friend. Jesus already died for those sins, so why not get the full benefit?"

"I don't know, Chris."

"Oh, man! If it helps any, you'll still be a sorry, stinkin' old sinner. Does that make you happy?"

I laughed there on sidewalk and a young black woman with skinny little braids falling to her waist glanced at us, shook her head, and then she couldn't help it, she smiled. "You all are crazy." But it felt like a compliment.

A minute later Chris plucked the flute from its case. "Seems to me, brother, after all the confessing you've done, just do some forgiveness asking, some turning away, and you'll be right with God."

Sounded like something Monica would say.

He lifted the flute to his full lips, pursed them downward, and the strains of "Be Thou My Vision" floated from the end of the silver tube, rising into the sky like a prayer over all the houses, office buildings, stores, churches, and people.

◆◆◆

The next week, a young man from Philadelphia visited The Hotel. Sister Jerusha, a jumbo-sized Sister of Charity, pulled the dreadlocked, skinny young man in her arms and said, "Frish, but it's been a long time since you've been down, Shelby."

Her face flushed and she ushered him into her apartment and made him a cup of tea. She invited me back, saying, "This is Augustine. He needs your help. He's a church boy who needs God again."

Lord, why oh why did You surround me with frank women? And who says they can't teach men a thing or two?

Shelby told me about his "monastery" in Philadelphia, and it sounded like a bunch of liberal radical idealists who couldn't find anything that satisfied them in normal church circles.

I liked it.

I liked the liberal part because it thumbed the nose at my father. I hate to admit that, but it's true. Even at the best of times it's hard to separate the policy from the purveyor. And it got me up there.

Before I left for Philly I sat by Chris and listened to his flute. "What do you hope to accomplish here?" I asked.

"A mega-church question if I ever heard one. But I'll bite. I like to make people uncomfortable on one level. A black man with Bible verses set up around him will do that. Especially these verses."

The verses broadcast messages of God's love and care for His creation. Verses like, "Taste and see the goodness of the Lord." Or, "Your heavenly Father knows what you need before you ask."

"Why would these verses make people uncomfortable?"

"It's hard to keep someone like that at arm's length."

True enough.

I went to Philadelphia and unrolled my sleeping bag on a cot. I prayed all the time, steeping myself in communication with God, feeling sorry for my sins, begging God to forgive me, and so gaining the healing I needed. Feeling like an orphan since the age of twelve, I found a loving Father.

Chris was right about a lot of stuff.

He's still on that corner, by the way. Stacy moved her racket down closer to the Inner Harbor.

And the love of God surrounded me, wound through the innermost portions of my soul. For two years I saw Him in the eyes of the people I served with and the people I served. I saw Him in a loaf of bread and a two-paragraph report that Chandra or Willis or Juan wrote. And we laughed a lot.

Did I tell you about the laughter?

It cleansed me.

I laughed with people who had nothing to laugh about. Who were free from the avarice and the power-hungry beast that still tried to free itself from inside me. I learned more than I taught and so took more than I gave, but for some reason it felt okay.

I realized we are all God's children. Every single one of us.

Val's in Shalom's kitchen with Bobby, a kid from the nearby trailer park. Bobby's fat and mean and by the usual definition, white trash. His parents both rely on welfare with no plans of exiting the system anytime soon, and although Bobby wears ripped, dirty clothing, they always have enough money for beer and cigarettes.

This is where serving the poor gets hard for me and I'll just admit it right now. Helping out the working poor, or the kids of a single mom who messed up but is trying to get her feet back beneath her is easy, even lending a hand to those so burned-out or oppressed they don't know how to rise above it. But it takes some supernatural interference when helping people like Carrie and Billy Morgan, who lie to get their checks and feed their habits rather than their son—Bobby's fat because Twinkies and frozen pizza are cheap. And the school meals aren't much better, burgers and potato nuggets or more frozen pizza, and guys like Bobby aren't about to take the green beans, and who can blame them? I swear they're plastic anyway. For white people, helping out in the ghetto holds a sort of glamour, but ministering to trailer trash with no jobs and a sense of entitlement—well, those people get no respect from anybody.

But there's a Bobby in that trailer who needs to know Jesus is in his corner because his parents sure aren't. They scream at him, yelling obscenities and put-downs for what I wouldn't even consider an infraction, more like a kid just being a kid.

"Shut the —— —— door, you little ————!" Carrie will scream.

No kid deserves that no matter how mean and annoying he is.

Serving the kids—that's my favorite part in all of this. I'd like to think it's the way to break the chain. Even for just a few.

From the darkened hallway I watch Val and Bobby sitting on the worktable as she patiently flips flashcard after flashcard in Bobby's face. He stumbles his way through. Then gets angry with her. He slaps the cards out of her hands.

"Okay, let's take a break." She hops down off the table and turns her back on him. "Want something to drink? We only have soy milk and tea. And water."

"I want Coca Cola."

"We don't have that."

He crosses his arms. "Well, that's all I'll drink."

She turns around and crosses her arms. "Go thirsty then, big shot. It's your choice." And proceeds to make herself a cup of tea. "Go home even. I'm sure it's more exciting there than this gloomy place."

Gloomy? What's so gloomy about Shalom?

I look around me. Cracked walls, buckled linoleum floors severely lacking that lemony fresh glow you see on TV commercials.

"Anything's better than that trailer." Bobby.

Now here's the thing. Bobby's been coming around here for a year and he's been nothing but trouble. Scares the other kids off. And when we have feasts, he fills his plate up like a mountain and eats only half of it. If you say anything to him, he flares up and makes a scene.

I guess he thinks he doesn't deserve any pity, or much of anything for that matter, from Valentine. Not with her face the way it is. Maybe she's the first person in the world he's ever felt sorry for. Who knows?

"So, you want that cup of tea?" she asks.

"I've never had one."

"I'll put lots of sugar in it."

What I wouldn't give for a cup of that stuff. Nothing but water since Ash Wednesday. What nobody else knows is that I've given up every other edible luxury. I'm so sick of beans and rice, that's all I've got to tell you. And I wonder if this is all really necessary, but I remember how much Christ gave up for me. It causes me to remember. My sacrifice seems pretty pathetic in light of that.

I'm dropping weight quickly. I should write a book, *The Lenten Diet: Just Give Up Practically Everything*. With my luck, it would give me the fame and money I always wanted back in the day. No thanks. I'm not that strong.

Sitting down on the couch in the main room, I miss the wave of gut that, until very recently, used to crash over my belt buckle. I sorta liked it. Drew was so thin. I don't want him to return in any way.

Fourteen days until Easter and then I've got to tell Val. I think. I've been praying and God's still silent. I decided not to ruin what Lent seems to be doing for her. The secret has kept for this many years; it'll keep for two more weeks.

I want to serve her. But I don't know what to do for her other than give her apple turnovers from the bakery over on the square, which I found out she loves. I give her funny cards and keep offering to go on her midnight walks, but she refuses.

Turnovers. God tells me to serve her and all I've got is turnovers.

I turn to Janelle and pick up her reader. She's a first grader with dark, ashy skin and a smile that pretties up even this place. "So, let's see what Al the Alligator is doing today, shall we, Janelle?"

She giggles. "You make Al so funny, Pastor."

Oh, the south, the south. I was trying to get away from that pastor title, but they just won't let it go! I pat her head. "Well, Al has a personality all his own, doesn't he?"

"He sure do!"

I point to the platter of snacks on the table. Val's doing. Cheese, crackers, and grapes never looked so good. "Did you get a snack?"

"Uh-huh. We all did."

Sitting around the room at card tables, seven other children do their homework. Charmaine Hopewell helps with the math and geography. Jessica with science and language arts. I'm the reading guy.

Laughter suddenly fills the kitchen. Bobby's laughing like tomorrow's never going to come. Val too. My eyes meet Charmaine's.

Not long until Easter and I'll have to tell Val the truth. It's not going to be pretty.

Janelle looks at me and says, "Where'd you get that crazy hair, Pastor?"

Before Val leaves she thanks me for the turnover. "And Janelle's question. Where did you get those dreads?"

"A lady in Philly, Celestine, from Haiti."

"Oh yeah?"

"She was a sweet person. She'd been involved in the dark religions and swore the demons still followed her. Part of me wanted to think it all her imagination, but many was the night I slept in my sleeping bag outside her bedroom door so she'd get a good night's sleep."

"That sounds like you."

"I told her I was going to Mount Oak—"

Val crosses her arms. "Why Mount Oak anyway? This isn't such a great place."

"God told me to."

"In an audible voice?"

"Almost. He wanted me to settle in a place that would constantly remind me of my wickedness and my foolishness."

She rolls her eyes.

"To keep me in a state of humility, Val."

She rolls her eyes again.

"Anyway, Celestine wanted me to take a piece of her with me. So she gave me dreadlocks."

"They're pretty crazy."

"My hair hadn't seen a pair of scissors in three years and was halfway down my back, so I thought, *Why not?*"

"I could give you lots of reasons."

"Well, while she was committing the dastardly deed, I could have told you why not myself. When she was finished teasing and rubbing, I was surprised a single hair was left on my head."

"You have good hair for it. Thick and curly, I'll bet. But don't you have to do something to keep them . . . you know . . ."

"A Haitian refugee keeps them up for me here in Mount Oak. She laughs and laughs at a white man with graying dreads. I swear Celestine put the gray in with all that rubbing."

"Good story."

"I've got a million of them."

"I'll bet."

"Really, Val. Doing this kind of work just gives you the best stories. It's kinda cool."

"I dunno, Gus. I kinda like stories of the rich and famous."

Say it isn't so. "Really?"

"Nah."

"Good."

Dad strikes again. This time by US Mail. Guess he realized the phone angle was a bust. He tells me he realizes what a terrible father he was and then gives the tired old quote, "Nobody gets to the end of their life and wishes they'd spent more time at the office."

Yeah, right, Dad, okay, fine.

Not word one about my mother, admitting his scheme bordered on the diabolical. I don't know. I don't know.

Great Drew, you're sitting here about to beg Daisy's forgiveness and you won't even give your own father the time of day.

Mother Teresa once said, "You only love Christ as much as the person you love the least."

Sometimes I can't stand that woman.

I read further down the letter.

"Please, Drew. Please," he writes.

The old Charles Parrish wouldn't have begged anyone for anything.

So we are all God's children. Isn't that right?

Val was tired so I told her I'd take tonight's Vigils. My father's letter crinkles in the pocket of the shirt I slide on over my head.

Will I tell him to come on down and bring his inoperable cancer with him?

I guess this thing we call faith is a climb. I always wanted to think of it as a big slide straight into the arms of God who waits at the bottom to catch us. But instead, He's a God who's on top of things—and like any mountain you climb, the closer we get to Him, the steeper the terrain.

Yes, yes. Jesus is the one accompanying me on the climb. I get it.

Huh. If you'd have asked me last year what my future would hold, I'd have said more of this. Just living simply here at Shalom, doing justice, loving mercy and all that. I didn't think my father would show up. I never expected Daisy would show up. I thought I could put the past behind me.

God's will be done. And it ain't gonna be pretty. I just have a feeling about that.

God's will be done.

I haven't any other prayer that makes sense.

I lean forward on the sofa and light a candle.

I lift the book of prayers into the circle of my gaze and I pray words I wouldn't think to pray on my own right now, but words I need, nonetheless.

Monica calls me as I sit down over yet another delectable bowl of beans and rice. For breakfast.

"We have to forgive him," she says.

"I know."

EIGHTEEN

◆◆◆◆◆

VALENTINE: 2009

I'm crankier than I've ever been and that's saying a lot. I point to the Apostle John. So John, wanna know why I've been hanging around the Laundromat so much? To keep from smoking, that's why.

And to pick up the turnover Augustine buys for me each day from the bakery on the town square. He says I deserve something sweet in life.

What a cornball!

My room, my window, what used to be something to look forward to, has become something to avoid. But where else am I going to go? Walking around town? No thanks.

And all these comic books.

Bartholomew smirks.

I'm sick of them. Sorry, girls.

I throw an issue of *Betty and Veronica* across the room just as Rick opens the door. It hits him in the chest. "Whoa, Val."

"Sorry. Nasty coincidence. I didn't know you were going to be there, and you know, a knock would be nice, Rick."

He holds out an envelope. "Sorry, Val. I guess I wasn't thinking at all, but you got a letter from Lella and I thought you'd like it right away."

He hands it to me.

"Thanks."

"You've been more cranky than usual lately."

See?

"It's this stupid smoking moratorium. That was just dumb. I've been smoking for five years and I thought I'd quit just like that?"

He shoves his hands in his pockets. "I dunno, Val."

"You dunno, what?"

"I think this is about more than smoking."

"Oh, you do, do you? And what could it possibly be, oh great psychologist?"

Man, I'm so mean to Rick. But it's just so easy. He sets himself up like nobody I've ever seen.

"You've been going down to Shalom a lot, spending time with all those little kids. Lella's gone and we both know she's not coming back. And you're in love with Augustine."

"What?"

He shuffles his feet a little. "You are, Val. Admit it."

"He's taken that vow, Rick. I just love him like a person. I'd be a gigantic, colossal, slobbering idiot to let it go farther than that. Get the message, Rick?"

His face reddens. "Yeah, Val," he whispers. "I get it. You know, I thought there was more to you. That underneath the rough exterior and the tough talk there was somebody kind and good." He looks down at his shoes. "I won't bother you again."

Dear Valentine,

It's been just lovely here with Aunt Dahlia. She's hired workmen to come in and do the house over with ramps and they're making the dining room my bedroom. I've decided to stay for the rest of the off-season. Aunt Dahlia, despite her talk about Uncle Joe, is so lonely. I feel needed.

You'll never believe it, Val, but I've been fitted with a decent set of prosthetics that I can control with my shoulder muscles, and I can now steer myself around in a motorized wheelchair. I've been given, as they say, a new lease on life! The only thing missing is you.

Aunt Dahlia says she'd hire you to come and live as my aid if you'd be agreeable.

Other than that, not much is new. I was considering whether or not I should go back on the road to earn my keep here at Aunt Dahlia's during the off-season, but she assured me she's financially able to care for me and would love to do so. She said the companionship far outweighs any inconvenience and she doesn't feel like I'm an inconvenience at all! I still have yet to make up my mind, however.

But I wonder how you're doing? Please write me soon. I long to hear from my dearest friend Valentine.

I do wish you'd come! Aunt Dahlia and I have such fun and you would too. We could go out to eat, to the movies, even on vacations together. We're already planning a Caribbean cruise!

Yours always,
Lella

An aid? Lella, you're my friend. I did all that because I love you, not because anybody paid me a dime!

I feel sick, like someone just propositioned me for sex or something.

Oh, Lella.

A Caribbean cruise? The movies? Going out to eat? Eat what, Lella? Mashed potatoes and gravy? What are you thinking? What are you thinking?

How can I go back on the road without you? Display myself like that without you displaying yourself like that? I'll be like the twins! We didn't swallow light bulbs or regurgitate keys or twist ourselves into pretzels, we were just freaks, Lella. FREAKS!

The door of my sideshow life closes behind me. Locks and bolts crash into place, soldered together by a situation beyond my control.

I press the tears back and rush out the door. I've got to get out of this room. I've got to get to the lake. I've got to sit and think. I don't know what to do. I can't go back on the road. I've got nothing anymore. No place to go. No future. Nothing.

Go! Peter says.

Yes, John agrees.

I slam the front door behind me, my coat open to the breeze. My skin burns. I burn.

A woman walking her dog gasps as I pass.

The dog rears up, tail wagging, and he jumps against me. I fall backward, landing on my rear end in the grass.

"I'm so sorry! Bibbers! Leave that poor woman alone!"

My scarf! I forgot my scarf! I grab at my neck, no scarf. No scarf!

I scrabble, gaining a bewildered stance, pressing my hands on my cheeks.

The only way to the lake is through the town square and beyond.

Oh no, I can't do this.

Go to the lake. Get to the lake, the words resonate within me. Bartholomew? Peter?

Jesus?!

No, surely not Him.

So I hurry. I quicken my pace with long strides.

"Oh, my gosh!" a man says. Then looks away, ashamed.

Dear God, please don't make this like a movie where the beast gets pelted with eggs and trash because people don't understand and when they don't understand they get scared and do all sorts of things out of character. I mean, there they were, hanging around the general store, caring for their neighbor, and all of a sudden a beastly person walks by and out come the pitchforks.

Okay, that thought helped.

"Mama! She's so ugly!" A little girl points to me. "What happened to you, lady?"

The mother's eyes open wide, beautiful brown eyes under finely arched brows. "Rebecca!"

She turns both of their backs on me.

But still stares and quick intakes of breath burn me as I burrow through the lunchtime crowd, and why did it have to be lunchtime? Each gasp strips something away from me.

"Look! It's one of the freaks!" A teenage boy reaches out his hand as I pass, makes contact with my shoulder, and pushes as hard as he can.

I lose my footing, watching him as he looks at his fat girlfriend in triumph.

"Oh!" I gasp, reaching out.

Everyone leaps away as I fall a second time, my spine scraping down the brick ledge beneath the window at Java Jane's.

The lake! The lake! Just think about the lake. That's all.

Forget where you are.

A young girl tugs my coat as I make it to my feet yet again. She stands with two of her friends. She's crying. My heart melts.

"Don't cry for me, sweetie. Cry for all these people who are frightened."

Resolved by her compassion, I chart my course, looking neither to the right nor to the left, passing through the square, finally turning onto Lake Shore Drive. Only a mile or so more.

My feet feel like lead. I pass the souvenir shops, still closed. Posters of perfect women in bikinis holding up suntan lotion, bleaching in the front windows, perfect, perfect women, selling something. The Dairy Queen. Joyce's Juicy Burgers. A small walk-in clinic only opened during the season. A Candy Kitchen. Josef's fine dining. Barnacle Bill's Seafood. They all slide by, these places of the normal, the perfect, as I hurry forward, the wind against me.

I stumble a third time, landing in the gravel at the side of the road.

A car pulls over as I gain my feet, rubbing my road-burned palms down the legs of my sweatpants.

"Lady! Are you all right? I saw you take that tumble."

I lift my face to him. "I'm okay."

"But your face. Did you fall on . . ."

"I'm deformed!" I scream as he leaps from his car. "I'm deformed! This is me! Get out of here. Leave me alone!"

The tears bite again.

No. No, no, no!

"But your knees . . . and your forehead."

The fall ate through my sweatpants. Blood drips down from a gash amid the abrasions. "Please!" I wail. "Leave me be."

"But you need help."

"I'm almost home." I lie. But then it doesn't seem like a lie. "Please. I'll be all right."

He pulls out a handkerchief and wipes the sweat from my face. He places it in my hand. "Please. Let me help you."

He looks like a nice young man. Sandy brown, curly hair, kind eyes. "I'm Robbie Fraser. I live on the lake. I can take you out there if that's where you're going."

"No. I can't. I've got to walk." I wipe my forehead. Blood imprints the white cotton.

"Are you sure?"

"Yes!" I want to yell at him like I yell at Rick.

He tries a few more times to convince me, but finally, shaking his head and looking like he thinks he failed me, he gets into his car and drives off.

I press forward.

The handkerchief!

I tie it around my face. Bless you, Robbie Fraser, for lightening my load.

I stumble onto my dock and facedown I beg God to come. Please, if You're only in my face just once in my whole life, God, let it be now.

Do not forsake me.

I turn over, lifting my face to the sky.

There's no condemnation to those who are in Christ Jesus.

I have held you in the palm of my hand. I have held you in my arms since before you were born.

I will never let you go.

Father, forgive me. I didn't know what I was doing. Jesus, take away my sin.

I can only feel and feel and feel, the verses from my childhood pouring into my head as I stare into the sky, the midday sun on my face, watching it as it begins to travel through the deepening blue.

I give up, Lord. Into your hands I commend my spirit.

◆◆◆

"Val?"

"Augustine."

"Jessica saw you tearing through the square a little while ago. I called Charmaine. She's taping for *Port of Peace* and said I'd probably find you here."

I sit up and I grab his hand, holding it to my heart.

"Val. What's going on? You're hurt. Your knees—"

"I was black inside, like tar. I've festered unforgiveness for years. Do you realize the ugliness of my face simply reflects who I am inside? I've been so mean to you."

"That's a little dramatic, isn't it? You were burned." His tone is tender.

"You know what I mean." I look out over the cold waters of Lake Coventry. "Baptize me."

"Right here?"

"Yes. Right now. Finish this thing. If you don't do it, I'm going to jump in the lake on my own and hope something takes. I'm that desperate."

He sits for several seconds and says, "I won't fail you again," and unlaces his boots. As he takes off his leather jacket he mumbles, "Oh, Jesus," over and over again.

I remove my shoes and my coat.

"Take off your socks too. You'll be glad they're dry. Do you have an undershirt on under that sweater?"

"Yes."

"Then take your sweater off too."

He removes his flannel shirt, folding it and laying it atop his jacket. He slips off his dime store watch and tucks it in one of his boots. Our skin raises up goose bumps. "Ready?"

Somehow, it all seems rather utilitarian, talking of socks and whatnot. Shouldn't we have just waded in without a thought, the Spirit taking such windy control we hadn't a thought for socks and whatnot? But it's mid-March.

We both gasp as we wade into the frigid lake.

"Oh, Val." He gathers me into the crook of his right arm. "Oh, Val. Just embrace me as I lower you into the water. It will be all right."

He touches my face and his eyes rest on me. He kisses my forehead, holds my nose shut with his bandana, then says, "I baptize you in the name of the Father . . ."

And under I go, the cold waters swallowing me whole. His arms supporting me.

"And the name of the Son . . ."

Yet another time, and into the waters of the lake my tears spill.

"And the name of the Holy Spirit."

I feel like I'm under for minutes. Years of tears gushing from my eyes and my body. Can a body cry? I die. As He died. Disfigured upon a cross.

He had no form or comeliness.

He died in ugliness, on display.

The holy freak, the Son of God, raised up for all the world to see, to laugh at, to mock, to despise, even to feel sorry for.

Augustine's arm tightens around me and he lifts me out of the waters.

He holds me in his arms, crying hot tears onto my face. "I don't deserve this. I don't deserve this. I don't deserve this."

Okay, it may not have been like the scene of a movie, but I was happy for the dry socks.

"You rode on your bike?"

He hands me a helmet. "I knew it was urgent. And I'm not in shape to go running to the lake these days. It's gonna be a cold ride."

He climbs onto the Harley and I climb onto the seat behind him.

"You know, a friend of mine, years ago, said he wanted a motorcycle someday. Well, he wasn't a friend. In fact, he was my enemy for years."

"He's not your enemy any longer?"

"No. I've forgiven him. At least I think I have."

Augustine twists the throttle and we head back to town.

Being forgiven is good, but forgiving is something even holier. I think John would agree with that.

NINETEEN

◆◆◆◆◆

AUGUSTINE

There's a verse in the Bible about God doing more than we could ever ask or think. That's what He did for me there at the lake with Daisy. For it was Daisy I baptized last week.

She went down into the water as Daisy and came up Valentine for real.

"I don't deserve any of it," I said to my mother on the phone, finally having garnered up the nerve to tell her who Valentine really was.

"Of course you don't. But you needed it. And God knows what we have need of before we even ask. He gave you the double-portion of redemption you needed."

"I'll still have to ask her forgiveness. I'm sure of that."

"Of course. It's going to be harder on her than it will be on you."

"I was hoping—"

"She's feeling all clean and neat right now, and you're going to drag up the muck she doesn't know is still there. But after that, and who knows how long it will take her to work through it, she'll be free of the grime. And so will you."

Spoken like a true prophet.

◆◆◆

When I left Philadelphia and returned to Mount Oak, I didn't hold much of a clue as to how it would work out. I felt somewhat like Abraham, blessed to be a blessing, called out of Ur. Only I was called back to Ur, I guess. Okay, the analogy falls flat if you take it across the board.

But to Mount Oak we came. Rachel, Jessica, and Justin in Rachel's little pickup truck with a small U-Haul trailer, me on my bike.

On the second day we were in Mount Oak we came upon the Laundromat at the end of Oakly Road. Upon inspection it seemed to be in good shape structurally, and the price was right. Thirty thousand.

Half of my remaining savings gone in one day.

With the plumbing redone and some work on the electrical system, hauling away the old machines, replacing the broken windows, adding kitchen appliances—used ones at that—another ten left my bank account.

I look around me now. We still need new floors and some paint these years later. But my account is emptied.

Now, I have no idea how many people I wounded with my avaricious messages at Elysian Heights. But I knew of the Rabinskis. Linda hadn't been assigned to a wheelchair yet when I went to the hospital and anonymously paid off most of her medical bills. She is now, though. And I visit her as Augustine from time to time. But really it's Drew who needs to see how she's doing.

It started small. Fixed-hour prayers, helping people with housework and yard work and homework, getting jobs to pay the bills and keep the place going. Then a money order started arriving for a thousand dollars each month. Monica thought she was being sneaky. But the Slade, Kentucky, postmark told the tale. I always act like it's such a mystery and she loves it. She knows I know, and it's a nice little game we play. Elysian Heights put us on their missions' roster after the New York pastor arrived and sends a check every month thereby cementing my belief that God, not man, created irony.

I quit my job as a short-order cook at the Waffle House about a year ago when the homework program really took root and my visits around the neighborhood used so much time, not to mention that our neighbors, realizing there was something missionlike going on, began to expect a sermon on Sundays.

I guess I really am a pastor.

But if I was a real, bona fide pastor, I'd probably take exception to that definition being placed on someone like me. They're a bunch given to exact terms, and who can blame them?

We're having a wedding today, by the way, in the little rundown park nearby. The ordination still comes in handy. After the ceremony the bride and groom want us all to paint the swing set and put some new boards on the seesaws. They invited the Hoovervilles to come down too. Personally, I think that's going a little too far, but hopefully they'll behave themselves. They're a pretty ripe bunch out there.

So maybe we're all a bunch of failures in the eyes of the world, and sometimes I feel that way all on my own. But a wedding's taking place today and the weather is fine.

We are on a bit of a holy high, I admit. The warm day, the dry grass, the orange and yellow paint, the beautiful bride with long brown hair curling down her back, and the groom with a recent short haircut looking ten years younger than a couple of days ago. The kids from all over the neighborhood stand on the sidelines and giggle. The glaring white gown sewn by Charmaine blows in the breeze.

And the food. Valentine made up three huge serving tins of pan-fried chicken. Add to that her mashed potato casserole, fresh green beans, a huge pan of Mandarin orange raspberry spinach salad—

covered with some kind of dressing she said she just put together using what Blaze had on hand in the kitchen—and we feast like Romans. Hey, I'm obeying the spirit of the law here. Joining in the celebration with the couple is what's most important today.

Justin is looking a little guilty—he's the ascetic of us all, but I tell him sometimes we have to accept God's lavish gifts as they come and we shouldn't put ourselves above His goodness. As long as you're not saying that about a Mercedes or a yacht, I think it's sound theology.

Miss Mildred's peach cobbler sits beside a homemade wedding cake brought by the bride's cousin, an extraordinarily large redneck, a term by which he describes himself, who likes to bake.

There's just no telling, is there?

Bobby fills up his plate fuller than he should, but I don't have the heart to say anything.

"Bobby, if you don't eat every bite of that, you'll have to go through your flash cards twice on Monday," Val says.

Val, because the bride asked her to, spoons up the mashed potato casserole, her dark pink scarf in place. She'd planned on just dropping off the food.

The neighborhood people are onto her though. The kids call her, "The nice lady with the scarf."

Maybe someday she'll remove the scarf. But that's got to come from her, not me. I'll never encourage Val to do anything she doesn't want to do again.

Easter's in two days and there stands my father, his suit hanging on him like a garment bag, his face drawn and gray. "Drew."

"Hello, Dad. I'm surprised to see you."

The understatement of the year.

"Can I come in?"

I swing wide the door. "How was your drive?"

"Tiring."

"I'll get you a cup of tea."

He nods.

"Have a seat on the couch."

So what do I do now?

Make tea. At least there's that.

I fill the teakettle to the top, giving me some extra time before the water comes to a boil. Man, my father showing up. He never went to anybody. People came to him.

Okay, so my pride flares as I turn up the gas burner on the stove. As bad as I thought I was, Charles Parrish was ten times worse. It doesn't seem so strange God gave me a chance at redemption with Daisy, but Charles Parrish is a different story. It's not that I don't think God is big enough. I just doubt my father's intent.

"You've got to forgive him, Drew," I say to myself. "You have no other choice."

No choice whatsoever.

I want him to squirm. He won't, though. Charles Parrish doesn't even know how.

I set the tea on the coffee table.

"You're not having any?"

"Just water for me."

"You didn't have to go to the trouble."

He's taken off his suit coat and rolled up the sleeves of his cotton button-down. He's loosened his tie. "I don't know why I'm even here."

"Because you're dying, Dad, and you want to make amends."

"Yes. I made so many mistakes." He leans forward, sips his tea, then casts himself against the back of the couch. "That drive took it all out of me."

"Hold on a sec."

I head back to my room, grab my quilt and pillow, and a while later my father sleeps like the dead right there on the couch.

God help me, I can't forgive him. I can't find it in my heart. It's not there. I pray for God to soften my heart. I was in rebellion for so long, I don't want to find myself there again. *Soften my heart.*

❖❖❖

Val enters Shalom with two aluminum serving pans in her arms and a tote bag hanging from her shoulder. "I noticed you ate your fill today. What about that fast?"

"What do you mean?" I take the pans from her.

"Oh, please, you've been eating rice and beans and nothing else. I'm a cook. I notice these things."

"Special dispensation for a wedding?"

"Sounds good to me."

I follow her into the kitchen where I set the pans on the worktable. She points to the first pan. "Okay, this one's got potatoes and green beans. That one chicken and salad. You all should be able to eat for a while on this. Want me to throw some in the freezer?"

"You should. With the Easter feast, some of that will go bad if you don't."

"Okay, good." She reaches into the tote bag and slips out a roll of aluminum foil. She shakes the box. "Like you guys would have any of this stuff in the most ill-equipped kitchen the world has ever seen."

I have to laugh. She's right.

"You know, you need a mother superior around here." She zips a sheet down the cutting blade of the box.

"Tell me about it."

"Who's the guy on the couch?" She spreads the foil on the table, grabs a few pieces of chicken, then lays them on the sheet.

"My dad."

She seals the foil. "Oh, wow."

"I don't know if I can do this, Val."

"What did he do that was so bad?"

"How much time do you have?"

"I'll stay until Vigils if that's what you need."

"You don't know what you're in for."

"Maybe not. I'm okay with that."

"Okay. Let me help you while we talk." I grab the roll of foil. "You probably won't believe it when I tell you."

"I don't know, Augustine. Life can be pretty strange."

I start right in. "My mother died when I was twelve."

"But, Monica . . ."

"Just wait, Val, it'll all make sense in the end."

Will it really?

I have no idea.

We're only promised today.

❖❖❖

I time line my life from the age of twelve until college. Pass over the midpoint saying I became disenchanted with my job (to say the least) and picked up in my quest to find Monica.

It's midnight when I finish. We've drunk two pots of tea.

"You know, you just can't tell what people are carrying around inside of them. I just . . ." Val looks down at her cup. "I'm sorry I gave you such a hard time at first."

"Val, no offense, but that's nothing compared to what I'm used to down here."

She laughs and her eyes light up in the gloom of the kitchen. They never looked like that, even when she was Daisy.

"Seems to me, Augustine, you're talking about forgiving him and all like it's impossible. And it is, with what you know right now. Have you ever considered you should hear the man out? It might make everything clearer and easier to navigate."

Oh. "There would be that."

"Why don't you go to bed? I'll just pray the Vigils in here and get to bed myself. It was a long day. But a good day." She heads into the main room and returns a few seconds later with the prayer book in hand.

"When do you all go back out on the road?" I ask.

She shrugs. "Late April."

"You excited?"

She picks up the prayer book. "Normally I'm ready to go by now. But I don't know, Augustine. Without Lella, I just can't imagine it anymore."

"You were a real pair."

"Yeah, that's it. I had Lella to take care of and that was that. That felt like my real job."

"Maybe God's calling you to something else."

"I can't imagine what it could be."

Really, Valentine? If you can't see it, you're blind.

I don't deserve to have her here, though. God knows I don't.

But Easter's coming soon, and Val might be happy to get back on the road, as far away from me as possible. And there isn't a person in the world, including myself, who'd blame her.

I stand to my feet.

"You know, Gus. It just feels like I've known you a lot longer than a few months."

"Yeah." I smile. Maybe she'll figure me out and I won't have to confess. Maybe she'll realize the truth, tear me apart, and it'll be over and done with. Lord, have mercy.

I transfer Dad to my bed, helping him shuffle along the floor. He says, "Thank you, Son."

Val's sitting on the couch getting ready to pray.

"Val, I want to serve you. What can I do to serve you?"

"Stop asking uncomfortable questions like that and stop being so weird."

Now that's a tall order.

Dad's just waking up when I walk into the bunkroom.

"I brought you some coffee from Java Jane's."

"I'm grateful."

He accepts the cup.

"Are you hungry?"

"Just a bit. It all takes away your appetite."

"The treatment?"

"Son, I'm refusing treatment."

"What?"

"They could stem the tide for an extra two or three months, but it's going to get me. Why go through all that when I'll die better and sooner without it?"

"You're done with life?"

"Completely. I've made a mess of it. Best to just call it a day."

"Why did you come?"

"Forgiveness."

I sit next to him on the bed. "Dad, there's a big difference between wanting forgiveness for yourself and wanting me to forgive you. As a parent, surely you understand the difference."

"Please forgive me, Son."

Dear God, please don't let him start to cry because I can't take theatrics. Not from this man. It would be way off course for him.

"Well, you've asked now. So you've done what you need to do. You're free and clear."

"It's more than that. I'm done with simply covering the bases. Being technically spotless. I had years of that."

"Really? What about the riverboat gambling?"

"Nothing happened there. I wasn't privy to the inside knowledge."

"But that night at the house? When I voiced my suspicions."

"I looked into your eyes and I saw myself in them." He sets the cup on my nightstand. "So I set you free to figure it out without me, without the pressure I constantly put on you. You were in such bad shape that night. You needed to be set free. I did what I thought was best. Maybe for the first time." He waves a hand. "I sound like I'm trying to get credit for it, Son. I'm not. I don't deserve that. I was only doing what I should have done all along."

"Why did you stay away from me then?"

"Because I didn't want to drag you down any farther. I figured Monica would do a better job with you."

"She did."

"That's what I gathered." He grabs my leg and shakes it. "Drew, I'm sorry for all I did to you. I was blinded by my own ambitions and being so important to people, and so much of what we were doing was with the best of intentions."

"Really? Even for you?"

He shakes his head. "Maybe not. Even those good intentions get tarnished by ambition and fear of losing influence. Power makes good men turn into . . . something else."

"Are your hands clean, Dad? Really?"

He reads my mind. "I didn't murder anybody. Does misleading people, lying, manipulating, sullying, taking advantage of others count?"

Whoa.

"I'll make us some breakfast. Is toast all right?"

"It's all I could stomach anyway."

"Is your suitcase in the car?"

"Yes."

"I'll get it."

"No. I can get a hotel."

"If you can handle it here, Dad, you can stay."

"All right. Thank you."

❖❖❖

I stand by his car, a black sedan, and long to beat myself over the head. What did I just do? Am I insane?

❖❖❖

After breakfast I give Dad the newspaper. He says, "No, thank you, Drew. I think I'll take a nap. Breakfast tired me out."

Once I'm sure he's asleep, I call Father Brian.

"Okay, Brian, I'm in serious trouble and I don't care when the NASCAR race is on."

"You sound like it."

"I don't know what to do."

"What's troubling you, Gus?"

"My father showed up."

"Oh. No wonder you're in such a state."

"How do I forgive him? He wants to make amends."

"Do you have a choice?"

"I don't feel it in my heart. I want to be obedient and more than anything, I want to be like Christ who forgives and taught us seventy times seven. But it's just not in there."

Father Brian clears his throat. "If we waited to forgive people until we feel like it, most sins would go unforgiven. Just forgive him, tell God you forgive your father, and let your emotions catch up later."

"But is it real?"

"Do you *want* to want to forgive him?"

"Yes."

"Then there you go."

TWENTY

Valentine

I arrange a basket of Easter eggs, the plastic kind, as I sit at the kitchen table early Easter morning. Bobby took a few bucks of mine and ran over to the Dollar General to pick them up along with a baggie of plastic grass. I told him to buy himself a candy bar. He bought two.

Inside each egg nestles a piece of chocolate and one word written on a piece of paper.

Kind
Caring
Friendly
Hardworking
Nice looking
Loving
Generous
Longsuffering
Gracious
Peaceful
Elastic
And finally . . .
Friend

Yeah, it's my peace offering to Rick who's been avoiding me, and rightly so, for a couple of weeks. In the refrigerator two dozen eggs wait to be hidden around the yard of the Laundromat.

I figure, *Why not?*

Coffee streams into the pot and Rick's head appears through the doorway. "Hey."

"Happy Easter, Rick."

"Same to you, Val."

I stand up and hold out the basket. "Happy Easter, Rick."

His eyes hold as much trust as a colander holds water.

"Here, take it. And I'm sorry."

His hesitation is as deep as the wounds I've given him. He shakes his head. "Nah. That's okay."

"Rick, I mean it. I'm asking you to forgive me."

He looks down at the basket. "And you think a little Easter basket's going to make up for all the insults and the shoo-aways?"

"Okay, this isn't going like I'd planned. Before you wave this away, just look inside each egg."

He lifts the basket from my hands like it's contagious or something.

"Save the white one for last. I'll pour you a cup of coffee." I turn my back as he opens the first egg.

As each egg displays its word, his face softens more and more.

"Elastic?" He laughs.

"Well. You know." I shrug.

He keeps opening until finally the white egg alone snuggles into the grass. "Okay. Here goes."

Friend.

"My friend," I say. "Rick, please forgive me. I am so sorry for treating you the way I have. I'm an idiot."

"Okay, Val, you're still my friend." He rises and puts his arms around me. "Of course I forgive you. You know, it was really nice of you to ask. Can I keep the basket?"

"It's Blaze's."

"Oh. How about the eggs, then?"

"They're all yours."

Roland busts through the door. "Happy Easter! Happy Easter! How's my favorite sideshow lady?"

He kisses me on the cheek.

"What about Lella? Isn't she your favorite?"

"You're all my favorite. But when you came up to me at that fair in Virginia, I knew you were special."

"Hey, I couldn't work in that cafeteria forever."

Roland's Wayfaring Marvels had set up at a fair just out of Lynchburg, in Madison Heights, and some of the ladies I worked with asked me if I wanted to go.

Lella was so kind when I went through the sideshow. "My, what a lovely scarf. And your hair is just gorgeous! I'll bet you can use grocery store shampoo because it's so naturally shiny and full of body you don't need the expensive salon products."

I laugh now as I slide a pan of broccoli cheese casserole into the oven. The hams are cooking over at the Laundromat. "You staying for dinner?"

"You bet. Three weeks and we're back on the road. Stuff to do! You excited?"

"How about a hard-boiled egg?"

"Sure."

When Roland pulled out of Lynchburg, I did too. My father bought me the pickup truck and camper. Roland loved the idea of Lizard Woman and the pay was enough to keep my truck running and propane in the tank of the camper. My needs are small.

"Maybe I don't need that seaside house after all." I hand Roland his egg.

"Now that's music to my ears. So you going on the road without Lella?"

"Is it for sure?"

"She called me last night."

I inhale down to my stomach. "Wow."

"So you still coming?"

"I've got no place else to go, I suppose."

"It wouldn't be the same without you, Val." He leans forward. "I'll even give you a raise."

"You must be desperate."

"Pretty much sums it up!" And he smiles at me like he would anybody else. Roland doesn't see my scars anymore.

I like that about him.

Who was I kidding with that seaside house anyway? "I mean, I love my little camper."

"It's a great little setup."

"And when I stop the sideshow, I can make jewelry, traveling around from craft show to craft show."

"Or we can grow old together."

"You're already old, Roland."

"You said it, Val."

I've got to leave here. I've got to go back. Maybe Charmaine's wrong. Maybe I can turn my making a living into a real life.

I pick up the kitchen phone. My father's on the other end.

"Happy Easter, Daisy!"

"Happy Easter, Dad!"

He said he was going to church with his wife today, it being the quintessential Christian holiday and the Episcopalians could do it up better than at his church.

"You got any plans?"

"Not really."

I don't feel like explaining it all.

Despite all of Augustine's pleadings, I'm not attending the Easter service.

"It's one thing for the kids to see me at the Laundromat, and I made an exception for the wedding, but Easter is about lambs and flowers and the Resurrection," I say on the phone as he pleads with me one last time. "My face will just be a distraction."

"No way. Oh, come on, Val, you'll have a good time."

"Nope. But you're coming over later on, right? Rick says we're all going to sit and watch *The Robe*. And I'm making caramel corn."

He sighs. "Oh, all right. Eating your food is such a chore."

We hang up.

"I feel like it's my first real Easter," I say to Bartholomew as I brush my hair. He says I should have seen the first one!

We were all scared to death, says John.

Phillip shakes his head.

I buzz downstairs and arrange the pans of food in a couple of cardboard boxes. Those Laundromat people want a feast? They'll have a feast.

"Ready to go over?" Blaze slides into the driver's seat of her station wagon.

"Yes. We've got everything."

"Great. Let's go." She backs out onto the street, the smell of corn bread filling her wagon. "Why not come in? I mean, Augustine's dad is there, and he's probably feeling uncomfortable. You can sit next to him."

"Wonderful. I'm uncomfortable enough as it is. Besides, he's been asleep every time I've arrived there for prayers. I don't even know the man."

Blaze turns onto the street. "Augustine's been a better son than I think I'd be if my father suddenly showed up with his tail between his legs."

"Well, my bad parent is dead. I swear, it was easier just having her die."

"Augustine is a kind of satellite around his dad, reminding me of a vulture circling an almost-dead body."

"Only Augustine doesn't want to pick at the body, he just wants to bury it and get on with his life."

"You really think that, Val?"

"At least that's my guess."

"Hmm." She pulls up to the Laundromat. "Sure you won't come in?"

"I'm just dropping off the food. I'll drive the car back home and pick you up when all is said and done."

"Nah. I'll get a ride. You just do, well, whatever it is you're going to do all by yourself on Easter Sunday morning."

"Thanks for that, Blaze."

"Hey, we all make choices."

We haul the food into the Laundromat and I escape through the side door before anybody can grab me and make me stay.

Charmaine won't find me on the dock this morning. There's always a lot of hoopla over at Port of Peace Assemblies, and Easter's her favorite day. She says God resurrects things all the time and it's easy to remember that on Easter morning.

Over the lake the sun beats down, turning the water to green.

"How are you?"

I turn at the words. "Hi."

"It's me. Robbie. From the other day when you fell."

"I remember. You were very kind. Thank you. I still have your handkerchief."

"My dad, he's the pastor over at the Highland Kirk, taught me well."

"Is that a Presbyterian church?"

"Yes. We live right over there." He twists his trunk and points to a small brown bungalow.

"Nice little house."

"Are you okay? From the other day."

"I'm fine."

"Mind if I have a seat?"

"No." It seems I can't ever be alone on this dock anyway.

"Are you new to Mount Oak?"

"I winter here. I'm with Roland's show."

"Makes sense. My mom met you all before Christmas. Poppy Fraser?"

"I remember. She's sassy."

He laughs. "So what are you doing here on Easter Sunday?"

"I tend to meet God here. He usually shows up in various shapes and sizes."

"I came out here a lot when my best friend died. It's a good spot."

"I'm sorry about your friend."

He shakes his head. "It was a long time ago."

"How old are you?"

"Twenty-six."

"Married?"

He laughs again. "No. Not even close. I'm teaching down at the middle school."

"Math? English?"

"Special Ed."

"Whoa."

"Nah. They're great kids. They're going to have a harder time in this life, for sure. But . . . well, I guess you know how that is."

"I do."

"You know, this may sound crazy, but—okay, I'll just come right out and ask it. How long has it been since you've had Communion?"

"What?!"

"I told you it was crazy."

"I'm getting more and more used to crazy. I don't know. Years, I guess."

"Want to take some now?"

"Are you a pastor?"

"Part-time youth pastor."

"Um. Do I have to go to your church, because I'm just not in the mood. And I have a hard time eating, so . . ."

He jumps to his feet and runs toward his house where a young teenage boy is feeding a yellow lab on the front porch. Robbie's younger brother, I guess.

Communion at the lake.

I laugh up at the sun. Well, stranger things have happened, I'm sure.

He returns a few minutes later, a dinner roll in his hand and a bottle of juice peeking out of his jacket pocket. "I brought a straw. I just thought . . ."

"You thought right. Thanks."

A straw too, Jesus? My goodness, You're going all out today.

He gives me the elements and I give them to him, and I swear I'm staring into the face of Christ here on earth, incarnated in this special ed teacher named Robbie Fraser.

He says a little prayer and sits with me until a voice calls from off his porch. "Robbie, come on or you'll be late to church."

"What my brother doesn't know is that I've already been there. But"—he lifts his body off the planking—"it can't hurt to go again."

"Thanks, Robbie."

"You're welcome. What's your name?"

"Valentine."

"I'll see you around."

"Well, probably not. I lay sorta low these days. But if you ever need me, I'm either at Blaze's or Shalom."

"I'll remember. Take care."

Yeah, I'll take care. Until I head back out on the road.

I don't want to go back out on the road. I don't say this to Peter, John, or Bartholomew, but right to Jesus, the guy in the middle, the one with the final say-so.

Blaze and Augustine bustle through the kitchen door around three o'clock.

"How'd it go?"

"Good. Good." Augustine sets a plate covered in tin foil on the counter. "I brought you some of the food."

"Thanks."

Blaze hangs her keys on the rack by the door. "Better than good. The music was beautiful."

"Really? Who sang?"

Augustine pulls out a chair. "Late last night an old friend of mine came into town. Surprised me. His name's Chris. Plays the flute. Anyway, your food was a big hit, Val. Not surprisingly."

"Nice. And now you can gain your weight back. You're looking almost svelte. Was Bobby there?"

"Yeah. And his parents."

"Maybe it's a turn around."

He shakes his head. "It's Easter. Everybody goes to church on Easter. I wouldn't get your hopes up."

"Augustine! What kind of an attitude is that?" I ask.

"Realistic. Not that I'm not glad they were there. Bobby looked miserable, though."

"See, Val, you should have gone." Blaze. "So what did you do while we were gone?"

I tell them about my lakeside Communion with Robbie Fraser.

"That's cool." Augustine. "Very cool."

Blaze takes off the silk scarf she'd tied around her neck for the day. "I'm bushed. I'll see you all later."

"So you doing okay?" he asks. He's tapping his fingers in rapid succession on the table.

"Yeah. I'm really not looking forward to getting back on the road, I can tell you that."

"Why?" The tapping continues.

"Lella not coming back is most of it."

"What else?"

I grab his hand and stop the commotion. "I don't know. I like it at the Laundromat, I guess. Bobby, the kids, and seeing Charmaine a lot. Even sorry old you down there!"

He smiles. "Yeah, I tend to bring down the place a notch or two."

"So anyway. There it is. I guess I don't have much choice. I've got to support myself. But it's going to be a real drag to say the least."

"I hear you."

He fidgets with a napkin.

"Are you sweating?" I ask.

"Yeah." He wipes his forehead with a bandana. "I feel a little sick to my stomach too."

"What's the matter?"

He takes a deep breath and blows out through lips formed into a small O. "Val, we have to talk. I've got a lot to say, and I don't know how I'm going to get through it."

"What could you possibly have to say to me that's making you sick?"

He inhales deeply, looks down at his hands. "Daisy."

"What?" I shake my head as the veil is removed in that single word. The inflection the same beneath the new rasp. Disbelief fills my stomach. "Drew Parrish?"

"Yes."

I hold my hand up to my mouth. This can't be. This man who saved me from myself . . . Drew Parrish?

He reaches for my hand, but I snap it back under the table.

"Daisy, please, I'm sorry. Oh, God have mercy, Val. I'm so sorry."

I can't think. I can't think. I've got to go. I run out the back door and into the yard. He's sitting there, at the kitchen table, looking like nobody I've ever seen before, some freak like me, and what's his angle now? Dear Lord. You made a big mistake here.

My heart heaves as its actual contents rise to the surface, blackening what felt new and pink just this morning.

I pull the scarf down and breathe deeply, wondering what goof suggested I quit smoking for Lent? Oh, Lord. Could someone else have baptized me even? Just that?

The entire story, my old life, washes over me. Trician. The endless auditions.

Hard . . . so hard.

I just wanted to sell my comic books and live in peace. To come home to a nice man who loved me. Maybe have some kids. Nothing grand. Lord, you know I wanted my life to be no big deal. My mother's ambitions propelled my own. I only wanted to get away!

Like I do right now.

"Daisy."

I turn. "I'm Val, Augustine. Drew. You're really Drew."

"I'm sorry. You can call me whatever you want."

"Why now? Weren't things bad enough? Lella's gone. I've got to go back on the road. I don't need this crap raked up. Anybody with any sense of compassion could see that!"

"I have to ask your forgiveness. I don't have a choice."

"Are you doing this for your sake? Or mine? I mean, why now? Why didn't you just let everything go on like it was going?"

"Because I had to do what was right. Confess my sin to you. Daisy, it's all my fault. Everything that happened—your face, your life. I know that. It nearly destroyed me as well when you disappeared and I saw what I had done."

"Good."

"You're right. I deserved everything I got. And I've been trying to make up for it ever since."

Yes, the overachiever returns. "Oh, I see it now! Your insane monastery, a monument to the great Drew Parrish's repentance and lifelong penance!" Rage boils inside me. I reach out with both hands, pushing him from me. "Your empire may have dwindled but you wanted to rope me in, just like last time, didn't you? You haven't changed at all. The packaging may be different, but the goods are just the same."

"No. I swear it wasn't that. Please, Daisy. Please."

No. Not like this! No, no, no!

I was just supposed to forgive him in my heart, feel like I'd done something great, just me and God. Not this.

TWENTY-ONE

AUGUSTINE

The words of Charles Parrish ring in my head. *Please, Drew. Please.*

Daisy turns her back on me and hugs herself. "Just go. I don't even know what to do with this."

"Okay. Daisy, I'm so sorry."

Her eyes glitter with rage as she turns back to face me. "I'm Val, Drew! Don't ever call me Daisy again."

"I won't. I'm sorry. I'm so sorry."

It takes me a while to return to the Laundromat. I ride my bike through the countryside.

Well, I asked forgiveness. I'm all clear, right, Lord?

Yeah, it doesn't sit well with me either. Truthfully, was there a way this was going to work out? Even asking for her forgiveness seems selfish after all I did. This was lose-lose from the beginning, as well as it should have been.

But the Bible, the Bible, the Bible.

Forgiveness is a strange bird. We seek it desperately, for ourselves yes. But it is impossible to demand it be given for the asking.

My heart is crushed, just as it should be. I deserve no less.

At times like these you wish you not only believed in the rapture but that it would happen right now. This is a tired, confusing world, and sometimes doing the right thing makes us feel worse.

Come, Lord Jesus.

Most of us, at the very least, agree on that.

Grind me to dust, Lord. Use me up and then take me home. Take away all of me.

My father sits on the sofa reading the old prayer book. "Hello, Son."

"Hi, Dad." I throw myself on the opposite sofa.

"It was a good time here today. I never knew church could feel like a party. You're doing a good thing."

I jerk my gaze across to him. "What?"

"Those kids. One little girl came up and showed me her Easter dress and said Pastor Gus bought up all the pretty dresses he could at the Goodwill and dropped them off on their porches in the middle of night."

"How did she know that?"

"She said her grandmother caught you and thought it was the most Christian thing she'd ever seen."

"Oh, Dad." I lay my head back on the cushion, looking up at the water-stained ceiling tiles of this dump. "Do you have time to hear a story?"

"I do."

I lift my head up.

He settles himself more comfortably. "Son, it's good to be here with you. I've got a lot to learn in this place. And unfortunately, not much time to do it. So tell me what's on your mind."

He hears it all, and with every word of self-indictment, I free him a little more.

In my heart I want some drippy emotional scene where I forgive my father and he hugs me and we weep together. But I don't see that coming. "How about a pot of tea? I don't know about you, but confessions go better with hot drinks."

He laughs. It's the first time I've heard my father laugh.

Several minutes later the tea steeps in a pot on the coffee table, mugs sit at the ready. "So Dad, I know what you're going through. Well, I mean . . . I don't know. I just . . . I forgive you."

Dad bows his head and folds his hands. He looks up. "Thank you, Son. It's more than I deserve."

"And I want you to stay here with me at Shalom. Just like you said . . . we don't have much time left, do we?"

"No. We sure don't."

My father is still a good-looking man, but his raw power is diminished, both in physique and in that aura he once possessed. I feel sorry for him.

Dear God, I feel sorry for him.

How strange.

He is one of God's children.

And so am I. And so is Val. And will we ever be able to grasp one another's hands with a joyful heart? I just can't imagine it.

The next day, I order a hospital bed from the medical supply company and set it up in the bunkroom.

He eyes it with suspicion.

"I know, I know you don't need that yet, but there's no sense getting a regular bed just to have to replace it."

"I know you're right, Son. Just seeing it there is hard is all."

"I know."

"It's funny . . . sometimes practicality can wound."

"Hey, we can get it out of here. No problem."

"No. No. I wasn't talking about the bed, Son. It looks like just what I can use. In fact, I'll use it right now. I'm beat."

It's 9:20 a.m.

"Let me put the linens on."

"I'll help."

"No, that's okay. Just keep me company while I do my work."

In those words I get a glimpse of what the next few months until his passing will hold. And I am grateful. I don't deserve this. But I'll be here.

I mean, I won't be heading back to Blaze's anytime soon. Val deserves to never see me again.

Blaze rushes into Shalom as I wash the supper dishes.

"Gus, Val's gone."

"Where is she?"

"I don't know. Her camper's gone. She left sometime during the middle of the night. What happened between you two after I left the kitchen?"

"Blaze, it's for Val to say, not me."

I've confessed to all the right people. Now it's time to do what Daisy suggested I should have done all along. Let it lie.

Blaze throws her weight on one leg. "Well, she's responsible enough. I'm sure she'll be all right."

"Did she take her things?"

"Not everything. She left behind her comic books and her costumes. Roland's heartbroken."

A week later Bobby enters Shalom, looking dejected and rougher around the edges than usual.

"Where's Valentine?"

"She went away on a trip, Bobby. Want something to drink? I've got juice." Val's influence is already making its mark. What kid wants tea to drink day after day?

"Apple?"

"Orange."

"Okay, I guess."

I pour us both glasses and hand him one.

"Hey, that's pretty good," he says after chugging it down in a few giant gulps. "Can I have some more?"

"Nah. Got to save some for the other kids."

"Shoot." He crosses his arms. "Maybe I should drink it slower next time."

I laugh. "It might be a good idea."

"Who's going to help me with my math?"

"How about me? I'm not too bad at it."

We settle down at one of the tables in the main room. After a while he looks up from his work. "You're not nearly as good at math as she is, Augustine."

I'm not surprised.

"Hey, Bobby, want to learn how to paint rooms?"

He shrugs. "Sure. You going to paint around here? Because it sure is ugly."

"Yeah. That's exactly what we're going to do."

"Just don't ask Mrs. Hopewell what color we should paint, though, because she'll say purple, and this place would look terrible if it was purple."

"I was thinking yellow."

"A nice goldy yellow. We don't want it to look like a girl's room."

"Definitely not."

Two hours later we've got the supplies. Dad even does a little taping around the windows. "This is a fine idea, Son. This place could use a face-lift. You know, you could start a halfway house or something here."

"That takes more cash than we have. We'd have to add on too. And you know, Dad, if we ever take this one step further, I was thinking about a place for kids. Older kids."

"You do well with children."

Charmaine buzzes in an hour later. "I heard you were buying paint down at the hardware store!"

"How did you hear that?" I tip some more golden paint into the tray.

"You can't do nothin' in Mount Oak without somebody seeing. You know that, Gus. I'm here to help! Like the IRS." She chuckles at her own joke.

Oh, Charmaine.

"How are you at painting around the ceilings?"

"They don't call me Sure-hand Charmaine for nothing! You got a ladder?"

I set her up. She climbs and starts singing as she cuts the paint in around the ceiling.

"I'm done taping the baseboards." Bobby.

"Good, I'm done scrubbing the walls. You go ahead and follow Mrs. Hopewell and paint down by the baseboards. I'll follow you with the roller.

Dad finishes the windows. "Nap time for me."

"You go on, Mr. Parrish." Charmaine. "When you wake up it'll look like the sun came for a visit and decided to stay."

Two weeks since Val left. I've caught myself thinking of her as Daisy, and I've forced myself to stop. She asked me to.

Blaze said she heard from her. She's just traveling around and is fine. She said she'll probably visit her dad for a while.

Dad offered to pay for new tile flooring in the main room and the kitchen and, not about to pass up a gift like that, I got the floor man in here the next day. Bobby helped pick it out.

"I like the stuff that looks like flower pots." He indicated the terra-cotta tiles.

"Nice choice."

It looks good in here now. Nothing fancy, but cleaner and more inviting. Who knows what God will do with this place?

It seems strange, drinking tea with my dad in the evenings. Sometimes we read quietly. If the time is right, we pray the offices together. I finally came right out and asked him if he was really a Christian. I know that's between God and him, but as I said, "I'll do so much better after you're gone if I know."

He smiles. He's been smiling a lot more and it changes him completely. I misused smiling back at Elysian Heights, but a genuine smile is the greatest thing. And if it's accompanied by a laugh, there's no telling what it will do.

"Yes, Son, I am."

"When?"

"Just before I got cancer."

"Before?!"

He nods. "Odd, isn't it? It's as if God knew what I'd need to get me through."

Okay, maybe it's not so strange after all.

"What happened?"

"You sure you want to hear this?"

"Positive."

He closes his eyes, then opens them. "I was taking Communion at the church the president goes to. I've been taking Communion for years, so I didn't think anything about it.

"All of a sudden, the wafer tasted like dead, rotting flesh, and the wine turned into sawdust. It was the most horrible thing I've ever had in my mouth. And I heard a voice inside say, 'This is what you've made of Me. What you make of Me right now.'

"I went back to the house and fell on my knees right there in the foyer. Thank goodness Malena takes off on Sundays. I wept like a baby and the words of your mother kept pouring over me, sin after sin, compromise after compromise.

"Son, I repented and I asked God to take me if He'd have me. I'd listened to enough sermons to know He would."

"Wow." Just one moment and he repented right away. He didn't take months like I did. "Wow."

"Pretty crazy, isn't it?"

"No. It was just right. It was your personal Pentecost."

"Yes. God meets us where we are, though heaven knows we don't deserve it at all, none of it. I stayed in my house for several months, only going out for medical tests, and I read the Gospels again and again. Hopefully some of it sank in." He lifts one side of his mouth. "Son, what you're doing here is what this country needs."

"Some food, God's love. I'd say you're right. Besides, I gave up politics years ago, Dad."

"Well, it's probably just as well. Look what it did to me."

And yet here you are.

"Want some more tea?"

"Yes, I'd like that. You make a good pot of tea."

TWENTY-TWO

❖❖❖❖

VALENTINE

I pull my camper into the narrow driveway to the left of Dad and Jody's house. It's actually Jody's house. They met on eHarmony, hit it off, and he moved up to Lexington after they got married.

Their downtown home is really a glorified shotgun shack. But it's been completely redone inside and they don't need more than one bedroom, or so Jody said when I called her and asked to visit. "You sleep on couch, okay? Very comfortable."

"I'll have my camper."

"Okay too."

As I extract myself from the truck, they pour down the front steps. I'm ashamed this is my first visit. That I've kept myself from the person who loves me the most.

Dad pulls me into a close hug and kisses the top of my head. Jody, black Asian hair soaking up the sunshine and holding it close, pats my back as he does so and says, "Is good. Is good. Thanks be to God."

I laugh as I pull back. I'm not foolish enough to think I'm home, but I'm so glad I've come.

❖❖❖

"Now you sure you sleep in that truck?" Jody lays out lunch meats, cheese, and bread for sandwiches.

"Positive. It's a nice little setup. So how's everything going, you two? You still selling your cards?"

Jody nods. "They going like pancakes! Stores can't keep enough in. I make 'em, cards cards cards, night and day."

"And your beads, Dad?"

"Revamped the Web sites, lowered the prices a bit, and it's going great! You got any more work you want me to put up? Everything else has sold. Well, except for that ugly marcasite one you did . . . with the carnelian."

"What was I thinking?"

"Don't know, honey."

"I've got a big box in the truck from this winter. And I'll make more while I'm here too."

"Good. You can go through the storeroom and pick out anything you'd like."

"Thanks, Dad."

We sit and munch on sandwiches. When we finish I help Jody clear the plates, after which she says, "Gotta work. Sorry, Daisy. Order due tomorrow. Fifty cards!"

"We'll finish up here." Dad hands me an apron.

"Who uses aprons anymore?"

"You'd be surprised."

"Oh, well." I tie it around my waist.

He hands me a dish towel. "You dry."

"I can do that."

He ties on his own apron. "It's good to see you, Daze. Quite unexpected, though. Not that it's a problem!"

"I just wanted to visit before I head back out on the road."

"Won't be long now." He turns on a stream of water, adjusts the temperature, then fills the basin, adding a shot of dish liquid.

"No. Next week."

"You sound thrilled."

"Lella left the show."

"Oh, honey. I'm sorry. You can always move to Lexington."

"And do what?"

He shrugs. "You could help me with the business, and Jody would welcome some help with her greeting cards."

The Laundromat comes to mind. "No offense, Dad, but I've got to figure out my own life."

"Good for you. I heard from your grandmother," he says.

"What did she want?"

He wipes a lunch plate with a soapy dishrag. "Your mother's been dead for three years now. She thought I should be reminded. Since she blames me and all."

I take the plate after he rinses it. "Hard to move on with her around to remind you all the time."

"Not at all."

"Really?" I set the plate in the drainer. "How is that even possible?"

"I don't know, honey. I guess we're responsible for our own moving on, don't you think? I've got a good life. Jody's wonderful. We have a nice routine, things to do, places we're known—like the coffee shop and what have you. Your mother's dead. She shot us all with her shotgun and now she's gone. If we keep picking at the scabs, it's our own fault."

"Like it's that easy."

"In any case, she can't make things right, and neither can we."

"Do you think she would have ever come to her senses and tried?"

"I doubt it." He sighs. "No. Can't picture it."

"I don't know, Dad. It's hard to move on."

He hands me a glass. "I know, sweetheart. But we all do sooner or later. Maybe we just have to figure it's where we're meant to go.

And it helps to have some gratitude for where we are, sometimes even where we've been."

"That's impossible in my case."

"Is it?"

"How could you stand being married to that woman?"

"I just did what I had to do."

"And me?"

"I wasn't much help at all."

"No."

"I'm sorry, honey."

For some reason it's easy to forgive my father. But I've never doubted my father loves me.

So much pain and heartache. Why couldn't Mom and Drew have just been content with what they'd been given?

I grab a pad of paper and a pen from the kitchen drawer.

Okay, Dad, I'll write down what I'm thankful for.

I begin to make a list and I find that almost every single one of them but Dad and Jody are in Mount Oak. And I've decided to go on the road? In black ink it makes little sense.

I show him the list.

"So what are you doing here?"

"Drew Parrish, that's what!"

"From everything you've told me, he's different now. I admit it, I can hardly believe it myself. But the kind of life he's living isn't some kind of act. Nobody would do all that for show. And not in Mount Oak! Sounds like he's undergone a real spiritual transformation."

"So what you're saying is that I'm doubting God's ability to transform a scum-sucking hypocrite into a man of God?"

"Well, not in those words exactly. But what about you? Have you been transformed?"

"I don't know now. I thought so, but when it all came slamming into my face . . ."

"Sounds to me you need to give yourself a little time."

"Can I just stay here a little while longer, Dad?"

"What about the show? Although, I have to admit, I don't know how healing that would prove to be. Not with Lella gone."

"Not to mention displaying myself."

"True."

"I'll call Roland and tell him I'm not going on the road."

"Stay as long as you like."

I make myself a cup of tea in my camper. Jesus looks down with His disciples from the icon I set up on the dinette.

"There's nothing more Drew can do to prove himself to me. So will you help me forgive him?"

You'll have to make peace with your mother while you're at it.

Oh, God! Why me?

I walk into a small church around the corner. An AME church, red brick, old wooden pews.

Empty.

'Fess up, Daisy.

I know, Lord, I know.

A black woman enters and sits down on the pew in front of me. She turns and I gasp. Her face. She doesn't smile.

Half of her face looks just like mine.

I pull down my scarf. "How did yours happen?"

"Bad boyfriend. What about you?"

"I did it to myself."

And there sits the truth of it all.

I wanted to get away from my mother. I didn't have the guts to do it on my own. I signed the surgical consent forms. I auditioned. I used sex to try and snag Drew. I let myself be led by the nose by two people who only wanted to use me.

"Have you forgiven yourself?" the lady asks me.

"I'm doing that right now."

TWENTY-THREE

◆◆◆◆

AUGUSTINE

I held his hand when he died. He hadn't spoken for two days, just lay there peacefully. The hospice nurses walked us through step by step and made the dying process somehow, well, godly.

And as I ready myself for his funeral, I can say I truly loved my father. The last five months of his life were a gift of grace.

Monica enters my bunkroom and pats me on the back as I face the mirror, tying my tie. "You look nice."

"I haven't worn a suit in years."

"You still look nice. Are you sure you can do this? Reverend Hopewell would be happy to fill in for you."

"No, Mom. Surprisingly enough, this is Shalom's first funeral. There'll be others, I'm sure. It's fitting the first was Dad's." I turn to face her. "Did you make your peace with him? In the end?"

"Yes, Drew. I did. It wasn't easy."

"I know."

"It's too bad he wasn't like this his whole life. It would have been a nice life."

"I know."

She adjusts my tie. "You don't match that suit at all."

I grin. "Yeah. I know."

She pats my shoulder. "Let's go. The musicians are setting up."

Some folks from the orchestra at Port of Peace Assemblies volunteered to help us consign my father to the ground. Charmaine's going to sing.

We've set up chairs in the main room. The funeral home delivered my father's body and now it's time to begin.

The casket remains closed, and the neighborhood folks file by and pay their respects. Somehow Charles Parrish made an impression all his own on them with his faithful appearances in the main room, lending a hand when he felt strong enough.

Bobby cries louder than anybody. My father reached out and gave Bobby a growing dignity. He made sure his lawyer left Bobby enough for a college education. In fact, that's what his estate's going for, a college fund for the kids here in the neighborhood. His idea. Not mine.

Finally, it begins.

Jessica leads us in the prayers. Justin in Communion. I give the eulogy, talking about his months at Shalom, realizing afresh that it was all we really had together over the course of my lifetime.

But it is enough. It has to be and it is.

Father Brian stands in the back, praying. He always says that's 90 percent of his job.

Charmaine sings another song at the gravesite. "His Eye Is on the Sparrow." One of her signature numbers.

His eye is on the sparrow, and I know He watches me. I sing because I'm happy. I sing because I'm free.

When the Son sets you free, you shall be free indeed.

I throw the first shovelful of dirt on the casket. Monica follows suit. We file away from the cemetery.

A flash of magenta scours the corner of my eye. I turn my head.

"Valentine!"

I run in her direction, dodging gravestones, jumping over markers. She does the same.

"Augustine!"

She slams her body into mine, our arms snapping around each other.

I hold her to me, embracing her as tightly as a mother grasps her hurting child. "I'm sorry, I'm so sorry."

Her eyes shine. "I know. It's done, Augustine. It's done."

◆◆◆

My father is in the ground, and I understand the final piece, why he came to me. We need forgiveness so badly. Maybe it's selfish to even ask, but in the receiving we are made free.

I will see my father again, when we are all raised as He was raised.

But the true miracle of the resurrection wasn't so much the raising. Is something like that too hard for the God who made the universe? The true miracle is in the forgiving. And though we are bruised and burned, blind and broken, we are forgiven.

Charles Parrish made terrible choices for many years, seismic repercussions swallowing us into its circle. I repeated those choices in my own fashion.

But all is forgiven now. All is forgiven.

◆◆◆

AUGUSTINE: ONE YEAR LATER

Val's bed is set up in the women's bunkroom these days. She made her formal vows, same as mine, a few months ago. Something good always bubbles in the kitchen, and word's gotten around that if you need food, Shalom's the place.

"Good morning, Mother Superior. What's for breakfast?" I ask.

"Oatmeal with cinnamon and brown sugar."

"Sounds like a plan. Do you know how blessed we are to have you here?"

"Hey, people need to eat. That's all I know."

"I thought maybe we'd get some more folks who wanted to join in on our work."

She crosses her forefingers like I'm a vampire. "That's enough of that, Gus."

She's right.

"And when did numbers replace mission? During the Great Awakening or Albert Finney or something? I have no idea."

"Uh, Val. It's Charles Finney."

"Whatever." She spoons me up a bowl of oatmeal. Smiles. I can tell because her eyes crinkle. She still won't get rid of the scarf.

One day one of the kids said, "Hey, lady, how come you look like that? It's kinda weird."

"Well, looks don't mean everything," Val replied with her characteristic snap.

That sure is the truth.

"Time for morning prayers, Gus. Where you heading?"

"Oh, just walking around the neighborhood, I guess."

"Good. That's very good." She turns her back on me and slides the pot of oatmeal into the refrigerator someone donated a few weeks ago.

Yes, it is. "If you want me to pray with you, we can walk together." I concentrate on the oatmeal as she wipes down the sink.

Side-by-side we enter the gathering room, sit on the sofa, and pick up our prayer books.

I look up. Her face is bare. "Did you take your scarf off in the kitchen, Val? Want me to go get it for you?"

"Nah. I think I'll give my face a trial run inside here."

"That's more than okay with me."

She opens to the day's prayers. "I've known that for a while, Gus."

And the morning sun shines upon us. Just as we are.

AUTHOR'S NOTE

Thankfully, these days there are other more humane and dignified ways to provide for the disabled, so you'd have a hard time finding human oddities like Valentine and Lella on display. Please forgive me a little stretching of the way things are in order to explore the metaphor of Christ's Body, His Church, in a deeper way.

ACKNOWLEDGMENTS

Many thanks:
To Ami and Allen and the entire fiction gang at Thomas Nelson—I appreciate you all for extending the freedom I needed to write this unusual tale. Your support and attention warms my soul. To Erin—you know what to do! To Rachelle—wow, this one provided you with heavier work. But let's hope it was worth it in the end.

To Phil Smith—for the book and for letting me know I wasn't the only person with an interest in human marvels.

To my friends and family, especially Will, Ty, Jake, and Gwynnie—I love and appreciate you all. And Will, thanks for helping me with the male voice.

To the people who have shown me the life of New Monasticism, this book could definitely have never been written without you. Particularly the people in my own intentional community, Communality, as well as those in The Simple Way.

To my readers—thanks for your love and support over the years! Please e-mail me at lisa@lisasamson.com.

And to the Father, Son, and Holy Spirit, who made and makes us all.

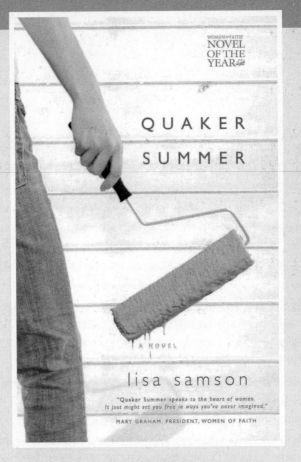

For all who know life isn't about busyness and stuff, experience the simple beauty of *Quaker Summer*.

THOMAS NELSON
Since 1798

Quaker Summer EXCERPT

CHAPTER ONE

Five months ago I raised Gary and Mary Andrews from the dead. I took a wrong turn trying to find a Pampered Chef party to benefit Will's eighth grade trip to New York City, and there it stood as close to the road as ever, their old house. Superimposed over the improvements of the recent owners, a small bungalow with cracked siding, smeared windowpanes, and a rusted oil tank figured into my vision. The mat of green grass dissolved into an unkempt lot of dirt and weeds supporting a display of junk: an old couch, a defunct Chevy, and rusted entities the purpose of which I never could say.

What happened inside that house remains there. All I know for sure is that Gary and Mary Andrews climbed onto our school bus every morning and never waved good-bye to anybody. We'd pull forward in a throaty puff of diesel, away from that little frame house, its once-white paint as gray as the dirt that always outlined Gary's hands and shaded behind his ears. As a sixth grader, I didn't realize children weren't responsible for their own cleanliness, that Mary's hair never glinted in the sunshine or smelled like baby shampoo because nobody helped her wash it; nobody thrust their fingers into her curls and scrubbed away the dust of a tumble in the yard with the dog; nobody applied a nice dollop of cream rinse to untangle knots from windy hours outside. I never stopped to think nobody in that house cared about them.

God help me.

So I sit now in the anonymity of my car, praying somebody steps out. Perhaps they'll look around, notice me sitting here, walk forward and ask if there's a problem.

No. No problem. I just knew the people who used to live here. Might you know where they live now?

No movement, no fluttering of the drapes, no shadows behind the blinds. Always quiet here. It always was.

I pull off the side of the road, the heavy tires eating the gravel. I turn for home. I'll find myself back here again soon. It's become the way of it.

I'm sorry. I'm so sorry.

I FELL ASLEEP last night to the eerie strains of "Blackbird," my last conscious thoughts of broken wings and sunken eyes. Waiting for moments to arrive when broken wings fly and sunken eyes see, waiting for that moment of freedom, flying into the light.

If I had to listen to one musical artist or band or composer for the rest of my life, I'd choose the Beatles. Their music encompasses all the emotions, all the moods, and all the tempos I'll ever need, taking me back to my childhood when my father would slip an album on the stereo, set the speed to thirty-three, and push the lever up to automatic. The fact that my father was younger and definitely cooler than the other dads around only helped the Fab Four become *the thing* to an elementary school girl who should have been listening to Bobby Sherman or the Osmond Brothers. I never really did go for the teen sensations.

Lying on my stomach, I would watch from eye level, chin resting on the back of my hands, and stare, gaze stuttering in and out of focus as the record fell to the turntable on the floor by the couch, the arm lifted, swung backward then forward, diamond-tipped needle poised with promise over the smooth outer rim of the vinyl disc.

As it dropped with slow precision, I held my breath wondering if it would really make contact with the disc this time. Those old hi-fi systems didn't miss the mark often, but they did enough to glue your eyes to the entire process and make your heart skip a few beats until the needle found its groove.

And then, after the static and scratch, Paul sang about his mother, Mary, comforting him, telling him to "Let It Be."

I was a daddy's girl, my mother having left him when I was two and then died not long after in a motorcycle accident with one of her precursor-hippie boyfriends. Nevertheless, I closed my eyes for the duration of the song, wishing she still existed and could lift her hand and rest it on my shoulder. She must have done that long ago.

Or maybe not.

During the strains of "Blackbird," I dreamt of my father for the first time in many months, his dark, winged hair breezing back from his wide forehead. Snuggled in the comforter freshly snapped down off the line yesterday afternoon, I wallowed in the numbness of slumber as he returned anew. Nobody told me how precious dreams of the dead become, how our own subconscious somehow gifts us with the time and space to once again be with those who have left us behind.

AND SO I lay basking in my father's presence, wishing so much for more time. But isn't that always the way? There he was, living in that little house in Towson, and I only saw him once a week. How differently I'd do things if I'd known he was slated for an autumn death. An accident at work. He was a plumber, a fact that used to embarrass me, an expert at redoing historical houses during his last decade. Nobody knew that wall was ready to fall down. They were just doing the initial walk-through. He was only fifty-five.

The cool morning air spirals the window curtains, and I inhale the breeze off Loch Raven to the bottom of my lungs. At the crest of the hill beside our home, earth—turned over and ready for planting by the farmer who lives next door—casts its loamy smell over the yard. As yet, the sun rests below a horizon unadorned but for the crabbed Dutch elm standing long past its expiration date. I hate that bleached thing. Why my neighbor, a sweet widower nicknamed Jolly, doesn't pull it down is as much a mystery as his very name. As far as I know, nobody knows Jolly's real name, and Jace and I wonder if Jolly even remembers. Maybe it actually is Jolly. Jolly Lester. I always figured it was John or Jacob or maybe James.

Jolly tries to live up to the name. Lord knows the man tries. But some days, especially when the rain falls in a light slick from a platinum sky, his sepia eyes tell me he misses his Helen with the longing of someone who loved one person all of his life and was content, even honored, to do so. And Helen loved him back.

The distant buildings of Towson peek over the trees, and farther yet, Baltimore lies hidden to me here. But life is beginning again in those places that formed me into this woman I've become, for good or for bad.

I should pray. My father taught me to pray.

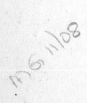